David Silas

First, giving a.. g.... .... whom all things are possible in my life. You have carried me through the the heartaches hard times and hardships. You were always present through the worst of my storms and I am eternally thankful...I give a strong acknowledgment to my loving grandmother. I know you're smiling down on me. To my patient aunts and uncles who never gave up on me. I love you all. To my cousins who believe in me even though time and distance keeps us apart.

My children: Nick, Mook, Heaven, and Lil David. I do what I do for all of you. To my sisters: Josey, Anna, Shone, and my brother LaDon. To my B.M. Tanisha, thanks for always riding with me. It'll always be love. To my day one niggas: Cash, Marcus, Short, Big bro Bruce, and Frank Lee. You got "Joker Jam" slamming just like you said you would. Now let's get on "THE COUNTY" and get this money. To Miles Cole, I appreciate all you did through "Corner Stone" to give me a smooth transition home. You're a good dude and I look forward to future business interactions. To my guys locked down state and federal, too many to name. (My niggas know who they are.) To Ms. Lela Cane, I thank you for all the time and effort you've poured into my project to ensure it would be the best possible work. You are greatly appreciated. And lastly; to my beautiful mother. You carried me into this world and held me down ever since. I love so much. And soon Lil lady everything you want and deserve you're going to have. I love you. Oh yeah, my bad.

I can't forget what made me into who I a today. I give a strong acknowledgment to the Windy City streets. Chicago niggas... Let's get this money.

CHAPTER 1

April 3, 2012 2:52 a.m.

"Man G', I don't trust that nigga' Twin."

"You trust me don't you?"

Shy grabs his phone, pulls his playlist up and glances through it as he speaks.

"Come on nigga', how the fuck you gon' ask me some shit like that? We go back since what? Forth, fifth grade?"

He finds a song and then connects his auxiliary as he goes on.

"Stop playing you know I ain't got but one nigga' and you him."

"Aiight act like it then and trust me..! Fuck dude."

Sensing a bad vibe, Shy looks over and Black is staring at him with the same serious face Shy had become so familiar with.

"Man, I don't know what the fuck you looking at me like that for."

"Because I'm saying nigga', you know I don't trust that punk either. I already know he's a snake and a coward."

"And!?"

"And because of that, you of all people should know since I don't do shit without thinking about it, that pussy gotta' be in the game for a reason."

Their eyes lock for a few seconds that seem like hours, then Black breaks the silence.

"That punk gon' play his part 'til I get through with him. Then don't even trip, I got something for his hoe ass and he gon' get it real early."

Shy nods and replies.

"You know I'm feeling you, but us being where we at, I'ma' say what's on my mind."

"Yeah...yeah...I know."

Black leans back in his seat, reaches in his waist line and pulls out a Glock 17 lemon squeeze with an extended clip. He taps it on his right leg as he stares out the front window then casually says.

"I've been putting this shit together for two years. This my lick, this our lick. For real homie, we on from here."

Black slowly shakes his head as he gazes at his own thoughts picturing the life he has in store for them. "And I'm telling you bro, there ain't shit that's gone fuck this up...nothing."

Shy turns the radio up one notch so he could hear Murda Mal get off a little better and without looking at his partner replies.

"All I'm saying is this here, I know what I'ma do. I never fucked a dollar up my whole life. But this other nigga, I can't honor dude at all. But like you say, this yo thang and you been putting it together for a minute. You my man and I trust you. Plus, you know me. I wouldn't give a fuck if the whole thang went wrong and all these niggaz got up outta there. I'm riding' with you till the wheels fall off this bitch and when they do, we bailin' together, pistols blazin' like fuck the world and everybody in it."

Black reaches over with his fist balled up and Shy daps his main man as Black says,

"You my nigga'."

"All the time, believe that."

Black looks out his side mirror, and as he tries to focus down the street, Shy speaks up.

"On the real though homie, it is something I'm kinda' trippin' on."

"Yeah, what's that?"

"What you think?"

Black takes a deep breath and blows it out.

"You mean Baby girl?"

"Without question."

Black nods. Then adamantly says.

"Yeah, I'm feeling you on that, but this that real shit, so ain't no room for loose ends, everybody gotta' go."

Shy shakes his head while letting out a slight chuckle.

"Aye man, this yo thang, do you."

"All the time,"

Black replies as he grips the steering wheel, then goes on to say.

"But on the real Shy, I can't even lie, I'm diggin' baby girl and been diggin' her for years. Plus if it wasn't for her we wouldn't even be sitting here right now. I hate to get down on her like this, but you already know the deal...if it ain't gangsta', it ain't me."

"Man G', you ain't gotta' tell me. I just put it out there because I know you feeling baby girl and I know she feeling you."

"Yeah I know bro, I ain't trippin'. I'm just talking."

Black pauses for a second, then goes on.

"It's just... man, I don't know. Hoes be funny sometimes and I ani't feeling going through that shit at all."

"What you mean?" Shy asks.

Black thought for a second then said.

"I don't really know how to put it, so I'ma' just use you and Nia for an example. Y'all been together like...Forever, so no matter what the fuck she was on even if she was getting down on you, and I ain't sayin' she is, but if she was. We both know, there's nothing in the world that's gon' make that girl go against you on some real shit."

Shy nods as Black goes on.

"So all I'm saying is this. No matter how a hoe get down, she gon' always have some type of loyalty to the nigga' she fuckin' on a regular basis, even if she is dippin'. Don't get me wrong bro, because I don't have a doubt in my mind that baby girl feelin' me, but the way I see it, is why even take a chance."

There's a short break in the conversation, then Shy replies.

"Right, right. I see where you at with that. I see exactly where you at."

Black and Shy were in a 1994 fully restored midnight blue with silver flakes Chevelle, sittin' on twenty-two inch chrome "Ashanti" rims and Pirelli low profile tires. It had a

350 under the hood with a dual exhaust and indeed it was a runner.

They sat on the custom midnight blue leather seats looking at the raindrops slowly fall on the front windshield. Jeezy's classic "Thug Motivation" now played low through the speakers as they waited for their five-man crew to pull up on the backstreet of Sunnyside, on Chicago's north side.

Black and Shy were both G.D.'s from the south side of Chicago. Shy was from "Killer Ward" off 77th and Paulina and Black was from the Englewood area off 71st and Green. They had known each other for almost twenty years and got money together for at least ten of those years.

Black was older, only by a few months, but when it came to the game he had years on Shy. Not as much the hustle part, more so the street side. Embracing the era when G's were G's Black believed in the words of N.W.A "Fuck the police!" And while you at it, the feds too, let them bitches do they job; catch me if you can, snitch niggaz get the fuck out the way and let the real niggaz check this paper.

He believed in that gangsta' shit, he was born and bred for the streets and honored everything about the game. He grew up in Englewood, which was like taking a crash course on gang bangin' 101. So by the time he had come of age, the streets knew without a doubt, Black would handle the business no matter what it consisted of.

He didn't mince words he said what he meant and meant what he said, and because he stayed about business, he addressed all business on the spot no matter what it consisted of. He was truly one of them dudes who didn't have an ounce of pussy in him.

So with all the characteristic traits of a natural born leader he finessed his way through the game. By seventeen, he had a regent slot for the G.D's in his area and was already touching at least a key and a half of cocaine. Niggaz was eating under his watch, and that kept the hood strong and loyal.

That was cool, but what kept niggaz honoring Black was the fact that he wasn't one of them niggaz who hid behind the mob. He was getting money and niggaz new it, but they also knew he was up with all the bullshit that came with the streets.

Black's cousin was a B.D from over east off 63rd and Calumet. While Black was getting' money in Englewood, the B.D's over east were warring with the G.D.'s off 57th Street. But because Black was Flinno cousin, Black could often be found rotating through B.D. land. That happened to be the cause of one of the most major shifts in his life.

In 2005 he caught two attempted murders and stayed in Cook County Jail from 2005 until the end of 2006.

The weather was just breaking in March. Black and Flinno were hittin' blocks blowing the loud when the G.D's off 57th shot up Black's car at the gas station trying to kill his cousin.

Later on that same night, Black pulled up on their block by himself and caught two of the niggaz lackin. He stopped right in front of their house and hopped out like.

"What's good G', where the loud at?"

One of the guys looked at him and started to say "right here," but before they could, Black was raising a sixteen shot black 9 millimeter lettin' it ride while he stood between the car door of a black Chevy. He shot three times from the car, hitting one in the shoulder and the other twice in the leg. While they squirmed on the porch, Black ran up and dumped seven more times hitting them in the back, chest, legs, and arms. But unfortunately; they both lived.

Two months later he was picked up on attempted murder charges, given a ransom for a bond, and was forced to sit down in Cook County Jail. It wasn't looking good for a while, but then the folks from Englewood started applying pressure to the victims and gradually the victims slowed up on cooperating until finally the State realized they wouldn't be testifying. So without a gun or witnesses, they were forced to let Black go. He spent almost two years in the County Jail though.

And that in itself was not only a test, but also a true lesson in survival. Because Cook County wasn't your average ordinary County Jail. It's one of the biggest and probably most dangerous county jails in the United States. It has 14 different divisions and holds more that fifteen thousand inmates. Ninety percent of the incarcerated population are gang affiliated with one of the many organizations throughout Chicago. All breeds of ganstas are found there. Some are recognized heads and probably have more money and power than political figures. So quite naturally even in this world inside a world cash still rules everything around them. So the same dope the streets got; the County got. You just gotta' pay more for it.

Black was in Division five. He had a little juice from the world, but more than that he was a recognized Gangsta'. Niggaz from out south knew his name whether they were folks or oppositions. He still had a little paper plus there were people on the outside who would make moves for him, so he was cool.

While locked up, Latrice stepped into his life. She was a five foot three, dark skinned stallion who favored Terrell Hicks only thicker, with silky smooth skin, deep brown eyes, a short Halle Berry style cut with burgundy highlights, and soft juicy lips.

Latrice was a correctional officer who worked division five. Originally from suburban Maywood, she worked her way to the Southside. She had been an officer at the county since 2003, and Black, whose birth name was Darren Lang, did what no other man could do in the three years she worked there; he got her attention.

Black had a Tyrese resemblance and stood six foot four inches. From the day he came on the deck, Latrice was feeling him. He had a sexy swag about himself that stood out as he stepped out the line with his mattress and brown paper lunch bag. So when she called his name from his I.D card, she took a mental picture as he stepped pass her in his tan D.O.C. clothes, and that picture stayed with her throughout the night, into the early morning, and carried her to work the next day with a little extra spice to her look and sex appeal.

Latrice sent out her female attraction vibe and once Black got a wind of it he started shootin' at her. After about three weeks of conversation, Latrice made a move and got him a job as a hall worker. Once she did, their conversation took on a more personal level.

Like the natural nurturer she was, Latrice began to take care of Black. She brought him food from the street everyday she worked, and made sure he had every toiletry hygiene product the county had, plus he stayed off the deck rotating through the whole division.

It wasn't long after he started working that the two started having sex. She would take her breaks while Black was mopping the hallways and they would dip off into utility closets. Latrice would peel down her tight ass county pants and bend over with one pant leg on.

"Come on boy, you better hurry up before you fuck around and get my ass fired." She would always say, knowing her girl was on security for her.

Black would knock her off twenty and thirty minutes at a time on a regular basis. Latrice loved it, and truth be told, the real thrill came from her fucking a nigga' at work she was supposed to be guarding. Sometimes just thinking about it got her juices flowing and for Black it was about the same. That and being one of the only inmates in the county jail fucking regularly. In any case, they were both digging their situation. It wasn't long before Latrice was wide open and sprung on Black. She watched him all the time and everything he did seemed to add to her attraction for him. She dotted on the way other niggaz acted towards him no matter their mob affiliation, and Latrice being a woman could see it clearly, and she loved it. It turned her on and kept her pussy wet. So the majority of the time, Black didn't even have to drive on the pussy, because she was driving on the dick.

They weren't even fucking a whole month before Latrice was bringing rocks, blows, powder cocaine, and weed into the county and Black was sending her back out with that paper. His hustle was crazy and she was feeling that too. Black became Latrice's regular man and she stayed loyal to him. He was her only sex partner, confidant, but most of all her closest friend. A short time later, she had fallen in love with him.

Nine months into them being involved, Latrice got pregnant and had a little boy two days after Black got out. They got married in March of 2007 two months later; Latrice was pregnant again, this time with a little girl and had the baby February of 2008.

Black was still married to the streets though and was deep in the game, but Latrice being twenty-eight, two years older than, Black had no problems with it. And it wasn't the game that fascinated her though; it was the way Black played the game and how well he played it that kept her hot for him. His ability to maintain a hustler's mentality while at the same time being an open loving husband and father kept her hooked and longing for more.

There was no place Latrice went in the whole City of Chicago that she didn't feel the safety of his presence. Black's name was familiar and Latrice and her children's faces quickly became associated with his name. Latrice ran dope, picked up money, cooked and bagged up cocaine while still maintaining a squeaky clean record as a correctional officer. The two shared everything, even some of the women Black had on the side.

Latrice was already into women, but not just any women, only the beautiful ones. And the more she understood the importance of women in Black's ability to stay informed and therefore safe in the streets, the more she opened up to his sexual relationships. Yeah, she occasionally had the opportunity to share the physical effects, but when it all boiled down to it, it was mainly because she loved him just that much. For Latrice it was always a bigger picture. So she not only allowed for other women to be a part of Black's life, but she also kept her eye's and ears open for any women who had well connected hustlas for men.

All Latrice asked was that Black brought no more babies in the world by anyone else besides her and that she always remained to be his leading lady. Black had no problem with that because Latrice was truly the ideal hustler's wife and no matter who he was with in the streets, his love and devotion was to her.

Shy was different, he was a playa'. He had a perfect resemblance of F. Gary Gray, all the way down to his brown skinned complexion, thick eyebrows, mustache, and chin hair. He wore a short fade with a razor lining and was five foot eleven. But unlike the film director, Shy didn't make movies about that gangsta shit; he lived it.

He knew how to get money and he got money all his life. He wasn't as gangsta' as Black, but together they made everything happen in the streets they needed.

Shy and jail didn't get along, so he never did a day there. The closest he ever got to being locked up was his weekly visits to Cook County to see Black, which he made from the first week Black got locked up until the day he came home. Black and Shy shared something that was rare in the streets of Chicago, and any other city as well; they shared loyalty.

The two were a lot alike, but unlike Black, Shy understood the importance of getting money with everybody. He didn't just fuck with the folks when it came to dope and paper, he fucked with all different mobs.

Shy got down with a Black Stone's from Moe-Town and a Four-Corner Hustla from out west. And because of Shy, Black and Flinno fucked with Moe and Solid as well.

Black did have a partner he clicked with though, and that was Dee. Dee wasn't mob affiliated, but in one way or another he always managed to be plugged with the right niggaz all his life. He was a master at cooking cocaine and shaking heroin. He taught Latrice how to do both and soon she was cooking whole keys on the stove like she was making pound cakes. Outside of Flinno and Shy, Dee was the closest friend Black had.

Now Twin, he was a different story all together. He was a coward type nigga' who had some good connects and that's the only reason Black fucked with him. But after tonight, Black wouldn't need him or his connects anymore.

Black and Shy were parked all of fifteen minutes when a black Ford van pulled up along the side of them. The window rolled down and a familiar voice sounded off.

"What up Cuzo?" Flinno said.

"What's good cuz, everybody there?" Black responded.

"Yeah."

"Aiight follow me."

Black pushed the switch to let his window back up, put the Chevelle in drive and slowly pulled off. He let out a little laugh while he shook his head leaning on the car door with his right hand on the steering wheel.

"That nigga' Twin is a certified pussy. On bro that bitch look like he about two minutes from crying."

"You ain't gotta' tell me fam, I already know."

A couple minutes later they pulled up and parked in front of a gray and red brick house that sat on the right side of the street, four houses from the corner. The block was quiet and motionless at 3:11 a.m. ideally at this hour, no one was expected to be up except crack heads, but unfortunately in a house on the opposite side of the street, three houses further down the block, a woman was up getting ready for her work day.

Meanwhile, Black grabbed a navy blue vinyl duffle bag off the back seat and he and Shy got out the Chevelle, walked to the van and stepped in by the side sliding door.

"What's good niggaz?" Black stated.

"What's happening Black?"

"What's up Solid?" Shy said to his homie.

"What's up Shy?"

"Aiight look, check it out."

Black said as he squatted in the back of the van.

"Everybody already know the deal. Dee and Solid, y'all in the kitchen, move the table and the rug; underneath it, the floor comes up. Its gon' be fifty books of yay there. Cuz, as soon as you and Moe get in the house, make the first right around the corner and go to the first door on your right. It's a dresser on the right side of the wall. Move it to the middle of the room and it's a latch on the ceiling, pull it down and in the ceiling it's gon' be thirty books of heroin. Me and Shy upstairs at the paper. Now when we get in, its gon' be more than likely three niggaz in the living room, and cuz, it's gon' be one nigga' in the room, but he might have a bitch in there with him. If it is, too bad for baby, because everyone gotta' go. Me and Shy gon' whack the bitch and the nigga' upstairs and handle our business. Everybody gotta' get their hands dirty on this one, so it's not shit left to talk about. Come through the door lettin' it ride - kill everybody! We can't afford no ghosts comin' back to haunt us, so don't wound 'em, don't just think they dead, Know they dead. Face and head shots, as many of 'em as it takes. Everybody got that?"

They all nodded in agreement. Black went on.

"Twin, you know if you see the twist, hit the phone. You got your phone on you?"

"Yeah."

"Let me see it."

Twin held his hand up and showed Black his I-phone.

"You got the number right there ready to send?"

"Yeah, it's already set to call."

Black stood up, bent over the back of Twin's seat and looked him right in the eyes with a serious stern face and poked his finger in Twin's chest.

"Muthafucka, you better hit that phone and you better be your ass out here when we come out, because I swear on my babies. I will kill you and every fuckin' body who look like you startin' with your grandmamma, all the way down to the baby your little sister just had. You understand me nigga'?"

Twin was terrified because he knew Black meant every word that came out his mouth.

"Yeah, don't trip. I'ma' be here - you don't have to worry about it, I got y'all."

Black nodded his head with a threatening look.

"Aiight nigga'."

He looked at him for a couple more seconds then went back to where he was squatting and unzipped the bag he carried in the van. Inside the bag were black leather gloves and guns. He handed a pair of gloves to everyone, then pulled out five mini 14's with screw on silencers already attached, and passed them out. Each man had a ski mask folded over his forehead, ready to be pulled over the face.

"All the bangers are throw aways, so if you gotta' drop 'em to get that shit, it's all good."

Lastly, Black handed them thin black vinyl jackets with gold letters on the back.

"What's this?" Dee asked.

Black held his jacket up and said,

"D.E.A nigga', you didn't know, we the feds. Now come on let's get this paper."

It was 3:15 a.m.

They all put on their jackets, pulled their ski masks down and bailed out the side door. They hurried up the walk way and up the five steps that led to the door with both hands on their guns like trained mercenaries on a retrieval mission behind enemy lines.

Black led the pack. Once at the door he put the strength and weight of his 226 pounds behind one solid kick to the left side of the door knob and the door flew open.

They stormed in following Blacks lead.

"D.E.A! D.E.A.! Everybody down! Everybody down muthafuckas!"

Black and Shy shot upstairs, Dee and Solid came in with their fingers squeezing the triggas; 'Fewt! Fewt! Fewt! Fewt! Fewt! Fewt! Fewt! Fewt! Fewt! Fewt!'

Silenced automatic bullets sailed through the air and into the bodies of the three Belizeans that jumped up from the couch in the living room, making failed attempts of reaching their nearby handguns. Bodies jerked back and forth as bullets went in and out of them. Blood squirted from their bodies, face, and neck splattering walls and seeping over them wetting their clothes and floor. Flames continued to shoot from the muzzles of the mini 14's while shell casings jumped out, clinking and clanking whiling dancing on the floor.

Once the Belizeans had fallen, Dee and Solid stood over them sending shots directly to their faces and heads, making sure they were dead.

In the bedroom, Flinno and Moe were doing the same thing to the naked man and woman who laid in the bed. Afterwards they slid the dresser over, Moe hopped on top of it, pulled the latch, a door dropped down, he then looked in the ceiling and saw the bricks of heroin.

"Hell muthafuckin yeah nigga'! That shit here my nigga!"

Flinno opened the bag and Moe began dropping the keys into it. In the kitchen, Dee and Solid found the same to be true beneath the floor and like Flinno and Moe, Dee, and Solid filled their bags.

Upstairs, Black and Shy expected to see a man and woman, but there was only a man. They quickly filled his body with slugs and then put another ten shots in his face leaving him lying in bed in a puddle of blood. They pushed the bed to the side and kicked through the dry wall behind it. Once they had a big enough hole, Black looked in and saw four clear plastic cases packed and sealed tightly with money.

He handed Shy two bags, then he took the others and they ran back downstairs. As they were reaching the steps, Dee and Solid were running out the door. Flinno and Moe were already in the van. Shy jumped in the van, Black threw him one of the bags of money, Shy slid the door shut and Twin pulled off. Black jumped in the Chevelle and fell in behind them. It was 3: 19 a.m.

CHAPTER 2

The Mahogany framed crescent headboard shined as Derrick Trumball lay in his king-sized bed. The silver and black printed mirror of two panthers staring at one another set in the headboard was smudge less. And the cool comfort of his black silk sheets against his naked body had him on top of the world.

The house phone on the far left night stand rang for the fifth time, and he continued to ignore it. Shortly thereafter, his cell phone buzzed, vibrating across the same night stand. Once it stopped, the house phone rang again.

"It's my day off, it's my day off, it's my day off."

Derrick muttered with his eyes closed. He glanced at the clock; it was 5:03 a.m.

The cell phone buzzed again.

"Fuck!"

He sat up and ran his hands across his face to the back of his head, cracked his neck, then looked down to his left.

"Mmm, mmm, mmm" was all he could say to the sight of the coco butter curve of the beautifully shaped round ass staring back at him. He let his eyes move down the long slender legs with red thigh-high stockings and laced garters until he reached the red four inch "fuck me" pumps on her feet.

Looking at the reflection in the mirror attached to the matching mahogany dresser, Derrick smiled at the hint of the little pink pussy tucked away between the legs of the woman who was lying next to him.

Three open magnum wrappers lay on the dresser next to a pair of red-laced thongs, along with two champagne glasses and a bottle of Moet. A red laced bra hung on the corner of the mirror and the smell of "Paris Hilton" perfume lingered in the air.

Derrick shook his head as he looked back down at the coco butter turn on. He slowly ran his hands over the soft backside and let his fingers slide between the crack of her ass until he felt the heat coming off her wet little kitty, then pushed his middle finger inside her. Candy squirmed a little bit as he slowly worked his finger in and out of her. After thirty seconds or so, she began to let out soft moans. A couple seconds later she spread her legs apart four or five inches and poked her ass in the air.

Still laying with her head on her hands, Candy turned to face Derrick. Her sandy brown hair covered her face wildly.

Derrick worked both his middle fingers in and out of her, soon the sound of her juices floated through the air. "Oh... oh... oh..." She moaned while gyrating her hips on his fingers.

Sliding down behind her, Derrick pushed Candy up by her butt onto her knees. With her ass high in the air and head on the pillow, Derrick was able to slide underneath her and guide her to his desired resting place; her pussy on his face.

He slipped his tongue inside her, and a chill shot through Candy from her silver dollar size light-brown nipples, to the tips of her polished toes dangling in the air of her pumps.

Derrick licked around her lips with the tip of his tongue, and then flicked at her clit. Palming her ass cheeks, he spread them apart and slid his index finger inside her butt. Candy let out a sigh, then softly whispered, "Yes."

Derrick pressed his lips around her clit and gently sucked as he worked his finger in and out of her. Candy moved anxiously back and forth pushing herself onto his finger, loving the feeling. Soon her thoughts began to drift.

"Shit... yes, yes, shit."

She whispered as the memory of her forty minute ass fucking settled on her mind's eye.

Candy licked her lips and shuddered, almost able to taste the inches down her throat as the warm water from last night shower sprinkled down on her. That thought took her over the edge. She began to cum, her hips buckled and she rose up on her hands, and then gripped the head board.

Her C-cup breasts dangled and swayed back and forth as she looked at herself in the mirror. She couldn't help but see her own disappointment, because Candy knew she not only wanted, but also needed the intensity of the whole nine inches running in and out of her, not just a finger; but what was a girl to do, she thought.

After she came and her juices covered Derricks face, she slid down and he slid up. Derrick put his back on the headboard and Candy put his rock-hard dick in her mouth.

Candy's head game was crazy; Derrick couldn't help but think if he not only would have known that, but also how much she loved to be fucked in the ass, he would have been nailing her a long time ago, but it didn't matter - he knew now, and he would capitalize on it from this day forward.

As she went to work, her head bobbed up and down, her ass swayed back and forth, and her red pumps danced in the air.

"How sweet it is?" Derrick mumbled as he took it all in through the reflection of the mirror.

"Work it baby. That's right."

"Hmm..." Candy replied looking up at him with his dick still in her mouth.

Derrick bit down on his lip and softly placed his hand on the back of her head. Candy took him out her mouth and licked him with the tip of her tongue from his balls to his head, and then asked,

"So how am I doing?"

Derrick chuckled, and replied.

"I'm saying, if you gotta' ask, then maybe you're not doing well enough."

"Oh yeah."

Candy twisted her lips.

"Well let me see what I can do about that."

She immediately deep-throated him, and jagged him off faster as she came up letting her spit drip down her hands while she stroked.

"Damn! Aiight then." Derrick said as he gripped her hair.

His cell phone vibrated across the table again, he reached over with his other hand and grabbed it. His partners name flashed on the screen.

'What the fuck he want this early?' Derrick thought.

When the phone stopped vibrating, he tapped end call on the screen and saw that all the calls were from his partner. The house phone rang again, but he told himself.

"Two more minutes, two more minutes, just two more m..."

Only it was more like two more seconds. He shot off in Candy's mouth in the middle of his words.

With a hint of surprise, Candy jerked back, but quickly regained her stride as she guzzled down the first half of the explosion she had been working so vigorously for.

Candy knew what she wanted, so she began to quickly jag him off until cum shot over her face.

"Yes, Yes. Shoot it baby, shoot it all over me. Shoot it in my face, I love it like that."

Then she put it back in her mouth and drank the remainder.

She looked up at him with cum all over her face dripping from her chin. She licked the corners of her mouth, wiped the cum off her face then rubbed it on her ass.

"I just love waking up to dick in my mouth and cum running down my throat."

"I see." Derrick smirked.

"You haven't seen nothin' yet."

Then like a good girl. Candy put his dick back in her mouth.

Derrick shook his head and tapped the screen on his phone. With one ring his partner answered.

"Man where the fuck are you?!"

"Where you think? I'm at home, it's my day off."

"Not anymore."

"Why's that?"

"Because right now I'm on Sunnyside, investigating a multiple homicide."

"On Sunnyside!?" Derrick said shocked.

"Yeah, your boy, his little brother, three of his guys, and some chick; all dead."

"Is that all?"

"Hell naw that ain't all!" Michael Mann's yelled angrily.

"All the shit is gone."

Derrick was speechless. He looked in the mirror no longer able to see the round coco butter ass swaying back and forth, or the heels dangling, or the head bobbing. Nope, all he saw was fifty keys of

cocaine and thirty keys of heroin where they should have been, and he knew that because only three days ago he and his partner watched them being tucked away nicely in their spot.

His dick went limp in Candy's mouth. "I'm on my way."

"How long?"

"Twenty minutes."

"Make it ten."

They both hung up. Derrick pushed Candy's head off his dick.

"Come on baby girl, breakfast is over, I gotta' get out of here."

"Nooooo." Candy reluctantly replied as she gripped him tighter sliding him back in her mouth.

"For real little lady, it's over with."

Derrick said as he pushed her head all the way back. Candy flipped his dick out her hand with a frown.

"Oh, that's how you do me right, cum all in my face and down my throat then put me out, huh."

"Hold on now. Just a couple minutes ago you said you love waking up like that, so the way I see it- you got just what you wanted."

"No, I didn't get it the way I wanted it though."

Derrick looked at her blankly.

"Come on now girl, I don't have time for this right now, so get your shit together." Candy pouts out the words,

"But I want some more."

"I feel you baby, because trust me, there is nothing I would rather be doing than fucking you in your ass

for another hour or two, but the truth of the matter is I got a multiple homicide to get to."

Candy folds her arms across her chest, and pokes out her lip like a stubborn child.

"Well, here go some more truth. You finna' have one right here in your house! Because I'ma' die if I don't get some more dick."

Derrick was up putting his clothes on, grabbing hers off the floor and dresser and tossing them to her.

"I guess you gon' be one dead bitch then 'cause for real baby girl, ain't no more dick!"

He looked her in the eyes with a stern face and added.

"Now get your shit on little lady because I gotta' go."

'Okay fine! Be that way then." She said snatching her bra. "You know you're an ungrateful muthafucka'."

"Yeah, yeah, yeah, aiight."

"Yeah, yeah, my ass." She responds with an attitude.

"Can I at least wash my face and brush my teeth?"

Derrick smiles. "Of course you can wash your face and brush your teeth if you got a toothbrush."

"Boy you know I don't have a toothbrush, why I can't use yours?"

Derrick starts laughing as he ties his shoes.

"Use my toothbrush? Come on baby, you know that ain't gon' happen."

"Why?!"

"What you mean why? Girl, you been suckin' dick all night."

"So! It's your dick I been suckin'!"

Derrick laughs.

"Aye, I ain't got nothing to do with that because on the real, to me, dick is dick. And since I don't brush my dick with my toothbrush you can believe this fo sho', you not either."

Candy twisted her lips and said. "Ha, ha, very funny," as she gives him the finger.

Derrick begins to snap his fingers back and forth.

"Chop! Chop! Now come on cutie, I gotta' get outta' here. Now I'm trying to be nice about this shit because I want to see you again, so don't make me get nasty and pull your pretty little ass out my crib by your hair because I will."

"Okay, okay, okay, I'm coming, damn!"

Derrick leans on his dresser while Candy rushes her clothes on mumbling under her breath.

'Look at this hoe.' Derrick thought, then said,

"Aiight, I see you upset, so I tell you what."

"What?!" Candy Snaps.

"Damn, slow down."

"Naw fuck that! This is bullshit Derrick and you know it."

"Right, I agree, so check it out. Call me later on tonight and we'll pick up right where we left off. How does that sound?"

Candy calmed down a little and looked at him with pursed lips. "You promise?"

Derrick smiled and put his arms out.

"Do I promise? Come on baby, look at you. You're five seven, beautiful face with the most gorgeous breast and body, and that mouth - whew!"

Candy blushes with a smile as Derrick goes on.

"You tell me why wouldn't I want you face down ass up in my bed for another night?"

"Awe, that's sweet Derrick. You really mean that?" Candy asks, adjusting her dress.

"Baby, come on now, look at me. I'm the police. If you can't trust me, who can you trust?"

Candy pauses to think, then replies.

"Wow, you know what, I never thought of it that way, you're right."

She giggles while putting her panties in her purse. Derrick shook his head while thinking,

'Come on now, this bitch can't be this fuckin' dumb.' They walked out. It was 5:37 a.m.

CHAPTER 3

Thursday, April 3, 2012 9:23 a.m.

Lisa Peterson has just finished her closing argument in the Cook County suburban branch court room of Rolling Meadows. Her client, Anthony Brooks, faces a possession with the intent to deliver four thousand four hundred and forty-eight grams of marijuana and two thousand-sixteen grams of cocaine.

While the jury deliberates, Lisa steps out the court room to call her significant others' home on Chicago's north side. She dials the number on her cell phone, it rings and a woman answered.

"Hello." Lisa looks at her phone to see if she has dialed the right number.

"Who is this?" Lisa asks.

"Who is this?" The woman responds.

"The woman who lives there." Lisa snaps with obvious annoyance.

"Now, like I said. Who is this?"

"Oh, I'm sorry ma'am. My name is Kimberly Anderson. I'm a crime scene investigator for the Rogers Park Police district. I'm investigating a multiple homicide that occurred here last night between the hours of 3:30 and 4:00 a.m."

Lisa's heart dropped to the floor and the blood drained from her face.

"What is your name ma'am?"

Still thrown off from the news, Lisa takes a moment to respond.

"Ma'am..."

"Yes, yes, I'm here." Lisa replied slightly shaken.

"What is your name?"

"Um, Lisa. Lisa Peterson. I'm a lawyer for 'Brickman and Edwards' downtown Chicago, but I'm in Rolling Meadows right now finishing up a trial."

"And you said you live here?"

"Yeah - no - well kind of. My mate lives there, and I stay there about three nights a week on a regular basis."

"What's your mate's name?"

"Tuko Dajanea. Is he one of the ones found dead?"

"At this time we don't know and truly I'm being honest with you. This scene is really bad. Six victims, all of them shot multiple times and at least seven to ten times in the face and head so identification isn't possible unless we get something from their prints."

"Well, Tuko would have been upstairs in the room."

"We do have a body upstairs."

"He has a tattoo of a lion on his right forearm."

A flash of the picture Kimberly took shoots across her mind.

"I'm sorry ma'am, if that is the case, then Tuko is one of the deceased."

Lisa pretty much knew that, but just hearing it caused reality to fall on her like a ton of bricks. Suddenly she felt light headed and had to balance herself on a nearby wall. Even though she didn't love Tuko, they had spent years in an intimate relationship - So grieving for him was inevitable, tears began to trickle from her eyes.

"Ms. Peterson, I'm sorry, I know this has to be hard for you right now, but listen, we're gonna' need you to answer a few questions."

Lisa, still trying to gather herself took a few second to answer, then finally says.

"Yes, I'm sorry. You'll have to excuse me because this is all such a big shock to me, but as far as answering question, I do understand."

"Good. And Ms. Peterson, I want you to know that I do understand how this can have you a little shaken, and I'm sorry for that, so I'll try to make this as brief as possible. First of all, how long do think you'll be at the court house?"

There was a short silence as Lisa closed her eyes and softly tapped her head against the wall while thinking. 'Man, what the hell did you get yourself into? Fuck Tuko, what the fuck.' She let out a sigh while rubbing her forehead and temple.

"Well, let me see. The jury is deliberating right now." She glances at her watch. "I don't know, three, maybe four more hours at the least."

"Okay, alright then in that case, let me ask you this. Do you know of anyone who would have wanted your mate dead?"

Lisa thought for a moment knowing damn well that with Tuko being one of the biggest drug dealers on the north side, a number of people could have wanted him dead. But her problem was that she was a lawyer for one of Chicago's most prestigious firms and her knowingly being involved with a person like Tuko would definitely affect her job, so she said.

"No, not at all. At least not right off hand I don't know."

"Was he involved in anything that would have warranted this attack on him and the other individuals in the home? Drugs, gangs, gambling?"

'Try all three.' Lisa thought, then said.

"No, not that I know of."

"And you say you stayed here two or three nights out the week?"

"Yes, that's correct."

"Where do you stay the rest of the week?"

"I have a condo in Oak Park off Harlem Ave."

"Well, if he was involved in something you didn't know about, which right about now it looks like he was, because this whole scene resembles gangland execution - I have to warn you, you may be in danger. So what I suggest is that you don't come back here at all and also remain conscious of everything and everyone around your Oak Park Condo. We're still going to need you to answer some questions..."

Lisa interrupted.

"Yes, I understand that. As soon as I'm done here I'll head directly to the police station. Addison and Halsted right?"

"Yes, that's correct."

"I'll head directly there and give a formal statement."

"Okay, the officer at the desk will direct you to a detective."

"Okay, that's fine, but if I may ask, is detective Derrick Trumball working this case?"

"Yes he is, he's the lead on it."

"Okay, thank you, I'll contact him."

"Alright ma'am."

After she got off the phone, she walked down the polished walnut color tile floor of the court building to the drinking fountain and took a drink. Next to the fountain was a wooden bench, so she sat down to rest her body and gather her thoughts.

The traumatic news instantly drained her mentally and physically, Lisa felt like she had been doing wind-sprints all morning.

She ran her hand up her beautiful light skinned face, then pushed her slender fingers through her long silky jet black hair, and put her head against the wall.

"Tuko, got damn it, Tuko, gotdamn it."

She muttered shaking her head.

Lisa was a thirty-three year old successful criminal lawyer who for the last eight years worked for one of the most prestigious law firms in Chicago.

From the very beginning she was a shining jewel. Brickman and Edwards recognized that, and in so doing, spared no expense in recruiting her right out of law school.

She was hands down the best criminal lawyer in the city of Chicago. She specialized in large scale drug cases, and every prosecutor in Cook County feared, respected, and admired her diligence and professionalism.

She was an absolute pit bull in the courtroom and hard to miss, because she only accepted high profile cases. Anything less than a key of cocaine, a key of heroin, three hundred pounds of high grade marijuana , a gallon of P.C.P., or two thousand ecstasy pills, got passed on to other lawyers in the firm.

Occasionally she took on female clients, but primarily she tailored her services strictly to males and that was solely because Lisa had an extreme fetish for drug dealers. And if it wasn't the drug dealer himself, it was the life style that came with the drug game.

Fighting drug cases was personal for Lisa. It wasn't about money; she had a much higher calling than that, which gave her, a deeper and more passionate commitment to her work.

Her natural beauty was passed onto her as a genetic gift. Her mother was a gorgeous Puerto Rican and her father was a tall, handsome, well-built, intelligent black man who was full of personality.

Through him, Lisa was blessed with an ambitious drive to achieve intellectually which she grasped on to at an early age. A resident of suburban Hoffman Estates while growing up, Lisa maintained a straight 'A' average from the fifth grade until she graduated from Hoffman Estates High School. And like most little girls who have good relationships with their fathers, he also set the standard for her of what an attractive man should not only look like, but also be like. Which for Lisa; meant successful. Her father alone did her a superb justice. But what her mother contributed made Lisa a polished diamond.

Through her mother she inherited her precious emerald green eyes, beautiful face, long silky jet black hair, soft shapely curved body, and natural sexiness. She was an only child, so her mother more so raised her as a girlfriend and not a daughter.

"The epitome of sexy."

Is what her father frequently identified her mother as, and indeed she was. Into all things elegant, Lisa's mother taught Lisa early on the importance of woman to not only feel sexy, but also not be ashamed to be sexy, so seeing her mother in lace and heels was an everyday thing.

Her father worked long hours creating, writing, and programing software. So Lisa and her mother spent the majority of the day together. It was nothing for her mother to walk around for hours only wearing panties and pumps. So having her body exposed was a natural thing for Lisa beauty was an absolute must.

"Always take timeout to pamper yourself little mamacita."

Her mother often expressed to her. So Lisa had been getting her hair, nails, and toes done since she was five. At six, she began walking in heels, wearing make-up at eight, and as soon as her breast developed her mother only bought her matching laced bra and panty sets.

Her mother was sexual, but not promiscuous. She was a loyal wife and instilled that in Lisa. So when Lisa finally reached high school she walked in aware of boys, confident, sexy, and dressed to impress.

As a freshman, she was five foot one, a hundred and seven pounds. She stepped through the door in black three inch open toe stilettos, a fresh pedicure, black miniskirt, black silk blouse, hair and makeup flawless, nails done and ready for class.

Hands down she was the object of everyone's desire who had ever imagined being with a beautiful woman. She got into track and tennis and before long her body developed into a young woman.

Her sophomore year, a senior name Angie Cummings took a liking to her and Lisa had her first girl-on-girl encounter.

She was invited to a party, got drunk for the first time and Angie began making out with her. Lisa was unbelievably turned on just by tongue kissing with Angie, but when Angie went down on her, Lisa was in awe. Her girl-on-girl encounter was good, but not good enough to commit Lisa to only women.

A month after that encounter, she met Dewitt. He was twenty-three years old and the biggest drug dealer in Hoffman Estates.

His dark-skinned complexion, low wavy cut, and six foot one muscular build captivated her from the start. He wasn't flashy, but had a confidence and swagger about himself that showed he had money.

He was simple though; diamond earrings, a chain, and a nice watch was all the jewelry he ever wore, but he always looked nice even when he wore jeans and gym shoes.

Dewitt wasn't aggressive, but like a true G, his gangsta' stood out amongst the crowd. He didn't have to flex it, it was recognized and honored. He had plenty of street knowledge and authority that was earned by being someone who took care of his business.

When Lisa and Dewitt met, he was driving a 1988 cream four door Park Ave. with 30's and vogues. He already had a female in the car, but as if she wasn't, Dewitt laid his thing down on Lisa.

By then Lisa had filled out wonderfully, grown two more inches, and took on the appearance of an older woman, but in all actuality she was barely sixteen.

Three days after they met Dewitt fucked her so good and so right that she came four times, lost her mind, and never wanted to leave his side. She had found love, she was sure of it, and nothing in the world could make her let it go.

She knew Dewitt was a drug dealer and the more time she spent in his world, the more it fascinated her. It was different, exciting, exhilarating, daring, and unpredictable - So much different from the secure life she had led up to that point. She went on road trips with him to cop dope, took Greyhound trips by herself with keys of cocaine, carried his guns, and he taught her to shoot. Some nights they set up for hours counting money, she had everything she wanted - because in all actuality, all she ever wanted was Dewitt.

Dewitt loved the fact that Lisa was smart more than anything else, and because she knew that, Lisa made sure she worked even harder at staying that way.

Missing school wasn't an option, anything less than straight A's wasn't an option, falling short of keeping herself up wasn't an option, so using drugs wasn't an option - not even weed. She drank occasionally, two, sometimes three days out of the month and only with Dewitt.

She was always expected to have a clear mind so any decision she made was based on sound rational thoughts. He instilled in her the importance of business and more so, keeping their business out the streets.

By the time she was seventeen; Lisa was weighing out and bagging powder cocaine into grams, sixteenths, eight-balls, quarter ounces, half ounces, and ounces. She never ever sold a bag, or even went with Dewitt during any transactions. It wasn't allowed, she was Dewitt's baby girl, so he kept her from that end of his dealings.

She knew Dewitt had other women. She had even been with some of them. But she also knew they weren't any thing to Dewitt. She was his number one and it was never up for negotiation. Her life was perfect by her standards, but her junior year, all that crumbled, and Lisa was faced with the hardest thing she would ever have to deal with and ironically, that situation ultimately shaped her life to be what it was today. Dewitt got locked up. He'd been selling cocaine and guns to an undercover agent for a little more than a year. Dewitt had known the guy for two years and it turned out that the whole time, Dewitt was the focus of a multi-jurisdictional drug trafficking sting in the suburbs. He had sold to the agent more than thirty times and was finally arrested after selling him five keys of cocaine and eleven handguns.

Deemed to be a flight risk, he was held without bond, and for three years Dewitt sat in Cook County Jail fighting his case. Although he had two of the best lawyers money could buy, there was no coming from under it.

During the entire time Lisa stayed faithfully by his side, always wishing she could do more than what she was doing. She wrote letters to the judge, researched case law at libraries, and stayed on top of his lawyers.

During visits with Dewitt, Lisa always said if she was his lawyer she would find a way to get him out. Her drive for that continually increased with each court appearance and by the time she finished high school, her mind was made up to become a lawyer and Dewitt supported her decision. He showed her anyway he could not knowing that the position he was in was enough fuel to propel Lisa forward.

She had access to all of Dewitt's money. She paid the lawyers and took care of him and anything he needed done. When Dewitt lost the trial, he received sixty years and Lisa was devastated. She was just about to turn twenty-one and she felt like her whole life was over.

Dewitt told her to take three hundred thousand dollars of the money and use what she needed to put herself through law school. She got into George Town University and was doing exceptionally well, but after her first year she experience tragedy back in Illinois, DeWitt was killed in Menard Correctional Center by some North Siders.

He was stabbed twenty-three times on the yard and died on the spot. When Dewitt died a part of Lisa died also, but his death was a martyr to her. She vowed to become the best criminal lawyer to ever fight a case so no other woman would ever go through what she had gone through.

She got the highest score on the bar exam in her class and was immediately picked up by a major law firm out of Chicago. Dewitt's aura was instilled in her mind and heart and that set the standard of the man she would always be attracted to. Anything less would never hold her interest. Dewitt taught her, 'Never go from sugar to shit, once you're ahead, never go backwards.'

Drug dealers didn't interest Lisa for the money. She had her own money and everything she wanted all her life, and now as a lawyer - she not only made real good money, but a real good statement as well. A statement that said she was her own person and whatever she wanted to do as a person, she could, and would do. And nobody could stop her.

Her three hundred and seventy-five thousand dollars paid for penthouse held, all white leather couches and love seats, which sat on plush white carpet. Six; forty thousand dollars oil painting hung on various walls, and she had a six foot long two hundred and fifty gallon fish tank built in her bedroom wall filled with exotic saltwater fish.

Her twelve foot long glass dining room table was the resting place for a ten thousand dollar crystal flower vase she kept white roses in. The oriental design on her dining room chairs matched the curtains in her living room and complimented the few pieces of oriental art positioned throughout the penthouse.

Flat screen TV's mounted the walls of both bedrooms and the living room. In her bedroom was a queen-size handcrafted cedar wood bed with oriental carvings and her name carved in Japanese along the top of the headboard. The dressers and end tables matched and her curtains did as well.

Her closet held over two hundred thousand dollars in clothes and shoes and her jewelry netted close to five hundred thousand dollars.

On an average, Lisa made forty-five to seventy thousand dollars for each case she accepted and some went close to a hundred sixty thousand, but she was the best and because of that she was also the most requested criminal lawyer in the State. So if you could afford her you were automatically her caliber of a man.

Never concerned with a client's money, because very few were doing as well as her, Lisa was strictly drawn to the life that came with the hustle. The streets, the guns, the drugs, the power, the women, and the gangsta mentality it took to not only survive in the game, but also excel above others. Anybody could become a drug dealer in her eyes, but only a few became true hustlas, and that's what attracted her - The true hustlas.

Lisa knew it took a different kind of nigga' to stand on top of a game that every shady, cut throat, and kill at will nigga' indulged in, and she found that those who did stand on top, all had the same mentality. And that mentality is what kept her hot, wet, and lusting for a part of the game.

She met Tuko when his brother got popped with twenty-six hundred pounds of cush. She saw the case in the paper and that same morning Tuko walked into her office with fifty thousand dollars cash and hired her on the spot.

During the course of Lisa winning his brother's case, Tuko and Lisa became involved. Over a period of time she grew to have feelings for him, but for Lisa those feelings never evolved to love.

The main reason was because she found out Tuko was in bed with Derrick Trumball. She was familiar with Derrick from the courtroom; he was a lead narcotics detective who also handled some homicides. She didn't know he was dirty until she became involved with Tuko, but it didn't surprise her, because Derrick came off not only to her, but almost everyone he dealt with as a certified gang chief.

Lisa was extremely disappointed to know Tuko worked for the police. It was a turn off to her. Her thing was the risk of the hustle, the excitement of the streets, the ability to out think not only the competition, but mainly the police.

So to her, Tuko was cheating. She didn't feel as though he deserved the street cred, and most definitely the dedicated loyalty she was willing to give a nigga' who was just doing his thing in the streets. By the time she found out, they had been messing with one another for two years and she had feelings for him, so she was just riding it out.

Two months after her revelation of Tuko and Derrick, she met Black at the Taste of Chicago. From the moment she saw Black she was reminded of Dewitt. His mannerism, his walk, hand gestures, the way he paid attention to everything while seeming as if he wasn't paying attention at all. His whole swagger was that of Dewitt as if they had the same spirit.

Latrice was with Black that day, so as Lisa examined Black from a distance, she also looked over Latrice. Latrice having developed a lot of Black's ways of being conscious of her surroundings at all times, picked Lisa off way before Black even noticed Lisa. Just being a woman helped it along because Latrice knew the difference between a casual look and a look of interest. So when her eyes met Lisa's, both women instinctively sized one another up.

As Black walked pass, he looked at Lisa and thought she was digging on Latrice, which was all good, because Latrice would make it happen if he showed the slightest interest in Lisa at all - But as they stepped off Latrice told him she popped Lisa off checking him out - So Black fell back and approached Lisa.

After twenty minutes of conversation, Lisa's thoughts were confirmed, it was official; Black was Dewitt in another life. She was already convinced but when she asked,

"Ain't your girl gon' get upset with you for spending all this time with me?"

And Black replied,

"Yeah she will, but she'll be cool if you decide to come home with us."

Lisa was struck with Dejavu and instantly it was 1998 again and she was standing ten feet from Dewitt's cream Park Avenue asking him that same question and remarkably she remembered the same exact answer had been given. She knew right then she was not only feeling Black, but more importantly, Black was her chance to have the life back with the man who was stripped from her.

Over the next few months she got confirmation after confirmation that Black was her man, the Dewitt who had been taken from her. She wasn't falling, she had fell, and fell extremely hard for him, which was cool; all except one thing, Latrice. She was fucking shit up for Lisa in her eyes. Latrice was to Black who Lisa had once been to Dewitt; his leading lady, and then some, because they were married with children.

Black, Latrice, and Lisa slept together twice and both times they fucked all night and laid up afterwards. It was nothing to Black and Latrice, but for Lisa laying in Blacks arms after being sexed so well, was all the comfort of the fairytale that had once been her life.

Eventually her womanly instincts kicked in and she began to convince herself she could get Black to stop fucking with Latrice. Her confidence in her sex game, plus her beauty was all she figured it would take.

Lisa thought she knew Black because in her mind she identified him as being Dewitt, and therefore knew everything about him, but what she found out was that Black wasn't Dewitt and he didn't really give a fuck who Dewitt was or who he had been to her.

Black felt the vibe of the emotional attachment Lisa was getting for him. Her attitude changed toward his relationship with Latrice; from there, he knew what was next.

Soon after that, Lisa got on some slick shit and Black blanked out on her ass hard. They were on the block in Black's truck and Lisa took her heels off, leaned against the passenger door and started rubbing his dick with her toes while saying.

"You know baby, you should to be doing so much better than this, and you could be easily. All you need is the right leading lady in your life."

For months she regretted those words because Black snapped.

"Look bitch! Let me tell you something right the fuck now. I don't know who the fuck you think you are, or who you got me fucked up with but you better understand real quick that I'm not that nigga' and you are not that bitch! I don't give a fuck what you have or how bad you think you are."

He shoved her foot away and her leg hit the console hard.

"I pop bitches off like you in my sleep and just like a dream slut, when I wake up, I forget about 'em."

Lisa's mind, and emotional state was scarred as she looked into Black's eyes and saw something she had somehow had missed; his loyalty to Latrice. Black was extremely protective of Latrice and she was finding out the hard way.

"No baby, I didn't mean it like that."

"Shut the fuck up bitch! You did mean it like that; you meant it just like that!" And Lisa knew she did too.

"And yo' ass lucky, because on the strength that we been fuckin' with each other for a minute, I'm not gone wrap my arms around your fuckin' neck."

"But what's gon' happen is this. From this point on you gon' miss me. If you happen to see me in traffic keep it the fuck moving. You better act like you got an allergic reaction to me and stay the fuck out my way. Now get the fuck out my truck before I smack the shit out your stupid ass."

Lisa couldn't believe what had just happened. She got out of Black's Expedition and got in her 2009 Benz CLS and cried all the way back to Oak Park. She felt so stupid, she would have never guessed that Black could be that much into Latrice from how he conducted himself in the streets, and from how open Latrice was with his sexual relationships, but she was wrong. Extremely wrong and the more she thought about it she felt even dumber. Because for the first time she realized that was exactly how Dewitt had been with her - So how could she have expected Black to be any different with Latrice?

Not only did he check her on the spot like a pimp checking one of his hoes, but he stopped fucking with her altogether. For three months he didn't call or return her calls. When he saw her in the streets, it was as if he didn't see her.

She couldn't believe she had messed up like she did, but she couldn't believe even more that he could just turn off like he did. She was shook. Tuko was nothing, she was drifting further and further away from him the more time she spent with Black anyway.

Then it came to her one morning, she woke up and realized how she could get back in grace with Black.

She called him from a new cell number. She was right in front of his house. Black had just bought a brand new 2009 black Yukon Denali and put 24' Dropstar Blades on it. She saw him in it the week before and now it was parked outside, so she knew he was home.

Black's cell phone rang and he picked right up. "Yeah." Lisa spoke as fast as she could without sounding unclear.

"Black, look before you hang up on me let me just say something to you."

"First of all, who the fuck is this?"

"It's Lisa, damn, you forgot my voice already?"

To her surprise, Black was cordial.

"Naw, I just got up, what's up?"

"Look, I'm parked outside in back of your truck; will you please come out and talk to me for a minute?" Lisa was being as sweet as she could without sounding as desperate as she really was.
Black looked out the window and Lisa waved.
"Aiight, here I come."
At this time Lisa was driving a white with burgundy interior Benz CLS 300 with black Giovanni 20" rims. She had on a red strapless Gucci dress with matching Gucci sandals, a one karat platinum band toe ring accessorized her freshly pedicured toes that were glistening with ruby red polish which complemented her one karat ruby studded earrings and her red snakeskin Gucci purse was sitting in her lap.

Her jet black hair was freshly pressed and feathered, her green eyes were shimmering behind the black onyx eyeliner, her lips looked like freshly picked dripping wet cherries sparkling in the sunlight, and for the first time in months, Lisa felt alive.

Her clit twitched at the first sight of Black. He came out wearing a pair of Tru Religion jeans with some all black air max , a white wife beater, white du-rag with a black white sox fitted cap to the back turned slightly to the right, with his diamond studded Jacob watch and diamond earrings.

Lisa watched him as he stood on his porch for a second, checking out the scene with his cell phone in his hand. His arms, chest, and shoulders seemed to bulge as she admired Black standing.
He trotted down the five steps of the porch, came to the car, and got in the passenger seat. When he sat down, Lisa's Miss Dior Cherie perfume filled his nostrils.
"What's up?" He said smiling.
Lisa turned and leaned back against her car door so she could look at her man. She missed looking into his deep dark eyes, at his dark milk chocolate skin, and thin nicely trimmed goatee. She took in the visual for a moment then said with pouting lips and eyes.
"I'm sorry."

"You said that before, so if you came all the way from the crib for that then baby girl you just wasted your gas."

"I know you're mad, but really Black, you gotta' believe me, I'm so sorry and it will never happen again. All I want is for you to be back in my life. I promise you, I know my boundaries and I will never cross them again. I'll play my part and never think I can play Latrice's ever."

Lisa's facial expression was one of wonder, anticipation, and nervousness as she fought to pick up any sign on Black's poker face, then he said.

"You look nice."

With those words the breath Lisa had been partially holding on to release along with the anxiety that had wrapped itself around her. Her nervousness subsided and she relaxed enough to be confident.

"I know I do, I meant to. I know red is your favorite color and look." Lisa lifted up her leg and dress.

"I'm not wearing any panties."

"Shit, when do you ever?"

Lisa flashed a cute but mannish smile and replied.

"Not even once."

Black grinned, "Well, probably once."

Lisa pushed him playfully on the shoulder.

"Boy you know I've worn panties more than once." Black laughed.

"So please baby will you forgive me." She repeated with the same injured doe eyes.

"Mommy just wants to spend some time with you."

Black looked at her, reached over, pulled her dress down around her titties, touched her right nipple, put her dress back in place and said, "Yeah man, we good."

Lisa's face and insides lit up. She felt brand new again. Smiling, she said. "Thank you, you don't know how much this means to me, but just to show you I brought you a little present."

She reached in the back seat and grabbed a black department store bag with Gucci written in gold letters across it and handed it to Black. She leaned back against the door and window biting on her bottom lip as she watched him go in it.

Black set the bag on the floor and moved the paper around so he could see to the bottom. When he did, he saw four keys of cocaine. He looked around unconsciously as his mind registered what was actually in the bag.

\ He grabbed one. It was wrapped and sealed with a roadrunner stamp on the front of it. He smelled it, and it smelled raw and strong even through the wrapper.

He looked at Lisa leaning against the window and she said. "I'm sorry baby; I hope those will help you out. I couldn't think of anything else to do."

Later on that night Black was nailing Lisa like never before. Afterwards she explained she got the keys from her man and he was super on, always had at least thirty keys at the house and more all over the north side.

Over the next year and a half, Black got a lot more information. He had been to the house when Tuko was out of town in Belize for a week. Lisa showed him where Tuko kept his cocaine and heroin while she hurried to change her clothes.

In an effort to impress him, she even mentioned to Black that he should hide his money in the walls like Tuko did, then she gestured with her head to the wall behind the headboard.

"It's three and a half million dollars behind that wall. I'm telling you this just so you will know that no amount of money he has means anything to me. I don't need him or his money; I'm only here because you're not available to me full-time."

Black thought about telling her to get that shit and they would be up, but he knew that would cause too much shit. This nigga' would be at her, and he knew he wasn't ever gonna' stop fuckin' with Latrice and the whole thing would be more of a headache than he wanted to deal with, but he also knew he had to have that shit, so it was on for real now. It was just a matter of getting it all at once.

Lisa told Black everything except that Tuko was working with Derrick Trumball and Black took it all in as if it was nothing. Two days before, Lisa sat in Rolling Meadows court house on the bench thinking about Tuko; she told Black about the fifty keys of cocaine and thirty keys of heroin, and now Tuko was dead.

Not one time did Black cross her mind though. Lisa knew Tuko and his brother dealt with a lot of people and any of them could have been the one to come in. Even some of the people closest to him.

It finally dawned on her how lucky she was, because if she didn't have trial court she more than likely would have been there last night, but it just so happened that she didn't want to make the hour and a half drive early in the morning, so she left from her house at 10:00 p.m. and instead of going to Tuko's, she went to her parents.

The case she was fighting had saved her life. She thought about that and said, "Thank you Jesus."

CHAPTER 4

April 3, 3:48 a.m.

Black pulled in the parking lot of 714 Burling and turned his lights off. Reaching under his seat, he pulled a chrome hair trigger .40 cal, sat it on the passenger seat, then looked up at the sixteen story white project building in Cabrini Greens and scanned the area.

No one was out but cluckers and the niggaz under the building working. He reached in the backseat, grabbed another black duffle bag, and stuffed the plastic bag of money he came out the house with in it, put it next to the .40 cal, grabbed his Glock 17 from his waistline, and waited.

Under the building, four niggaz watched the Chevelle waiting to see who got out. After a minute one of the youngins' said. "Who the fuck is that?"

"I don't know G'. I've never seen the car before."

"You think they're on bullshit?"

"I don't know, but if they want it."

C.G reached into his waistline and pulled out his nine,

"They can get it."

Nip pulled his pipe as Black Boy was saying.

"Niggaz ain't crazy fam, you can believe that."

"Right, right." C.G replied.

They looked for another minute then C.G. and Black Boy faded back near the stairwell where two chairs sat in front of apartments 107 and 108. Black Boy reached in the pocket of his Polo Jeans and handed C.G. a lighter.   C.G. ran the flame back and forth across the back wood until it was dry.

"Aye Nip?"

"What up?"

"You wanna' hit the blunt?"

"Yeah."

Nip holds out his hand as he stares out the gate to the parking lot. Black Boy turns to C.G.

"Look at this muthafucka." C.G. laughs and Black Boy yells to Nip.

"Nigga' you better come get this muthafucka if you want it, because yo rock smokin' ass baby mama upstairs."

"Come on G' bring it here, I'm watchin' these niggaz in this car."

"Them niggaz still out there."

"Yeah on bro them and nobody got out either."

C.G. and Black Boy walk to the middle of the gate.

"Man, they not on shit. A nigga' probably just getting' knocked down."

Just then a tall light-skinned slim dude with bulging eyes comes around the corner wearing a pair of old scuffed up green air force ones, some dirty blue jeans, and a white T-shirt that said 'Get Rich or Die Trying' on the front with a picture of 50 cent on it.

"Y'all workin'?"

"Yeah Daddy-O, What's good?"

"Can I get seven for sixty-five?"

"Yeah, come on with it."

He handed C.G. the money and Black Boy hollered.

"Comin' at you seven times Chris."

"Gon' upstairs Pops." The clucker sped off.

C.G. looked at him, chuckled and said,

"Slow down Pops." Then resumed his conversation.

Upstairs on the third floor, Nikki Page lit her crack pipe next to the incinerator. The smell of piss and garbage was strong, but Nikki didn't notice it at all as she held her lighter to the end of her glass pipe and listened to the sizzle of the rock melting into smoke through the brillo. She watched as the smoke slowly drifted down the tube and entered her mouth.

After holding the smoke for a few seconds she blew out a cloud that filled the air. Momentarily dazed as the effects of the crack ran through her, Nikki stood there stuck, unable to move.

A second later she stepped back onto the porch, eyes bucked out, clutching her pipe in one hand and her lighter in the other as she watched a black van pull up and park behind another car and turn off its lights.

"Who the fuck is that?" Black Boy exclaimed.
"I don't know. Lil Chris, take it up to the five!" C.G. hollered.
Without a response, Lil Chris who had over five hundred crack rocks in a clear plastic baggie, shot upstairs.
Black got out of the car and walked toward the van. As he was walking C.G. Nip, and Black Boy saw the D.E.A. letters across the back of his jacket.
"That's them people!"
All three shot upstairs yellin'.
"Heads up!"
"Here they come!" Lil Chris shot up more stairs.

"Everything all good?" Black asked as Twin stepped out the van.
"Yeah." Black walked to the back of the Chevelle and popped the trunk.
"So them niggaz made it to the truck?"
"Yeah, they should be pullin' up in a minute."
Black pulled out two gas cans. He handed one to Twin.
"Hit the van and make sure you get everywhere, all in the front, and the whole back."
"Okay." Twin replied.
Twin walked around, opened the sliding door of the van, hopped in, and started dousing the front with gas.
On the third floor Nikki Page took another hit off her pipe as she watched Black and Twin. Black put the Glock 17 in the front of his waistline, walked around, opened all the doors of the car, grabbed the duffle bag, set it a safe distance away, put the .40 cal. in his back waistline, and started wettin' down the Chevelle. When he was done he threw the gas can on the backseat and walked to the van.
"Bro you almost done ?"

"Yeah, just about."

Twin stopped pouring and looked at Black with a smile.

"Damn homie we on for real, it's no turnin' back from here, I'm finna' get right."

Just then Shy pulled up along the street in a dark blue four door Tahoe. Black looked over and saw him.

"You get the whole van?" Twin was just turning over the gas can.

"That's good and look, check it out."

Twin looked at him smiling.

"This what's up, I appreciate you driving and that's on the real, but man playboy, I got some bad news."

Twin's smile faded. "Some bad news, what you mean?"

Black reached around his back, pulled the .40 cal. and said.

"Just what I said pussy; bad news. You staying here."

"Wha..."

Black pulled the trigger and it sounded like a bomb went off in the Greens as the explosive sound echoed throughout the building and the back courts. The slug hit Twin in the chest and went through him and the van. Twin's body was blown back; he slammed against the inside of the van and rocked it a little. Black stepped up, hit him again in the stomach, and then dropped the gun in the puddle of gas.

Looking over his shoulder, Black pulled out a match book, lit one, stepped back, threw the match and instantly the van went up in flames. He stepped to the Chevelle, did the same, and grabbed the duffle bag, trotted to the Tahoe, jumped in and Shy pulled off. They hit it down Burling to Halsted, turned off, and headed toward Chicago Avenue.

"You got some blood on you." Shy said. Black looked down at himself

"Where?"

"Right there on your hand." Black wiped it on his pants as he glanced at the clock, it was 4:03 a.m.

"Was everything there?"

"Hell yeah cuzo, everything was there."

"So we good then?"

"Fo sho'." Dee said.

"Damn what happened to Twin?" Solid asked.

Without turning around Black nonchalantly said.

"Don't worry about that; just know he got what he had comin'."

"Got what he had comin'? Oh that's how you getting' down huh?"

As soon as the words came out Solid's mouth, Shy shook his head and thought 'What the fuck that nigga' say that for?' as he glanced over at Black. Black turned and looked at Solid with piercing eyes and said.

"What the fuck you mean, that's how I'm getting' down?"

"Man, I'm just sayin', dude rode wit' us and it just seem like you pulled it on him."

"Like I pulled it on' em?" Black said with a frown.

"Solid, leave that shit alone." Shy interjected as he sat up in his seat looking in the rearview mirror to make eye contact with his guy.

Black waved his hand at Shy while still looking at Solid.

"Fuck that! I wanna' know what this bitch ass nigga' mean. What the fuck you mean nigga'?"

Black said aggressively while staring into Solid's eyes.

No one in the truck said a word, Flinno, Dee, and Moe all looked at Solid, and Solid was looking at Black, suddenly feeling out of place.

"Naw, I was just...you know... I was just...saying..." A nervous ball of fear was mounting in his stomach, and like a little kid who was caught on the spot, he didn't know what to say.

"You was just what nigga'?!"

The look on Black's face was something Solid had never seen before and without question it scared the shit out of him.

"Man for real bro, I don't know what the fuck I was on. I was just trippin' my bad."

Black kept his eyes locked on him for a couple more seconds and then shook his head.

"Fuck around and give me a bad vibe about your ass if you want to and you gon' find out real muthafucka fast what happened to Twin."

"He cool Black", Shy said, then looked in the rearview mirror...

"Ain't that right nigga'?"

"For real I'm cool, so, so very cool. I'm so muthafuckin cool back here. I'ma' fuck around and spit out a fuckin' ice cube. Straight up, that's how cool I am. Man, you don't gotta' say that shit but one time playa'."

Flinno looked over at him and started laughing.

"Aiight, damn nigga'! We get it, you ca-ca-ca-cool! Wit' yo sca-sca-sca-scared ass."

Moe began laughing so hard tears graced his eyes. He then playfully touched Solid's chest to see how cool he really was.

Solid slapped his hand. "Get yo muthafuckin hand off me vic!"

Moe laughed harder.

"Oh, but you ah Gangsta' wit' me though right?"

Black turned around as Shy was saying. "Y'all niggaz cool the fuck out back there." He looked at Black and put his fist out, Black dapped him and Shy said.

"You good?"

"Yeah man I'm good." Black replied.

"You know you my nigga' right?" Shy went on.

"Fo sho'."

"Until this bitch bust right?"

"No doubt."

Shy then nodded his head as he said,

"Don't let that shit throw you off." Black looked out the window as Shy went on.

"I gotta' give it to you. You put that shit together and straight up, everything fell right into place too."

"Not everything."

"What you mean?"

Black turned to him,

"Baby girl."

Shy leaned back against the door and window then nodded.

"Right, right."

"Well the way I see it, you probably just didn't think that through good enough in the first place; because on the real, you may fuck around and need her."

Black let out a sigh.

"Yeah I been thinking about that, but fuck it, I can't do shit about it right now anyway.

"Heads up playboy, here I go right here."

Shy slowed down and stopped at a midnight blue 2009 Chrysler 300c with 22" Savini rims.

"Now look man, go straight to the spot. Hop on the E-way, don't get on the phone, do the speed limit, wear your seatbelt, and don't move until I get there."

"B, why the fuck is you talkin' to me like I'm some type of shorty who don't know what the fuck he doin'. Remember, I'm the one who ain't ever been to jail before, and it's a reason behind that."

He pointed at Black. "You be careful."

Black looked at him with a smile.

"I love you nigga'. Aye cuz, hop in the front."

Flinno got out, shook his cousin's hand, hopped in the front seat, and Shy pulled off.

Black opened the door of the 300c, tossed the bag on the passenger seat, got in, started the car, pulled out a cell phone, touched the screen a couple times and scrolled to save numbers. There was one, it read, 'Hit'.

He pressed the send, on the second ring someone picked up but didn't say anything. Black said four words.

"I'm on my way."

The other line hung up. Black got out the car, smashed the cell phone on the ground, got back in and pulled off.

CHAPTER 5

April 3, 2012 6:05 a.m.

Derrick Trumball ran his finger over his nicely trimmed goatee and stepped back in the house on Sunnyside not believing the mess he had to deal with. The light brown skinned, six foot one, two hundred and eleven pound, well built, thirty-six year old head detective for the Rogers Park police district was hot and wanted some answers. Derrick had been a detective for fourteen years, recruited right out of the academy with high expectations of undercover work. He was that new breed of officer, so to speak; young, street-smart, knowledgeable of gangs, and relaxed amongst the criminal element.

His first two years on the force resulted in seven large-scale drug seizures, sixty-five arrests, and the apprehension of hundreds of automatic handguns and assault rifles. The next four years of his career was spent moving up the ranks in the department, but in his seventh year, things changed in Derrick. His perspective on the war on drugs shifted and suddenly he developed a different outlook and ideology for his retirement plan.

He had the streets locked, niggaz talked to him, and he could get at all the gang chiefs. So starting with ten keys of cocaine and two keys of heroin, Derrick began securing his future. Soon every major drug dealer and gang chief from Chicago Avenue to Evanston was in his pocket.

It was ideal, because after all, Derrick had tactical command in seven out of every ten major drug seizures in his district. So with each one, he made sure he got his off top. And no sooner did he get it, it was in the streets. He kept his ear open and feet in motion and niggaz knew it was a whole lot easier to just fuck with him, than it was to go against him.

Yeah, some niggaz got on that 'I ain't fuckin' wit' the police' shit, and those same niggaz became examples. Their joints got raided and they ended up with the type of time that it takes seeds to grow into full grown trees. And then there were those couple times when Derrick put that bread on a few heads, and like clockwork the streets cashed that shit in.

See, Derrick had that more than throwback dough, he had that old school colonial cash, and like with all things, money made shit happen. Niggaz didn't try him because he kept the big hats well supplied with the best dope, guns, and information from city to federal investigations. He took care of his guys. They ate good, their team ate good, and the police in their area didn't harass them much unless a war broke out and bodies started piling up. When that happened, everybody understood, somebody had to go down. But still, Derrick made sure it was never any of his guys - So niggaz pretty much stayed loyal to him.

Tuko was one of his guys, in fact, one of his major figures and he wanted to know who killed him. But not just for the sake of catching his killer. Nope, Derrick wanted to know who had his dope. Somebody walked out of Tuko's house with close to seven million dollar's worth of his work and bullshit ain't nothing, he had to have that back. So when he pulled onto Sunnyside, he had his eyes and ears open.

Blue and White police cars, ambulances, detective cars, plain clothes and uniformed officers flooded the scene. Bystanders and gawkers watched intently at the early morning action that brought about yellow tape.

Derrick grabbed his cell phone and pressed send, his partner answered.

"Where are you?"

"Out front." Derrick replied.

"I'm on my way."

Michael Mann's had been Derrick's partner for seven years and his friend even longer. He was just as filthy as Derrick, only he didn't have the street savvy to deal with the niggas - so he just made sure all the dope got seized and their tracks stayed covered.

As Derrick was walking up the front porch Micheal saw him.

"What's up?" Derrick asked.

"Not much at all."

"What it look like in the inside?"

"Bad, real bad. Whoever it was made sure everyone was dead. Everyone got shots to their faces, back of the heads and body. It's like they were making a statement."

"For who - us or them?"

"Who knows, this one is hard to call."

"That bad huh?"

Michael shook his head and replied.

"Man it's so many holes in their heads, literally their brains are leaking out of the skulls. Two of the victim's skulls are cracked in pieces, and nobody is identifiable by face. They're gonna' print 'em all, but we know who they are. The female in Tuko's brother's room, I don't think is Belizean, maybe Hispanic."

"Maybe she put this little caper together and ended up with the short end of the stick."

"I don't know." Mike said as he paused to let some officers pass by.

"Everybody got it with mini 14's, all throw away's recovered at the scene. We're gonna check 'em against other murders, attempts, or random shootings that casings were recovered from. Whoever it was knew what they were here for and where to find it."

"What makes you say that?" Derrick asked as he continued to survey the crowd that formed behind the yellow tape.

"One witness."

"Who?"

"A lady getting ready for work lives about three or four houses down; said she saw a black, blue, dark red, or green colored van and a four door car with rims on it. Said they pulled up, but when the guys in the car got out and got in the van she thought it was strange, maybe a drug deal-so she watched."

"Thank God for nosey women." Derrick commented with a smile.

"Right, in any case, she said they were in the van for two or three minutes and then five or six guys got out and ran to the door with duffle bags. She said one of them had a jacket on that she thought said D.E.A."

"D.E.A. huh." Derrick smirked.

"Yeah, same thing I said. So anyways, she said they ran in the house and she saw what looked like gun fire lighting up through the window, but wasn't sure because she didn't hear anything."

"Silencers."

"Right. So she watched and about two minutes later they all ran out with the same duffle bags, all of' em but one got in the van, the one guy gets in the four door and they ride off. They rode pass her house but she still couldn't get a color or make on the vehicles. The only thing I'm confused about is upstairs in Tuko's room."

"Why?"

"Because the walls are all kicked in. What were they looking for?" Michael asked curiously.

Derrick stood there taking everything in his partner said and then walked inside the house. He looked at the scene and shook his head. Blood and bullet casings were everywhere like it was a fallout at a terrorist convention.

Derrick had to give it to whoever it was, especially for the thoroughness in making sure there were no witnesses. Police techs and crime scene investigators carefully gathered anything that could remotely be considered as evidence, but Derrick knew there was none to be found and he also knew something else they didn't know. He knew, fifty keys of cocaine and thirty keys of heroin walked out with whoever murdered everybody in this house, and that was what he was concerned about and that would be his ace in the hole. Because whoever it was would try to get it off and no matter where in the city it surfaced he would know and then, surprise niggaz, the police.

Derrick laughed to himself and then that faded, because whoever it was had balls and he wondered how come he never met these soon-to-be-dead pros, or had he. Every nigga' he knew was finna' be put on alert.

He stepped out on the front porch and looked at the crowd. One by one he examined each face, searching for any type of sign or look of satisfaction. Because inside of him he knew that somebody out there knew what happened. So he wanted to spot the face, the eyes, the mannerism, because when he did, it was on.

"Yeah niggaz...You got away - for now. But the horse that shit's fast doesn't shit long. You can run, but you can't hide and when I find you, I'ma' touch yo ass in such a way, you gon' wish you never knew what dope was, and that's a promise...Yeah niggaz, that's a promise."

Derrick stepped back in the house...

CHAPTER 6

April 3, 2012 4:23 a.m.

Fire trucks were pulling up in front of 714 Burling in response to two burning vehicles. Once the vehicles were extinguished the charred remains of a body was discovered in the burning van.

The fire department notified the police at the Larrabee and Division station that a homicide was associated with the burning vehicles and ten minutes later the Cabrini Greens project building was infested with police and squad cars.

Homicide detectives Frank Pateel and Donathan Gates were in charge of the crime scene.

The gun shots that echoed through the projects brought many residents out of their apartment onto the gated porches where they stood captivated by the burning vehicles until the fire trucks and police arrived and gave them something else to look at.

By the time the police arrived, people were standing around by the dozens spectating. Residents had come from other buildings in the Cabrini Greens development and a number of people had moved from their porches to the entrance and parking lot.

Officer Kenneth Bateman secured the area of the vehicles with yellow tape, officially making it a crime scene.

Frank Pateel and Donathan Gates looked into the van at the charred body still clutching the gas can. The interior of both vehicles were burned completely down to the metal frames and springs in the seats. Soot and ashes stained the windows of both vehicles and settled in the water used to extinguish the flames.

"So what do you think Frank, drug deal went bad?"
"I don't know, but I don't think so."
"Why's that?"
Frank Pateel looked a little further in the van.

"Whoever this guy was is still holding the gas can which means he probably wet the van down. There had to be at least two people because he didn't shoot himself. So I figure drugs were involved, but not a drug deal - something different"

They walked from the van to the Chevelle and looked in.

"Another gas can. So maybe the other guy hit this car and then hit our vic."

"Then what?" Donathan questioned.

"He ran off?"

"Not likely." Frank answered and went on.

"I'm guessing there had to be another person involved."

"Another driver?"

"Yeah."

They walked back to the van.

"Check this out Frank."

As the water drained from the van through the side door and the hole in the bottom of the van that was made when Black stepped in and shot Twin a second time sending another bullet directly through him and the van, the .40 cal. appeared from underneath the blackened water.

"So much for chasing down a gun huh?"

"Yeah, you know what it is Donnie?"

Donathan bent down to get a good look at it.

"A .40 cal."

Frank called one of the uniformed officers over.

"Bag that firearm."

"Yes sir."

"And start interviewing everybody in the crowd. Somebody saw something because these buildings never sleep."

"We've already started interviewing. Myself and four other officers."

"You come up with anything yet?"

"Not yet, at least not from me. Pretty much everyone claims they heard the shots, woke up, looked out of windows, or stepped out on porches and saw the fire."

"Keep asking. This is a twenty-four hour dope spot, somebody was out."

"Okay sir."

True enough the 714 Burling building was a twenty-four hour rocks and blows spot, but even if someone had something to say they wouldn't be doing it right then. Never in a million years; especially when the murder didn't involve anyone in the Greens. Nobody's son, man, uncle, cousin, friend, or father had been shot - so nobody had a reason that concerned them enough to step up with anything.

Information was precious on the streets, especially information about murders. Given the right circumstances, that information could be used to barter someone out of a tight spot. So if someone did know something, the information wouldn't be passed along to the police right then. Maybe to a friend, who would tell someone else, who would tell someone else, until finally the information had been added and taken away from to the point that it wasn't what it was to begin with anyway.

Then somewhere along the line someone might get caught with some dope or guns, be facing a parole violation, or just not ready to go to Cook County jail. So in an effort to save their own ass the faithful words that make every Chicago detectives ears sound off would be said.

"I know about a murder."

To close a murder investigation, almost anything is negotiable. So information would be held onto until a circumstance like that occurred. Either that or a shady detective would put the murder on someone and force their hand or deal with the alternative, which was taking the case. And niggaz ain't trying to do fifty days for a nigga' let alone fifty years. So of course niggaz get real long winded in their coversation...

Frank Pateel and his partner stood in front of the van thinking of scenarios. Frank walked to the back of the van, looked at the plates and ran them through to the dispatcher, then did the same thing with the Chevelle.

"It's a long shot, but I just ran the plates."

"Yeah, longer than a long shot." Donathan answered.

"Okay, let's see what's up shall we." Frank said and began.

"Okay, this guy has a hole through his chest and one through his stomach. A .40 cal. at close range will definitely do that, but this is Cabrini Greens and I doubt they would have risked so much heat coming to the building by blowin' a couple holes through a guy and burning his body up. They know how hard we're gonna' sweat the area, and they're making too much money to have us around here anymore than we already are."

"So they're not from the area?"

"That's what I'm thinking Donnie boy."

"Well if that's the case then check this out. Let's say it's not a drug deal, but a drug or money heist."

"Or maybe not drugs, but jewelry or other large sums of money."

"Yeah, I had'nt thought of that."

Frank Pateel called another officer over.

"I want a city-wide check on any and all jewelry stores being robbed, homes that were reported to have large sums of cash, banks, currency exchanges, armor trucks, anything where large amounts of money was involved and get it back to me."

"Okay sir."

"Alright go ahead." Frank said.

"Where was I?"

"Some kinda' heist."

"Oh yeah, let's say these guys hit whoever and then head here to ditch and blaze the vehicles. While they're here one of the guys gets greedy."

"Or already had planned to take the other guy out."

"That too, whatever the case, they come here, soak the vehicles and our char-broiled friend here gets the short end of the stick."

"Or the long end of the barrel." Frank added with a hint of humor.

"Right. The other guy has another ride and they ride off into the sunset."

"The sunrise Donnie boy,"

Frank taps his watch.

"Its 5:05 in the morning."

"Okay the sunrise. You're such a shit for details."

"Yeah and one of those details is this."

Donathan looked at his partner and Frank said.

"Where the fuck are they watching the sunrise at?"

"That's why we get the big bucks Frankie baby, to figure that type of shit out."

"Big Bucks! Shit, who the fuck is giving you your check? It can't be from the same city."

"Oh but it is Franky, the good ole Windy City Chi-Town, my kind of town where there's seven murders for every one officer and more guns on the street than stop signs."

"Hey, you ever stop to think how these assholes get all these fuckin' guns?"

"Yeah, all the time."

"Enlighten me."

"It's easy, the same place they get all the dope from."

Frank rolled his hand over as a gesture to say 'spit it out.'

"The government." Donathan says as if he had unraveled a true conspiracy theory.

"Noooo shit. That explains it all."

Donathan laughed and added.

"No I'm serious. Man, don't you know they recovered some rocket launchers and hand grenades out south. What the fuck do gang bangers need with rocket launchers?"

"Or hand grenades?"

Frank and Donathan walked away from the van as Crime Scene Investigators took over.

The detectives stepped under the yellow tape and walked to the entrance of the project building. Frank saw officer Bateman.

"So how we doing?"

"Almost the same."

"Almost?"

"Yeah, almost, I have one person who says she saw the car pull up first, then the van. The guy in the car gets out with a D.E.A. jacket on. He then opens his trunk as he's talking to the guy in the van. A minute later she hears a gunshot and a second or two after that, she hears another one and runs inside her house. She doesn't know exactly how the fire got started."

"Fuck that sounds pretty damn good."

"Yeah, I would have thought so too, but the lady looks like she's been up for two weeks straight smokin' crack. When I walked up on her she looked like she had just taken a blast into outer space."

"Where you find her at?"

"Third floor, back by the incinerator I was walking up, she was walking out, eyes wide as owls and could barely talk."

"Fuck! I hate it when our only witnesses are crack heads. You get her name and apartment number?"

"Yeah, it's Nikki Page, apartment 304, but like I said she's higher than a kite, so even if what she said is true, what good could she be as a serious witness?"

"Let me get the information anyway, just in case."

Kenneth Bateman tore off the piece of paper from his notebook and handed it to Frank.

"Aye Frank."

"Yeah."

"I just got the make on those plates back. The van comes back to a Dolly Madison truck, the Cevelle plates are to a '83 station wagon out of Peoria."

"Well like we said, a long shot."

Frank and Donathan assisted with interviews over the next hour and came up with nothing. After running into continuous dead ends." Donathan said.

"Why don't you get Trumball down here, he usually does pretty good with this area?"

"You're right."

Frank pulled out his cell phone and dialed. Derrick Trumball picked up on the second ring.

"Trumball."

"Derrick, this is Frank from the 1-8."

"What's going on?" Derrick asked.

"Same shit that's always going on in Chicago, dead bodies."

"Tell me about it, I got six over here, a whole house full of Belizeans done up pretty good. All multiple shots to the face. Only witness says she thinks she saw one person out of five or six wearing a D.E.A. jacket, but she's sure they were in a van and a four door with rims."

"Best thing I've heard all morning."
"Why's that?"
"I got a burnt up van and four door at 714 Burling. One witness says a guy had a D.E.A. jacket on. We have one vic bar-b-cued with two .40 cal. slugs right through him. Only problem, no one's talking."

"I'm on my way."

CHAPTER 7

April 3, 2012 5:55 a.m.

The Goodyear tires on the rims of Black's 300C rolled onto a cobblestone driveway in west suburban Barrington Hills. He touched the volume button and Twista's Kamikaze lyrics faded to near silence as he rolled up the forty-yard driveway. Off to his left stood a tan cobblestone house built with two tone light and dark shades, and although the well-manicured bushes that lined the front of the house, nicely trimmed deep green grass, weeping willow trees, multicolored crystal chipped landscaping rocks with mulch worked in and around them were appealing to the eye, Black had no desire for it all.

His only desire was the business, and the business didn't consist of checking out the old man's house, it only consisted of dropping the dough that would be needed to secure his ass. As he rolled up, the third door on the far right of the three car garage opened. Black drove in and the garage door closed behind him. Black had only met the old man five times. Two dinning occasions; one lunch, one dinner, once at Chicago's Antiques, and the other two times were right here in the garage of the old man's home.

Both times Black was there he couldn't help thinking how no one could ever imagine such high levels of illegal business was taking place in such a well-kept community.

It kinda' pissed him off, but at the same time made him laugh, just to know how the police sweated the blocks in the inner city, when the true crimes were taking place far from the city. But now wasn't the time to dwell on that. There had been much talk about today, now it was here - And that's all that mattered to him.

The garage had no cars in it, instead, it housed surveillance screens that monitored every section of the house and driveway, a computer, fax machine, phone, a modest Sony 30" TV, a black leather sofa, glass coffee table, two work desks with rolling comfortable cushioned chairs, a four foot tan file cabinet, refrigerator, microwave and at least five handguns that were easy to get to no matter where the old man was in the garage.

Black sat patiently. He was in an area that was sectioned off from the "business office" as the old man often referred to it as. Finally, Black got out the 300C, duffle bag in hand, and walked through the door connecting the two rooms.

The old man sat in one of the blue swivel chairs with his Burberry slippers and pajamas on, remote control in his hand watching CNN.

"This goddamn world is going to hell in a hand basket."

He said without looking away from the coverage on ISIS.

"Don't these assholes know they aren't going to win this shit? It's a goddamn holy war and Israel is God's chosen people."

"Hey, you can't stop prophecy." Black commented.

"Huh." The old man said, still not looking away from the TV.

"Prophecy, all this was prophesized to happen in the bible. Check out the book of Daniel."

Black sat down in the other swivel chair and put the duffle bag down in front of the old man. The old man looked good for sixty-five. He always had a nice tan as if he flew to Florida weekly. His blue eyes were as good as they were when he was thirty, his hair was gray, but he always made the comment that it was a crown of wisdom and his sharp mind was evidence of the truth in his words. This is what Black admired.

"How's Latrice?" The old man asked.

"She's doing good, real good."

"Did she take my advice on the investment tip I gave her?"

"The agricultural one or the Home Depots?"

"The agricultural."

"I heard her talking to someone on the phone about it, but we haven't discussed the outcome yet."

"Oh, it'll turn out fine; I can truthfully say I've never made a bad investment."

"Yeah, I can believe it. Latrice respects your advice a lot."

"That's good, she should, Latrice is a fine woman, her father and I were friends for over forty years. He was my closest business partner before he died. He was a low tolerance for bullshit type of guy and I always respected that in him, I respect that in any man."

John McKay acknowledge as he looked at Black with eyes that said 'I'm exactly the same.' Black understood completely.

"I was at the wedding when Curtis and Margaret got married, at the hospital when Latrice was born, and at the funeral when Curtis died. Latrice is like my daughter and Margaret is like my sister. That's why I know Latrice really loves you. A father knows these things, and over these last four years I've grown to understand why. You take care of your business Darren, and as long as you continue to take care of your business you and I will continue to be on the up and up, but just understand, bullshit breeds bullshit – You know what I mean?"

Black looked at the old man like he was his own father passing wisdom down to him and answered. "Yeah, I know what you mean."

"Good. Now, I'm assuming you have something for me?"

"Yeah it's right here."

Black pointed to the duffle bag. "We have to count it out, but it's more than enough."

"I don't have to count out anything." John said as he nonchalantly flicked through the channels.

"Right, what I meant to say is, I gotta' count it out."

The old man nodded and Black grabbed, unzipped the duffle bag, tore through the plastic and started counting the twenties, fifties, and hundred dollar bills until he reached three hundred thousand dollars. When he was done he had thirty stacks with ten thousand dollars in each stacked line neatly on a mahogany desk.

With more than four hundred thousand dollars left in the bag, Black felt good to have taken care of his business. He zipped the duffle bag back up and rolled his chair next to the old man who was still watching CNN.

"It's no way in the world I'd be over there fighting in that shit."

The old man's words were bitter and distasteful. He turned the TV off, got up, walked to the file cabinet, grabbed six manila envelopes and handed them to Black.

"I will never have to worry about Latrice, Lil Darren, and Tamar, but business is business and I like the fact that you even thought this far ahead concerning your security."

"Actually Latrice did."

"Well I can understand. Now, you do know that the moment you drive away from this house nothing can stop this other than the designated kill switch?"

"Yeah, I know."

"So you're sure this is what you want to do?"

"It gotta' be like this because this is just the beginning and by the time I get to where I want to be, one thing will be for certain."

"Yeah, what's that?"

"That the world would never have imagined that a nigga like me existed."

"Ambition, that's good, that's actually the first thing I noticed about you."

"Thanks."

"But listen Darren; always remember slow and steady wins the race. You rush, you get anxious - You get sloppy, you make mistakes. Ambition is nothing without wisdom, wisdom comes with understanding and you will never learn to understand without patience."

The old man tapped his temple with his index finger.

"Use this, the more you use this - the less you have to use this." He reached under his right thigh and pulled out a .38 automatic with a pearl handle.

"If you use your mind, you'll almost always find a way to eliminate the problem without using these. Slow and Steady. Anticipate the problem before hand, so you can eliminate it before it becomes a problem. The more problems you anticipate, the less you'll have. So remember always use your mind. From what I know of you, you're a good thinker and Latrice is a special breed so I'm confident you'll reach your goal."

Black sat there listening carefully, soaking up the old man's words like sponge.

"But always remember, not everyone is a thinker. A lot of guys believe they are, but they're not. Yeah sure, they think, but not about the right things. Their mind is clouded with useless thoughts. They'd rather visualize themselves being on top of the block instead of on top of the world. That block mentality keeps them on the block; they limit themselves because they can't see pass cars, jewelry, and women. So instead of learning from the mistakes that their so-called chiefs made, they make those same mistakes. They don't know how to listen; they only know how to hear, so therefore they don't learn. You learn from listening not hearing."

Black nodded, fully understanding the difference in the two. The old man went on.

"Because they don't learn, they never grasp the understanding of leadership - which is simple; every great leader was once a great follower who knew the importance of paying attention to his leader's mistakes.

The old man shook his head. "You know what one of the biggest problems is Darren?"

"No, what's that?"

"Too many chiefs, not enough Indians. Everybody wants to be the shot-caller. Darren, you make sure that everyone you deal with knows who the chief is and that all the Indians know their role, even the squaws."

Black nodded again while the old man's words seeped into his heart and soul. As he did, the realization of what was not only taking place, but what would also take place in the future set in on him. He was ready. And all he knew was those who weren't had better get ready, because it was on. He was rising to the top and he wasn't playing no games with nobody; including the niggaz he was fuckin' with.

"Now as far as the farmhouse is concerned." The old man went on.

"It's secure, Latrice and I have been out there and she knows how to operate all the surveillance and she's aware of every entrance in and every exit out."

"Yeah, me, her, and Shy took a couple trips down there. It's good, it's perfect."

"Well." The old man stood up and held out his hand. Black stood up, put his hand in the old man's hand and John said.

"Good luck."

"Thanks."

"Tell Latrice to call me in a few weeks, I might have another investment for her."

"No problem."

Black grabbed the duffle bag and envelopes, walked to the car, got in, the garage door opened and he backed out the cobblestone driveway.

Black knew he had just made a series of moves from 3:15 a.m. to now, which was 7:41 a.m. that no nigga' he knew of had ever made. He saw his Gangsta' shining like the north star in the blackest night, set apart from every star in the sky. It was symbolic for him, because he knew he was not only born to shine, but to outshine all others.

This was just the beginning and when it was over everyone would say 'No one ever laid it down like him.' He felt good. And then he remembered the old man's words and like music to his ears.

"Slow and Steady " circulated through his mind in a way that he would never forget.

He pressed the disc changer as he backed out to the street, put the car in drive and

drove off as Kanye West spoke to him.
   "Drive slow homie - Drive slow."

CHAPTER 8

April 3, 2012 6:35 a.m.

Derrick Trumball was pulling into Cabrini Greens. The fire trucks were gone, but police cars and unmarked detective cars still had the area flooded. He stepped out of his blue Caprice with a toothpick in his mouth, Chicago White Sox fitted cap on, and his badge hanging from a platinum chain around his neck. His black short sleeve T-shirt hugged his upper body and arms as he strolled over to Frank Pateel and Donathan Gates. While he walked he thought to himself, 'Yeah muthafuckas I'm here, and somebody gon' tell me something.'

He walked with fearless confidence like he had been raised in those projects. He knew almost every face out there and without a doubt every face knew him.

"What's up Frank?"

"Derrick, how's it going?"

"You tell me?"

"If I had something to tell you I would."

"Well just let me know what you don't know then."

"That's easy, nothing. I don't know shit."

As they talked, they walked over to the van. While walking Derrick examined the face of every person he passed looking for that small hint of secrecy that may lay behind their eyes.

They ducked under the yellow tape, splashed through the puddles of blackened water, walked up to the sliding door of the van and checked out the seared remains of Twin.

"Well meet our vic, formally known as Bar-B-Boy."

"No shit and well done at that. Has C.S.I. been here?"

"Yup, not much to gather though, anything that could have been something went up in flames. So basically we're hoping dentals can ID this guy, and then that he has record so we can sweat the area where he lives and try to find out who he runs with because whoever he was with crossed him."

As Frank talked, Derrick looked in the van and at the Chevelle.

"So I figure, if it was a big enough deal, heist, or whatever for somebody to put two holes in him and burn him up, then it had to be someone who trusted him enough to bring him along in the first place. You just don't hit big licks with anyone - You gotta' be comfortable with him, or them."

"Right, right, true that."

Derrick said as he leaned over into the van being careful not to get the blackened soot on him. He looked at the body and took the toothpick out of his mouth.

"Damn, what the fuck they hit 'em wit'?"

"40 cal, close range, and obviously with murder on the mind, because one shot would have done it, but they wanted to be sure." Donathan answered.

"Well if they're not sure, I sure the fuck am. What you guys think?"

"Sure as shit." Frank said, Derrick gestured with his left hand and said,

"Okay, give me what you got."

Frank began. "The fire department was called at 4:15 a.m."

Derrick immediately calculated the time it takes to get from Sunnyside to the Greens and factored in the time it probably took to gas up the vehicles, pop bar-b-cue boy, and ride out. It added up to the time the witness said she saw the vehicles leave, give or take a few minutes.

"We got a call from them about 4:40 a.m. about bar-b-cue boy. We get here, check him out, put our super detective thinking caps on and come with a scenario."

"Which was?"

"Big heist: Drugs, jewelry, money, or all of the above. But instead of ole bar-b-cue boy gettin' paid, he got slayed."

"Yeah, that's what happens when you don't choose your friends wisely." Derrick jokes.

He looked at the burnt corpse and shook his finger at it.

"Betcha' next time you use better judgment in picking the people you rob with."

"So anyways, we figure it has to be at least three people involved. Bar-b-cue boy, hit-man, and driver."

"Try six or seven."

"That's right; your witness said she saw five or six."

"That's right, she said she saw at least five or six run into the house, plus the driver."

"No ID, huh?"

"Nope." Derrick answered then asked.

"What about the plates?"

"Bogus."

"You know that for sure?"

"Yep," Donathan answers, then adds,

"Yeah, you see, the van's not really a van at all, it's a Dolly Madison truck, at least that's what the plates register as, and the car is actually a station wagon out of Peoria."

"Sure wish we could have got a make on those plates before all this." Derrick said.

"Yeah, I know right. But one thing we got goin' for us is that it's so many of 'em. Niggers make mistakes."

Derrick looked at Frank harshly, letting him know he didn't approve of his word selection.

"Come on, you know what I mean D-man."

"Yeah, and you know what I mean Franky boy."

Just then Frank recognized the gang chief in Derrick. "Sorry."

"Don't worry about it. Go ahead, finish."

"Well, people make mistakes, especially when they're so many involved. Because of course you got the people who can't keep their mouths shut, then there's the ones who are in such a big rush to show what they got, which is always good for us, because that means that word is traveling through the streets. The more involved, the faster the word is traveling."

"Yeah, but what if bar-b-cue boy is only the first of a couple more to get it?" Derrick mentions. "Then I guess we're fucked." Donnie says.

"Yeah, not exactly what I wanted to hear, but you're 'bout right."

"So what were they after at your scene?" Frank asks.

"Don't know. The house was clean with the exceptions of a few guns that did the vics no good, the upstairs bedroom wall was kicked in so they were looking for something."

"Probably money. A lot of these guys hide their money in the walls."

A light went on in Derrick's mind that had been out until Frank said that. Suddenly things were a little clearer.

"So you said someone saw a D.E.A. jacket, who saw it?"

Frank fished through his pockets for the torn off piece of paper he received from officer Bateman and finally found it in the breast pocket of his shirt. He glanced over it while they walked toward the building.

The sun was up and with sunrise, many of the young hustlas came to life, so early morning wake ups had started and because the police don't stop no show when it's time to blow, weed smoke was in the air.

"Her name is Nikki, Nikki Page. She stays in apartment 304, but supposedly she was so cracked out she could barely talk."

"Jaws movin' all crazy and shit." Derrick said.

"I don't know, but I guess."

"So she's our only so-called witness?"

"So far, but we still have to do follow ups with the rest of the uniforms and see what they got, so..." Derrick cut him off.

"Aiight, you guys get on top of that and I'm gonna' see if I can shake somethin' loose."

"No problem."

They all dispersed going their separate ways. Derrick walked into the building and as he did everyone acknowledged him as more than the police. The building welcomed him with the type of reverence that the hood only gave to guys who were getting' it, or who were known for handling nation business.

Derrick was the police, which was no secret, but the biggest kept secret from the police was that Derrick was getting' more money, and callin' more shots than the niggaz they were after.

On a scale of one to ten on keeping your game tight, Derrick was bona-fide twenty-five. He kept the upper hand on everyone he dealt with. He had something on all of them that would bury them either in the courts or in the streets and he made sure they knew.

He made sure they understood at any given second he could launch a full scale raid that connected them to any place dope was found, any murder that had taken place, or any conspiracy that unraveled. He covered his ass in the streets while at the same time keeping himself in good standing with the police department.

As Derrick entered the building he got head nods, and nothing but respect and admiration from the project drug dealers. He walked along the ground floor to the stairwell. Along the way, all sorts of twenty-five cent chip bags, candy wrappers, small brown paper bags, cigar wrappers, Hennessey, Remy, Seagram's, and beer bottles lay scattered on the ground and between the grated gate that went from the first to the sixteenth floor of the project building.

The smell of cush filled the air, but didn't drown out the ever present smell of piss.

As Derrick entered the stairwell, the scene changed to Graffiti covered walls. Scattered in the corners and along the steps were empty crack bags, aluminum foil wraps that once held heroin, and empty weed bags. Like the rest of the residents, Derrick paid it no mind as he made his way to the second floor.

Before stepping foot on the stairs leading to the third, he was stopped in his tracks at the sight of Nikki coming down the stairs. She was still high, but now out of money, Nikki was no doubt on her way to find a dick to suck. Still tweaking from the hit she got from pushing the brillo through her pipe, Nikki didn't even notice Derrick.

"Nikki." She jumped nervously. Then with her hands close to her chest she focused on the face the voice belonged to.

"Damn, Derrick, you scared me, shit!"

"I scared you?" Derrick repeated smiling.

"Yeah, I guess I just didn't see you."

"Yeah, that's all it is, you gotta' slow down baby girl. Where you running off to?"

"Nowhere I ain't did nothin' Derrick." Derrick's smile turns to a chuckle as he leaned over and rested his forearm on his leg that was one step higher than the other.

"I haven't said you did anything sweetheart."

Nikki looked nervous as fuck, but eighty percent of it was the crack. Her eyes were buck and her once pretty light brown complexion had deteriorated into a dark lifeless mask of skin.

Her jaws were slightly sunk in and what remained of her once pretty silky hair was tucked under a pink dirty Baby Phat hat. The pink and white Enyce T-shirt she had on for the last four days hung off her and barely showed a print of her once beautiful round breast, that now sagged from years of neglect, lack of nutrition, and never wearing a bra. Her jeans hung off of her and her shoes looked run over - She was a mess.

Nikki didn''t care though, crack had long since stripped her of her spirit, knocked the life out of her, destroyed her self-esteem, raped her dreams, and killed any ambition she had. So in a short time, life; as precious as it is, had been stolen from her one hit at a time.

It was sad too, because Nikki used to be a beautiful woman, but during the eight years of her smoking career, anything and everything that produced the light of life was melted on a piece of brillo and turned into a cloud of smoke that disappeared into thin air.

Like a lot of people who smoked crack, Nikki dreamed of being released by the demon that chained her, but also like most smokers, she didn't possess the will to free herself.

The longest she'd ever gone without smoking in the last four and a half years, was three days. In those three days she saw a slight change in herself, but being constantly surrounded by the drug, she was quickly drawn back.

Some nights, she'd wake up wanting a hit bad. So knowing she could do something better than almost any woman in the projects, Nikki hit the streets in search of some dick to suck. She would line 'em all up, knock 'em down, and collect her ten dollars or rock after she swallowed every drop of cum each one shot down her throat.

If she was lucky, she would get two bags to let 'em fuck her in whatever hole they
wanted - Many nights for Nikki was spent bent over in stairwells, abandoned apartments, or on the side of buildings having trains ran on her. It didn't matter though, the only thing that mattered to Nikki was crack; everything else was secondary.

"Naw, you didn't say I did nothin', I was just tellin' you that's all."

"So what happened this morning?"

Nikki had to think for a moment because so much happened in her life while chasing that shit, she could have run down a list to him, but then she realized what he was talking about.

"Oh - you mean with the car and van?"

"Yeah - what you see?"

"I didn't really see anything."

"You didn't really see nothing is not the same as not seeing nothing. So let me know what you really didn't see."

"I was on the three and you know me Derrick, I smoke. I don't mess with nobody I just smoke my little crack. So I was takin' me a hit by the incinerator and when I came out a car was pullin' up. I didn't pay it any mind, but then a few minutes later I took another hit and this time a van pulled in behind the car. The guy in the car got out and he had a D.E.A. jacket on."

"You sure?"

"Yeah, from the three I can see good to where the cars are at."

"Did you see what the guy looked like?"

"Nope."

"Not anything - light-skinned, dark-skinned, afro, low-cut, anything?"

"I didn't see him Derrick; I swear to you, I wouldn't lie to you, if I knew I'd tell you."

"Okay, go ahead finish."

"The dude got out his car, walked to the van and then to his trunk and got something out then the other dude got out the van."

"You didn't see him either?"

"Nope."

"Was he wearing a D.E.A. jacket too?"

Nikki thought for a second.

"Nope, I don't think so."

"Aiight, then what happened?"

"Then the one who was in the car opened the trunk and handed him something."

"Did you see what it was?"

"Nope, I don't know what it was, but after that he started opening all his car doors. He grabbed a bag and put on the ground, then he was doin' somethin' in his car."

"Could you tell what he was doing?"

"I couldn't tell what it was. Next thing I know I hear a loud ass gunshot that sounded like a bomb. It scared the shit out of me; I dropped my lighter and almost dropped my pipe."

"Almost huh?" Derrick chuckled.

"Yup, then I heard another one, so I just went in the house and finished smokin' in the bathroom."

Derrick digested what Nikki said then asked.

"Who was workin' last night?"

"Lil Chris had the pack and C.G. was collectin' the money wit' Black Boy and I think Nip was on security."

"So C.G. was downstairs?"

"Yeah, Chris was in the hallway wit' them big ole bags. I bought four wit' my last forty dollars. I was only gon' spend ten, but they was so big I figured I'd better get 'em while the getting was good."

Derrick laughed. "But C.G. was downstairs when the car pulled up?"

"Yup."

"You seen him?"

"He on the nine."

Derrick reached in his pocket and peeled off five twenties, handed them to Nikki and said.

"Go run up to the nine and tell C.G. I said come here right now. Not in two minutes, but right now. That's yours because I don't want you out here suckin' no dick for bags, you hear me?"

Nikki nodded.

"Yeah I hear you, I only do it when I don't have any money."

"Well, now you got some money. Gon' do what I told you to do now and hurry up."

"Okay Derrick."

Nikki turned around and shot upstairs. Ten minutes later she was on her way back down stairs with five rocks in her hand.

"Here he come Derrick. I told him exactly what you said, and look,"

She showed him three twenties,

"I didn't even spend all the money. I got five bags for forty dollars, so I still got sixty dollars."

Nikki held out her hand with a bright smile as if she had something of value and not something that gradually stripped the life from her.

"You need anything else?"

"Naw, I just want you to be careful smokin' that shit and make sure you get something to eat with the rest of that money."

"I will, as soon as I get done. I been smokin' for three days and I'm thinking about quitting too."

Derrick laughed.

"You thinkin' about it huh?"

"Yup, and I think I really can this time."

"Okay baby girl."

"Alright Derrick, I hope you get everything worked out, thank you, bye."

Nikki went in the house. As she was walking off, C.G. was coming downstairs.

"What up D'?"

Derrick looked at C.G. like he had some type of involvement in what had taken place. Not that he thought he did, he just wanted C.G. to understand the seriousness of the matter.

"That's what I wanna' know? Niggaz getttin' shot, burnt, and fucked up all on your watch my man, what's goin' on - talk to me - what happened last night?"

C.G. looked at him like he was being held responsible for something he had no control over.

"Man Derrick, I don't know what the fuck happened. Chris was workin' the pack, I was checkin' the dough, Black Boy and Nip was on secuirty. Some nigga' pulled up but never got out the car. A few minutes later a van pulled up, then the nigga' in the car get out. He got on a D.E.A. jacket, so we hit it upstairs thinkin' they finna' smack the buildin'. We get to the seven and look down, next thing we know the cannon go off two times. After that the nigga' set the car on fire and bailed in a truck."

"A truck?!"

"Yeah, it pulled up on Division and waited on the nigga'."

"What color?"

"Couldn't tell, but it was dark: black, blue, green, or something like that."

"What kind of truck?"

"Shiit... a Tahoe, Suburban, Denali, somethin' like that - a four door."

"You sure it was a four door?"

"Yeah."

Derrick stood there pulling on his goatee.
"You good D'?"
"I will be when I catch these niggaz. Look, check it out; I want you to keep your eyes and ears to the streets for anybody who comes up on some keys of yay or heroin. Let the guys know whoever comes up with the right information got a brick comin'."
"Get the fuck outta' here."
"Nigga' do I play games?"
That was good enough for C.G.
"Damn, don't even trip, I'm on it."
"Yeah, I know you are. What that paper lookin' like?"
"It's good."
"You know it's almost check-in time right?"
"Do I ever forget check-in time?"
Derrick smiled as he took a step back and pointed at C.G.
"You my Nigga'. Don't forget! Eyes and ears to the streets."

Derrick trotted downstairs feeling like he was hot on the trail. He saw Frank and Donathan outside.
"We're lookin' for a dark color four door truck. Tahoe, Suburban, Escalade, Denali, or something along those lines that's what our shooter got picked up in."

He said with a shit eatin' grin. Frank and Donathan thought to themselves, 'How the fuck does he do that shit?'

By the time Derrick made it downstairs, Twin was in a body bag on his way to get his dental records checked. The tow trucks were removing the cars, the yellow tape was being taken down, and officers were dispersing.

Derrick hopped in his car and sat for a moment piecing together the new information.

"They come in, kill everybody, and know exactly where all the dope is and now this money shit."

He nodded his head as he stared aimlessly biting his lower lip.

"Damn! I didn't even know that nigga' had money stashed and if it was in the walls then it had to be a pretty penny."

He thought it out some more talkin' it through out loud.

"Now, the type of money you go through the trouble of hiding behind walls, you don't just go around tellin' niggaz about, but you told somebody Tuko. Who? Who?"

He dug a little deeper in his thoughts, a minute later a smile broadened on his face.

"Who do niggaz talk to about shit they don't talk to no other niggaz about? Their bitch. You muthafuckin' right. That hoe know something. Yes siiirrr!"

He started the car and that old Beanie Sigel sounded off.

"I speak the truth - Every time I step in the booth." Derrick pulled off.

CHAPTER 9

April 3, 2012 9:08 a.m.

"What's up baby girl?"

"Hey baby." Latrice responded relieved. "I'm so glad to hear from you."

"Are you?"

"Boy stop playin' you know I am."

Just hearing Black's voice lifted the ton of worry Latrice had been carrying for the last week, finally she could relax and let herself unwind.

"How did things go?"

"Everything went alright."

"Good, that's good, because I was worried."

"Were you?"

"Yes, more than you know, I'm so glad it's over."

And she was because this whole ordeal had been eating at her for the longest. When Black left out that morning, even though Latrice knew what he was doing went against every Godly principle ever written or instilled in her heart. She still rolled out of bed, got down on her knees, repented for her involvement, and asked God to forgive her and Black. She prayed for the Lord to protect her husband and above all to bring him back home to her. So at the sound of his voice she couldn't help but to say "Thank you Jesus."

"So where are to you?"

"About twenty minutes out from the farm."

"You already spoke to John then huh?"

"Yeah."

"How is he?"

"He's good."

"Alright then, I'm glad. As a matter of fact I need to call and thank him."

"Yeah, you do that."

"Don't worry, I will."

"You know baby, it's a trip."

Latrice snuggled into her goose down pillow and pulled her silk sheet over her.

"What's that?"

"The old man, I don't really know how to explain it, but it's a trip because I've never felt the way I feel around him with anybody before. He got it all the way together and it's somethin' about that old man I feel is gon' be a part of me one day."

Latrice rolled over and looked at her and Blacks wedding picture on the dresser. "Not one day baby, it already is, why you think I love you the way I do?'

She let out a sigh.

"What?" Black asked.

Latrice grabbed the picture and gazed at it as she spoke.

"Baby I have seen them all: Chiefs, Board members, Universals, Generals, Field Marshals, Hustlas, Gangstas, and hitmen, but none of them have what you got. You got that; it. And I know you got it because I was raised seeing it."

She set the picture back down.

"Baby when I look at you I see a part of my father and if no one else had it, my father had it, and so does John."

A warm feeling stirred inside Latrice.

"I look at you the way my mama used to look at my father and until I met you I didn't understand what the look in her eyes really was. I grew up seeing it, but now I understand it. I also understand her complete loyalty to him."

Latrice sat up, placed her back on the headboard, crossed her legs, and got comfortable.

"My father has been dead for eight years now and my mother has never as much as looked at another man, let alone entertained the thought of being with one. No one could ever fill my father's shoes for her just like no one could ever fill your shoes for me. I love you so much Darren - So if you don't believe nothing else, believe this. As long as I have breath in my body baby, you gon' have somebody by your side who is gonna' sweat, blood and bleed tears for you. No one can, have, or ever will love you like I do. I'm your wife, and the downest woman you will ever have by your side and you can believe that."

Black listened to Latrice, feeling her love seeping through the phone, into his ear, and going straight to his heart. He didn't have to question if she meant it, he knew she did, because he felt the same about her.

They had that ghetto love, and without a doubt, that ghetto love has to be the strongest and most misunderstood love of all. And that's just because those who don't live in the ghetto, or know about the ghetto, can't relate to the ghetto - And since they can't relate, they can't appreciate the ghetto, and therefore they will never understand that ghetto love. But hey, everything ain't for everybody anyway.

"Yeah baby, I'm feelin' you, and I'm feeling every word you said' and just know that your man feel the same way."

Soft and sweet, Latrice replied.

"I know baby."

Just then Tamar, their daughter who was laying in bed with Latrice opened her eyes.

"Hey baby, you up?"

She nodded her head while looking up at her mother with her beautiful brown eyes.

"You wanna' talk to daddy?"

Her eyes lit up and a smile came across her face as she nodded again.

"Okay, come up here with mommy."

She made her way up the bed and Latrice put the phone to her ear. With a soft raspy whisper she said.

"Hi daddy."

Black's insides tingled at the sound of his daughter voice. He smiled and said.

"Hey baby, what is my pretty little angel doing?"

Tamar was overjoyed, because to her there was no one more special than her father. She knew no matter what, she could always get whatever she wanted from him.

"Nothin', I just woke up."

Yeah, you hungry?"

"Yes."

"Okay, well I'm gon' tell your mommy to get you somethin' to eat. I'm out doin' something right now, but I'll be home a little later and we gon' do somethin' alright."

"Okay daddy."

"Okay baby, I love you."

"I love you too."

"Let me talk to your mommy."

"Okay...Here mommy."

"Hello."
"Yeah, my exit comin' up, so let me get off this phone."
"Alright, I need to get myself together anyway."
"Yeah, Tamar says she hungry."
"I know, I'm gon' feed her now."
"I'ma' hit you later on."
"Okay baby, be safe."
"I will, I love you."
"I love you too."

Black hung up the phone, turned up the radio and let Tyrese's 'Sweet Lady' bump through his speakers as he got on the off-ramp in Clinton, IL. After about ten minutes of riding down back roads where the only scenery was trees, high bushes, dirt, and open fields, Black saw the Tahoe parked in front of the three bedroom ranch style farmhouse.

Moe, Solid, and Dee sat on the porch in white cushioned deck chairs blowin' Dro. Shy was in the Tahoe listening to some underground drill music by 'Murda Mal'.

They all looked up when the midnight blue 300c came into view. Shy thought to his self 'My nigga'. Yeah it's all good now' and got out the truck. Black pulled next to the Tahoe and got out with the duffle bag and envelopes.

"You good nigga'?" Shy asked as they slapped hands and cuffed one another's four fingers in a handshake.

"All the time."

"What's that?" Shy asked pointing to the envelopes.

"A little bit of business I had to take care of to make sure niggaz act right."

Black had his game face on - because to him the stang was just preseason conditioning, just a little something to get everybody ready for the season. He had a vision, and his vision wasn't limited to inner city drug trafficking, it didn't stop at being an untouchable mob figure, it was much bigger than fifty keys of cocaine and thirty keys of heroin, it went beyond millions of hidden dollars.

No it was much, much, deeper, much bigger much more complex than that. This nigga has a dream. A dream he had dreamt since his first eight ball of cocaine got mixed with baking soda and water. The moment the ice hit that thick yellow oil and rocked up, Black whispered,

"I'm gon' be the largest King pin to ever step foot on U.S. soil."

That's when it was decided and now it was on.

He looked at the rest of his crew and thought, 'I got a squad and they hungry, but they ain't got my ambition. That's cool though, because I got enough for everybody.'

Then the old man's words flashed through his head. 'Make sure everybody knows who's chief, and all the Indians know they part, even the sqaws.'

Black nodded as if he was sitting in the garage next to the old man again.

I hear you' he thought, and indeed he did.

"Check it out" Black yelled as he held everyone attention. "We finna' get this paper, and we finna' get it the right way so understand its rules to this shit. But if everybody stick to the script its gon' be gravy. Niggaz gon' eat, and our grandchildren's grandchildren gon' still be tastin' the gravy off our plates. Ain't no room for no bullshit though, because any of us could easily be in the same boat them Belizeans in, y'all feel me?"

Everybody reflected on the bloody mess they left behind and Black's words set in with meaning and importance.

"It's time to turn it on, so check it out, we in the barn. Y'all grab that shit because it's game time."

"Fo' sho', I'm feelin' that." Solid said as they all got in motion.

As they walked to the barn, Black looked at the trees that literally surrounded the two acre land the old man gave to him and Latrice for this sole purpose. The trees seemed to be intentionally planted fifty yards out in a perfect circle and then fade another hundred to a hundred and fifty yards out into a small forest.

Beyond the forest was a pond, and throughout the forest, a series of cameras with short and long range digital zoom lenses watched day and night and relayed back to two-six small circuit screens, one in the farmhouse, the other in the barn.

From the moment you turned on the dirt road headed to the farm, you may as well had started smiling, because your fifteen minutes of fame was on. No one could approach the farmhouse from any direction without a ten minute heads up being given to anyone who sat in front of the screens.

The farmhouse itself appeared to be clean. A small modest kitchen, with an oakwood kitchen table and chairs, oak cabinets with matching tile. The living room housed a 36 inch color TV that sat on a brown rollaway stand.

A comfortable leather La-Z-Boy recliner sat in the corner just far enough off the wall to kick it out. A small glass coffee table sat in the middle of the room on the raspberry Shag carpet which laid throughout the entire house with the exception of the kitchen and bathroom. A raspberry colored knit couch sat along the wall next to a glass end table, with a love seat on the other side.

The master bedroom had polished redwood dressers with a matching Queen-size bed. Over the bed was a window where a camera sat outside just beneath the gutter.

On the dresser in front of the bed sat another TV with a six-split screen that alternated from each of the twelve cameras set up around the premises. From that room you would eventually see everything that moved in the vicinity in twenty second intervals.

The other two bedrooms only had beds in them, but in the closets, the floors let up and were deep and long enough to store three A.K. automatics, two S.K.'s and a couple tech nines.

The old man and Latrice's father used this farmhouse before Curtis died. Since then the old man had rerouted everything he was involved in to a more convenient location. The farmhouse was designed to be a secure location for him and Latrice's father, and now it was a secure place for Black.

The barn had five horse stalls lined to the right when you walked in and hay lofts on top. To the middle left of the barn, bales of hay were stacked a top one another. Scattered hay covered the floors of the stalls and two cameras were tucked in the far back corners of the top of the barn.

Black walked toward the third horse stall with his duffle bag in one hand, the envelopes in the other.

"Hold this."

He handed the envelopes to Shy, put the duffle bag down, kicked the hay away from a spot on the floor, and pulled on a black metal latch.

A six foot section of the floor pulled up revealing ten steps that led underneath the barn.

"Damn - Double O' seven four." Flinno joked.

"You on some super secret squirrel shit, huh cuz?" Black ignored the comment and started his descent downstairs.

"Whoever last make sure you drop the latch back."

Once downstairs Black hit a light switch on the wall and the entire room lit up. As each man made it downstairs they looked around in awe.

There were four medium sized rooms a large kitchen with vents that sucked air out above the stove. There was a small deep freezer and refrigerator in the kitchen as well as a sink and stainless steel cabinets lined the wall above the sink which had stainless steel countertops.

In one of the medium sized rooms there was also a stainless steel countertop and cabinets. On the countertops were six large blenders and on the far wall and ceiling vents were also installed for removing the air from the room, and a glass table with four chairs sat away from the wall in the left corner on the white tiled floor.

Another room had cabinets along three of the walls and along the floor. The room was air conditioned and carpeted with gray plush carpet.

The next room had two black leather couches, a 50 inch Sony flat-screen on the wall, a glass coffee table that sat in the middle of the room on gray plush carpet and a 40 inch screen in the corner with six-split screens that displayed the surrounding area of the farmhouse as well.

The last room which they all followed Black into had a ten foot polished cedar conference table, eight cedar chairs with black leather cushioned seats, and a computer in the far right corner.

"Have a seat."

Black said and everyone grabbed a chair. Black pulled out a chair at the head of the table which was symbolic to a C.E.O. in a boardroom. Black didn't sit down, instead he walked around and handed each man an envelope with their name and a single digit number on it. When he was done he was left holding one that had Darren Lang and a number 1 written on it.

Each man's full birth name was on the outside of their envelope and when they opened it they saw various eight by ten photos of their children, their girls, their mothers, fathers, grandmothers, brothers, and or sisters.

The pictures showed various shots of their kids being picked up from school or walking home from school or playing outside, as well as their grandmothers and mothers at church and walking into their houses and their brothers or sisters on the blocks or at work or in different places they frequented in the area they lived, or in the cars they owned.

Each of them looked at the pictures in wonder, amazement, and speculation.

"Man what the fuck is this shit?" Solid a.k.a. Michael Thompson commented, still staring at his people in the pictures.

"Look here this is the deal and I'ma' start with me so y'all don't think I'm on some bullshit."

Black took his pictures out the envelope and spread them out on the table so everyone could see them.

"Everybody know wifey, everybody know my shorties. Cuzo and Shy, you two know moms, and Cuzo this your moms my auntie."

Everybody looked on intently.

"This what's up. In the event that I get knocked and in the process of them people puttin' that pressure on me, I fold, and decide' to work wit' them y'all don't have to worry about hittin' me - Cause what's gon' happen is this, somebody gonna' hit my whole family."

Everybody's attention level went up a few more notches.

"There's no big I's and little U's on this hit list. Anybody get out there and start singing gon' get it, but not before they see everybody in their family get it first, from the babies to the first ladies."

Solid stood up.

"What the fuck you talkin' bout nigga'?! You den snapped! What the fuck is wrong wit' you?!"

Black instantly went in his waistline, pulled his Glock 17, and pointed it right in Solid's face and with calm intensity, through gritted teeth said.

"What!? What nigga'!?" He slid the chamber back.

"You got a problem bitch!? Cause if you do I'm gon' knock yo shit the fuck back right now and save all your people a trip to the morgue. You know how I get down punk! Anybody can get it, so act like you don't know bitch!"

Black's temperament had risen to the point of no return.

His eyes blazed with anger and in his mind he heard 'Anticipation of potential problems, the more problems you anticipate the less problems you'll have.'He was on the verge of blankin' out for real.

"Now I told you, this shit don't go down unless a muthafucka decide to be a snitch bitch. So if you got a problem wit' it then you must got some bitch in you, and can't hold water. And if that's the case then pussy you better start prayin' you can take fifty shots cause I'ma' dump this whole clip in yo ass!"

Black's eyes and face got more furious as he went along. Everybody in the room knew he don't have a problem giving it to a nigga', so everybody sat quiet. Everybody but Solid, he stood there petrified, truly understanding that he was looking in the face of death.

He humbly spoke

"Black my man, there's no bitch in me but you gotta' understand them my peoples you flashing pictures of and shit."

"And?!" Black snapped. "What the fuck do that mean?! These my people too!" He waved the gun at Flinno and Shy.

"Yeah I know, but I'm just sayin'." Solid added

"What? What the fuck you just sayin'?! Gon' say it! Let everybody in the room know what's on yo mind."

Solid shook his head and looked down at the table not able to peer into the eyes of his angel of death any longer.

"Look man I'ma' ask you this and I ain't gon' ask you this again. Do-you-got-a-problem-wit'-this-shit?"

Everybody in the room looked up at Solid, and his discomfort grew.

"I'm good I was just trippin' man. That shit just threw me off that's all."

"This the second time today you done got thrown off. You my man's man, but don't get it twisted. I will knock you off and I won't lose a wink of sleep about it. You better stop playin' with me nigga'."

Black lowered the pistol, put it back of his waistline and just as quickly as he flipped out he was back cool.

Black was a livewire, true gangsta', but he made shit happen, made niggaz step they game up, either that or fall to the waste side. He looked around the room, and then calmly went on.

"I done seen too many niggaz go down. Thoroughbred niggz who had that cake, but look at 'em now, where they at? FED joints like A.D.X, or doin' time underground in Colorado somewhere, Tams, the Yak, and down there fuckin' with them white boys in Menard. Don't get me wrong I slip, I fall, I get popped, I get down wrong then I 'pose to get what I got comin' as well. I knew what the fuck I was gettin' into when I did the shit."

His face got serious as he shook his head.

"But I ain't goin' out like them other niggaz who doin' a thousand years because another nigga' too scared to go to jail because he worried about whose dick his bitch gon' be suckin'. Man I'm on somethin' and if y'all wanna' get this dough, then trust me when I say, you lookin' at the blueprint. But we can't play games because these people not gon' play wit' us if we get knocked. So if you ridin', we ridin' this bitch all the way out, but man – I'm not responsible for what happen to you if you flip bitch in the middle of the race."

Everybody sat quietly.

"So we all in? We all good?" Head nods went around the room. "That's what I'm talkin' bout."

Black put his banger on the table and sat down.

"Now these hits already bought and paid for. The only way they get canceled is if you die. So, that's that. But look, we got fifty keys of yay, thirty keys of blow and everybody at least three hundred and fifty thousand to the good right now. That dope we got, we ain't fuckin' wit' for two years and look, Chicago – That's over wit'. Let them niggaz have the city, we gon' kill everything that surround it. This what I want y'all to do."

He leaned forward.

"Solid. You and Dee, y'all finna' take over the west suburbs: Elgin, Aurora, Carpentersville, Schaumburg, Hoffman Estates, Palatine, Bolingbrook, and everywhere else. Cuzo, you and Moe, y'all takin' the show on the road down south: Centralia, Carbondale, Shawnee, Vandalia, Charleston, and Mount Vernon. Me and Shy gon' kill Central IL.: Decatur, Peoria, Bloomington, Normal, Clinton, Springfield, Champagne, etc.

"So this the deal. Go find a spot in one of these small towns and set up shop. Use that three hundred and fifty thousand to start you a small business. Something real low-key that you can start wit' less than twenty stacks. Every two or three months put some more of that dough into your business so it looks like it's growing on the paper side. Keep good detailed books, cause trust me, it's gon' come a day when the feds come knockin' at our door wantin' to know how we got so much paper, and it's all gon' stem back from that business."

Head nods went around the table as Black went on.

"Keep your bitch involved in everything, because I'm tellin' you your bitch will make or break you, depending on the place she feels she has in your life. Put her in school, do what you need to do, but take care of her and be up front wit' all yo business. Let her know that you gotta' rotate wit' other hoes because hoes know who doin' what, and how much they doin'. Make her understand. Me, I ain't got that problem because my girls know the deal - so make sure your girl know the deal too.

"Every nigga' here been fuckin' with the same female for years - so if y'all can't get a understanding by now – y'all won't ever have one - so leave her ass in Chicago. Over these next two years all I want is for us to become niggaz who the police see as legit small business owners raising families: Peewee football, little league, P.T.A., bake fuckin' cookies if you got to, but get yo name and face right with them people."

Black paused for a second to look at the screen on his phone and quickly went back to his conversation.

"And look, don't floss. You gon' have plenty of time to shine. Don't bring no attention to yourself, but on the low, keep yo eyes and ears to the streets. That's where the bitches on the side come in at. Everybody here got enough playa' in 'em to pop the right bitches and get 'em to tell you what you wanna' know wit' out exposin' your hand. Find out who sellin' bags to bricks. See who's capable of doin' what, then slowly start cuttin' into 'em. Everybody like to eat, once they find out you can feed 'em, they wit you. And the last thing is this. Be lookin' for a connect! Not no little petty ass twenty or fifty keys either. We need a connect who can touch a hundred or better. I know its gon' be hard, but we all know them niggaz out there. Stay all business! Whoever comes up let 'em know you a package deal.

"You got niggaz you eatin' wit', don't rush it though, it's gon' come. Just make sure you in position when it does, cause when we get ready to move this shit, it's over wit', we on and it ain't no looking back. From this day forward we getting it. MONEY TEAM and the whole State of Illinois is our muthafuckin block..."

CHAPTER 10

April 3, 2012 11: 17 a.m.

Lisa needed to clear her head so she stepped out the courthouse, began to stroll, and soon found herself staring at the Arlington Park Race Track. After a moment of looking at it she realized there was symbolism in the track and her life. Because to Lisa, her life had been a series of circles she'd been running around only to end up where she started; the death of another mate.

Although Tuko was not like Dewitt, Lisa still felt the pain. The feeling of loss brought on a flood of memories about Dewitt, and that in turn made her think of Black.

"Thank you Jesus."

She softly whispered as she thought about how blessed she was to not be grieving the only other man she had ever truly loved.

"Black, I love you." She softly exhaled.

She felt compelled to call him, but before she could, she received a call from the

Court room clerk saying the jury had returned with their verdict. Lisa let her know she would be in the courtroom in ten minutes and started her walk back up Arlington Heights road.

With Black and her situation on her mind heavily, Lisa stepped back in the courtroom. The judge, the stenographer, State's Attorney, courtroom clerk, and Bailiff were the only ones present.

The judge looked at her and asked. "Are you alright Ms. Peterson, you don't look well?" He was so use to her over all professionalism releasing an aura of confidence in the courtroom that he was actually concerned.

"Yes, I'm fine your honor. I just have a few things on my mind."

"Well I hope everything will be okay."

"They have no choice but to be. Some things are irreversible."

The judge nodded cordially, and then went on to address Lisa and the State's Attorney.

"Are both parties ready to proceed with the verdict?"

They both agreed with a

"Yes your honor."

"Good, let's proceed. Bailiff, bring in the defendant."

The Bailiff walked out a side door of the courtroom and a minute later returned with Anthony Brooks from the holding cell. Once Mr. Brooks was seated, the Bailiff retrieved the jury from the deliberation room and they all filed in, in the order their seats were assigned.

"Before the jury gives their decision I would like to take a moment to thank you all for your time and effort in servicing your community. Upon giving your verdict, your obligation to the community is over. Do not concern yourselves with any sentencing in the event of a guilty verdict. You have all been wonderful and on the behalf of everyone in my courtroom I thank you."

The jury nodded in appreciation.

"Have you reached your decision?" The foreman of the jury answered.

"Yes sir we have."

"Is everyone in agreement with the decision?"

"Yes sir, we are."

"Would the defendant please stand."

Anthony stood up without showing any signs of the nervousness coursing through his body. Lisa stood next to him confident of her defense, but mind elsewhere. All she wanted was to be riding down I-90 with the top down on her Benz SL 500 letting the warm air blow through her hair while she allowed for everything to sink in more.

"What say you?" The judge asked the jury.

"On the charge of unlawful possession of a controlled substance with intent to deliver, we the jury find the defendant Anthony Brooks - Not Guilty."

Anthony bubbled over with joy, but once again didn't show it. Lisa was pleased with the verdict and normally would have been more enthusiastic, but truly she was weighed down. She turned to Anthony, shook his hand said, "Good luck," and walked out the courtroom.

A moment later Lisa stepped out of the court building and just stood there a few seconds letting the warmth of the sunshine sooth her face. It was an out of the ordinary beautiful seventy-nine degree April afternoon.

"A great day to be alive." She muttered.

Lisa held her arms out, looked up to the clear blue sky, and counted her blessing, because once again she was reminded of how easily she could have been laying next to Tuko.

"Thank you, thank you thank you," she said and stepped off.

Walking to the parking garage, all she could think of was Black and for some reason it was frightfully and undeniably strong. Sure, Black was always the center of her thoughts, but not like now.

First she couldn't understand it, but then it came to her and it was crystal clear. Tuko's death' she thought, and then whispered. "Right, that makes sense."

Lisa realized that Tuko's death gave her an understanding of how easily a love one could be snatched from her. Nodding her head, she thought about how strong and so full of love Black was.

The streets knew little of this, but she did, and Lisa definitely envied Latrice for that very reason. Why? Because she knew. She knew Latrice had to not only be feeling it, but also feeling it on a higher scale than she was. Just knowing that made her want to kick Latrice's ass sometimes. Lisa was jealous no doubt, but nothing in the world would dare make her express it, hell naw, she swallowed that shit time and time again, because never would she risk losing what she had with Black.

Yeah, maybe he didn't love her in the same capacity as Latrice, but he did love her and that was good enough to provide hope that one day she would be more to him than she was now, and until then, she would have to be satisfied with being second, because at least second meant Black loved her enough not to hurt her.

Lisa got in her SL, took her Gucci heels off, untucked her white silk Prada blouse from her black Prada skirt, looked in the mirror at her beautiful green eyes and said. "You'll be alright girl," and went in her purse to get her keys. When she opened it a picture of her and Black was the first thing she seen.

She grabbed it and thought about that night. As her mind drifted she felt as if she was reliving the evening.

It was her birthday. Black was wearing a blue and white Armani button down with a white long-sleeve V-neck Armani sweater. A pair of black Louis Vuitton jeans, camel Louis Vuitton loafers, and the Ulysse Nardin watch with two karat blue diamond earrings she'd bought him.

Lisa had on her light green Louis Vuitton body dress that matched her eyes and came down just below her ass and thighs, with her Louis Vuitton emerald for inch heels. And three karat diamond charm that read 'Baby.'

In the picture Black stood in back of Lisa with his hands wrapped around her waist, their cheeks pressed together. It was a magical night for her, and like a child at Disney Land, she would never forget it.

Lisa touched Black's face on the picture as if it would give her the same warm feeling of his skin and whispered.

"Damn, why do I love you so much?"

She grabbed her keys, stuck them in the ignition, started the car and Mary J. Blige came on singing to her heart.

'If you look in my eyes, you'd see what I see.' "You know that's right girl." Lisa commented to herself and pulled off. It was 11:49 a.m.

"Aye Dee let me holla at you for a minute"

Black and Shy were in the kitchen leaning against the stainless steel countertop when Dee walked in. The cocaine and heroin had been stacked in the cabinets of the air-conditioned room. Solid, Moe, and Flinno were in the office counting the money, and Dee was giving the yay a test run to see how good it would come back.

"Dig Fam, check it out." Black said with a smile.

"Awe shit, I den seen that smile before." Dee joked and Shy laughed before repling.

"Yeah, you know that nigga' too huh?"

"Yeah I know that cat."

"What you know then Playa'? Why am I smiling?"

"Man I ain't even finna' get into it, what's up? What you wanna' holla' about?"

Black's smile broadened as he shook his head, walked over, put his arm around Dee's shoulder and said.

"How about something simple like... I don't know, let's say, dollars in weight and grams."

They all sat down and Black started.

"What you think about the yay?"

Dee nodded, "It's good, real good. I only cooked a couple grams, but that shit jumped back nasty."

"I'm sayin', talk to me Dee, what's it looking like?"

"Man it's decent, I cooked about two grams or a little less and it came back to a little over a ball."

"But it ain't garbage though, right?"

"Naw, naw, it look right. What I"ma' do though is take that back and let somebody check it out, but on the real, I already know its butter. But you know we can't be for sure until somebody hit it."

"Right, right." Black added then paused to think for a second.

"So if you only cooked two grams and it came back like that, what you think it will come back like if you do a whole thang without beatin' it up?" Dee bit down on his lip while slowly shaking his head.

"I'ma' have to say two, two and an eighth easy."

Black nodded while he pulled at the hair of his goatee and Shy spoke up.

"Yeah that's gravy. That'll send us through the door with a little more than a hundred and twenty books."

"Yeah I know." Black added and went on.

"So Dee, let me ask you this. Can Latrice cook good enough to bring it back like that?"

"She cool."

"Yeah I know she cool, but can she cook good enough to bring seventy-seven ounces back from thirty-six?"

"Yeah she can."

"Well you know that's you and baby then right?"

Dee shook his head smiling. "See nigga', I knew yo ass was smilin' for somethin'. Every time I see that smile, I end up getting' the shit worked out of me."

"Well you must not see me smile much because I don't be workin' you."

Shy cut in. "Nigga' you always talkin' bout you don't be workin' nobody. You be workin' the shit out of niggaz."

"Well just know. When you be getting' the shit worked out yo little ass, it's on purpose."

They laughed, and then Dee spoke up.

"Yeah Black, I already figured I was gon' be cookin'."

"But you're not gon' be by yourself. Wifey gon' be here and Shy gon' be here too."

"See, that's the shit I'm talkin' about. Where the fuck you gon' be at nigga'." Shy protested.

"If you slow yo little dirty ass down you would know."

Black looked at Dee, pointed at Shy and said.

"See, that's why I be workin' his ass. It's his mouth. That little nigga' think just because I won't put that heat on his ass, I won't touch him up."

"Aye Dee, don't let that nigga' fool you, he ain't crazy, and he know I ain't goin' for no touch ups."

"Oh, I'll touch your little ass."

"And what I 'pose to be doin' while you touchin' me up?"

"I don't give a fuck what you go' be doin' it won't stop nothin'. I'm the big brother round here."

"Yeah aiight nigga'."

Black flagged Shy off and got back to Dee.

"But look, like I was sayin'. I'ma' be here some of the time."

Black turned and looked at Shy.

Shy said,

"Fuck you nigga'."

Black continued.

"While you and wifey cookin', me and Shy gon' be baggin' up. I figure if we start in about two months, that a give everybody enough time to find 'em a spot and get settled in where they at. Once we start we gon' take it nice and slow. Do about six to eight books every couple months until we get 'em all done. The D', we can't really fuck wit' until we get ready for it."

"Yeah, I was lookin' at that too, and all those bricks aren't brown. I know at least ten of 'em China-white, and it might be some more of 'em." Dee pointed out.

"Shiit, that's even better." Shy said.

"No doubt." Black agreed.

"In any case, we'll check that out when we start shakin' the dope. I just wanted to touch down wit' you so I can get these figures right. Everybody gon' be at the table when we start choppin' – So everybody gon' know what they got to bring back anyway. But me, you, Shy, and wifey need to be on top of the business before then."

"Yeah I feel you." Dee replied.

"Aiight that's what's up then. Come on let's help these niggaz count this dough so we can get the fuck outta' here."

It was 12:08 in the afternoon.

April 3, 2012 7:50 a.m.

Derrick went back home and took himself a long hot shower. Afterwards he made scrambled eggs, French toast, bacon and sausage, ate then took a nap.

At 1:15 p.m. he woke up and called his partner. He found out that Lisa had been to the station, gave a statement, went to the coroners, identified three of the six bodies and left. While at the station she asked to speak to him. Since he wasn't there, she tried his cell phone but got no answer.

When Derrick got the message, he started to call Lisa's office, then saw that he had a missed call and checked his voice mail first. It was Lisa.

"Derrick, this is Lisa, Tuko's girl. I don't really know what's going on, but I need to talk to you. Please call my cell phone." She said as she read out her number.

As soon as Derrick listened to the message he called her back "Hello. Lisa?" "Yes this is she - is this Derrick?"

"Yeah."

"What's goin' on?" Lisa asked with calm concern.

"I don't really know much yet I was hoping you'd be able to help me out."

"Help you?" Lisa questioned.

"How's that?"

"Well, who do you think would have come in on Tuko."

Lisa thought to herself 'that's a dumb ass question.'

"Let's see Derrick, how about every stick up man up north and God knows where else. You know Tuko, everyone knew what he was doing. I wouldn't be surprised if it was some of his own guys."

"Yeah that's what I'm thinkin'."

"Why's that?"

"Because they knew what they were looking for, and where to find it."

"They did?" Lisa said surprised.

"How do you know?"

"Because they were only in the house a couple minutes."

"So you have a witness?"

"Not a good one, she only saw the car and van pull up and drive off."

"Did she get a description?"

"Not a good one, just dark colored. We found both of 'em dumped and burned in the Greens, and one dude shot and burned inside the van."

"By the police?"

"I wish, but no by one of his guys."

"Serves 'em right." Lisa commented with genuine anger.

"Well let me ask you this, who knew Tuko had money in the walls?"

Lisa was caught off guard by the question and suddenly it was silence. Derrick picked up on it instantly and thought. 'Yeah, I knew this bitch had somethin' to do with it.'

After a few seconds Lisa spoke in a questionable tone.

"Money? What do you mean money in the walls?"

"The bedroom walls, they were all kicked in. They kicked 'em in for something and the only thing people like our guy put behind walls is money, because I doubt they were there to get a dead body." Derrick responded with a chuckle.

It had been a while since Lisa had told Black about the money and it was such a drive by conversation she barely recalled even having it, plus Black was the last person on her mind. But she was really racking her brain wondering who would have known though, because she thought only her and Tuko knew.

"I don't know Derrick, that's news to me."

"So you didn't know it was there?"

"I never saw any money."

'Typical lawyer response, evasively honest.' Derrick thought.

"Well, we're on top of it. I got the streets watchin' so somethin' will turn up, and when it does you know everybody involved is gon' get what they got comin'?"

"I'm sure they are."

Derrick changed his tone to show implication.

"You understand what I mean when I say everyone right?"

Lisa picked up on it. Not only the change of tone, but also what he was implying, but since she literally didn't know what happened she paid it no mind.

"Yes, how could I not."

"Okay then Lisa, try to stay in touch and I'll see you around."

"I sure will Derrick."

Once the call ended, Lisa put her phone on the bathroom sink, took off her robe, and stepped into her nice hot bubble bath. She laid back and let the hot water and Bath and Body Works stress relief bubbles take effect as she thought about what Derrick said about the money.

The water was relaxing and the stress relief bubbles were soothing. She sat there thinking a couple moments, and unknowingly drifted off to sleep.

Derrick looked out his window nodding his head replaying every word of his and Lisa's conversation making sure that what he felt from Lisa's pauses and evasiveness was warranted.

He decided it was, and since it was, he would have to keep a close eye on Ms. Peterson.

CHAPTER 11

Black and Shy were already on top of where they would be staying. Latrice and Shy's girl, Nia had done their homework on Bloomington, Normal for a month before Black and Shy even hit the lick.

Black had a, "I will not lose" attitude so not one time did he ever think he wasn't gonna' be able to pull the stang off. So Latrice and Nia started hitting the Central Illinois area for a place they thought would be good for them and their kids.

Bloomington, Normal a.k.a. The Twin Cities was the up and coming area for blacks migrating from major cities in IL. From the tip of the north to the bottom of the south, Bloomington became a resting point.

Peoria, Springfield, and Decatur were all a reasonable drive from the Twin cities, but for what Black and Shy were on those three areas didn't fit the format.

A lot of niggaz had already branched from all over Chicago to those three areas so the land was set up pretty much the same as Chicago as far as getting' money was concerned. The projects, blocks, and backstreets had already been claimed by different mobs and niggaz kept 'em flooded with rocks, blows, and weed.

That wasn't the problem. The problem was Black wasn't about to get involved in any messy long drawn out wars over little pieces of land to lay his shit down. Naw, he was much smarter than that. Wars bring police, and police investigations turn into federal investigations, and when the feds get down everybody usually ends up with a gang of time.

So other than a war, Black wasn't really concerned with the feds, because if things stayed on track he wouldn't have to see them for a while, and when he did – he'd be ready.

The main problem that Peoria, Springfield, and Decatur posed for Black was the inability to be low-key. That was extremely essential to his plan; they had to maintain a well

-developed reputation in the eyes of the police, surrounding neighbors, schools, and business owners of being a family that wasn't rooted to the streets and in no way involved with gangs or drug traffic.

Peoria, Springfield, and Decatur couldn't afford them that luxury, because all three places had a murder and crime rate that kept new faces under close scrutiny by powers that be. Bloomington, Normal on the other hand was different. Yes, every major mob affiliation had taken up residency in the area, and heroin, cocaine, Loud, good-green, ecstasy, and meth was being pushed through at an alarming rate, but it was low-key, and more importantly, it offered lots of small business opportunities and options.

It was a college town, home of the I.S.U Redbirds and many corporate company offices such as: State Farm, Mitsubishi, Diamond Star, Nestle Bites, and Afni. Jobs were available, schools were good, and it wasn't out of the ordinary for a black person to have his or her own business.

Blacks owned property, C&D and B&R construction was the first black-owned roofing company in the town. Barber shops, detail shops, entertainment companies, and clothing stores were black-owned and rampant in the area. So it wouldn't be unusual for Black and Shy's family to develop a prosperous business, but the main thing was blacks were doing it without selling drugs so police involvement was minimized.

Latrice had an impeccable work history as a correctional officer with Cook County and had already looked into becoming a C/O for McLean County Jail. Her years and experience would put her in the door as a sergeant and she would be able to identify every person who was getting' money not only in Bloomington, Normal, but also Peoria, Springfield, and Decatur by word of mouth.

Nia and Shy already owned a beauty salon on the Eastside of Chicago off Cottage Grove which did every kind of braids, hairstyles, and had barbers. Shy and Nia already had plans to make the place bigger and add pedicures and manicures to what they offered.

Nia had two sexy females who were the best at what they did from braids to styles working for her. She propositioned them on making the move to Central Illinois and they accepted. They knew nothing of what would eventually take place, but they would be keys to finding out who was in the game. They were cut from that street cloth and were attracted to and attracted street niggaz who got money.

She would hire two more stylist, three barbers, two manicurists, and some shampoo girls from the town, pay 'em good so they stayed in the shop and eventually all their clientele would shift to Nia's place.

April 25, 2012, Latrice and Black moved to the Eastside of Bloomington in a nice low-key area off Walnut Street. Not many blacks were on their block, and the ones who were had jobs and working reputations.

Nia and Shy moved to the Eastside of Normal off, Fell Street in a similar environment. They both rented with the option to buy three bedroom houses with full basements and backyards which was typical.

Little Darren was only four, and Tamar was three, so they would be in daycare and kindergarten at Irving. Shy and Nia had a daughter name Niya who was five and would attend the local elementary school.

Black decided on opening a small used car lot. He had some connects with car auctioneers, and because Latrice had been filtering dope money through stock investments, taking the lump sums of short-term investments and banking the money, they had enough money to legitimately buy enough nice cars to start the lot and offer good prices that would attract young and old customers, and Latrice still had money in long-term investments that she had for years. So on paper, anything Black, Latrice, Shy, and Nia wanted to do would look good.

Their choices of business and Latrice's job put them right on the forefront of the streets without having to be in them. So over the next two years all the pieces would come together.

Around the same time Black and Shy were settling in, Flinno and MOE were doing the same in Centralia, Illinois. Flinno brought Kasandra down with him. They had been together on and off for eight and a half years. She loved him to death, but Flinno was too much into females, had plenty of 'em and Kasandra wasn't steppin' down or playin' the back for no hoe. Even though she didn't play the back, she wouldn't be with anyone else either. They had two kids; Devon who was five and Chanel who was three. The kids alone were enough to keep them with one another on a regular basis. Flinno got money on the land and Kasandra was recognized as his girl by the whole area, so no matter what was goin' on, they both knew where home was. Kasandra was twenty-seven, a year younger than Flinno. She had an associate in business, plus was a certified registered nurse. Nursing was her job, but singing was her dream. She could sing like a nightingale, resembled an angel who took on the appearance of Nia Long and was without question a rider who was down for her man.

She kept his pistols, dope, and money. And was more than willing to take the case if it came down to it, because she knew Flinno would never leave her out there, just like he knew she would never put him out there. Out of all the years they had been together the best thing Kasandra had ever heard him say was they were moving out of Chicago. She knew finally, she would have her man without all the bullshit. Kasandra knew the deal and what the plan was so together her and Flinno came up with an entertainment company. Their plan was to take the city life entertainment to the small southern town. Not that it was something that wasn't already there, but Kasandra's business education, natural talent, angelic beauty, and ghetto mentality placed her in a unique position to offer what wasn't being offered, as well as do what was already being done, only better.

She had a gang of hood-sick girls who were ready, willing, and had the body and looks to be top notch strippers. They could all dance and hood life removed all restrictions concerning getting a dollar. These hoes had a mentality that they'd been suckin' dick and fuckin' niggaz and hoes for free or for outfit money - so a chance at doing private parties and being on stage for the dough was a chance of a lifetime.

Kasandra figure Flinno and her had enough legit money to put it all in the company and Flinno's three hundred and fifty thousand would keep 'em comfortable.

She would advertise the company, rent out nice spots three or four times a week, and give the town a place to go on a regular basis. Change it up to cater to all age groups and eventually get live artist once it was creating a good buzz.

Moe had a girl in Centralia, that's why they went there in the first place. They had five years under their belt and a two year old little girl name Lacy. Latoya, his girl, cooked better than anyone he ever tasted food from, so they planned out a restaurant. Latoya was thirty-one, a year older than Moe. She had been a bank teller for six years with a spotless record. On many occasions she moved dope up and down the highway for Moe and counted thousands without even considering taking a dollar. She knew how to bag up and keep money in order, and more importantly, she was loyal.

Moe had been taking care of her from a distance since they met, so she was able to save a lot of her own money. Latoya's family all cooked extremely well so her mother, father, grandmother, and two sisters would help with all the cooking while she and Moe actually managed the restaurant.

Like Kasandra, Latoya knew what the bigger plan consisted of and since she was born and raised in Centralia she already had a lot of information on the dope dealers, and everything Kasandra needed to know for the entertainment company.

She was familiar with the surrounding towns, and was looked at as an upstanding citizen in the public eye. Her family was rooted in the community because they were all from Centralia, so Latoya gave Moe and Flinno the edge they needed to filter in without the suspicion that comes with big city niggaz moving to small towns.

The police know eight out of ten niggaz hit small towns because they're sweet on the money and they don't have to go through the big inner-city drama so they watched them, checked them out, and seen who they were associating themselves with. The moment the connection is made between them and local drug dealers or users the investigation starts, but that connection wouldn't be made, at least not for a couple years and by then, any interaction with drug dealers or otherwise could be purely coincidental. The restaurant and entertainment company would bring about a lot of interactions, but they would all be legit.

CHAPTER 12

May 25, 2012

Black hadn't seen Lisa in a month and a half and had only spoken with her twice since the robbery homicide. He told Lisa, Latrice's grandmother was really sick, so they were going down south to help and support the family for a while. He left it at that so he could determine when he wanted to get at her.

Even though Lisa felt an extreme need to be with Black, she was also touched to the heart that he would be willing to set aside the game to support not only Latrice, but her family as well. Just the thought of that being a part of Black's character moved her deeply.

No doubt, her own need for that comfort and support intensified the nobility of his
alleged actions, but even if she hadn't needed it, she still would have been impressed.

Black called her early in the afternoon on May 25th.

"What's up baby girl? How you feel?"

Excited just to hear his voice, Lisa's heart beat increased. "I'm fine, but a lot better now though."

"Is that right?" Black replied feeling himself.

"Yeah that's right."

"So how you lookin' for time?"

"Why?" Lisa questioned giddy as a school girl with a crush.

"Because I might want to take you out for lunch."

"You might? Well what do I have to do to change that might, into I want to take you out to lunch?"

Black didn't say anything for a second then replied.

"Take your panties off and meet me downstairs."

Lisa's clit twitched and pussy moistened instantly.

"Well, I'm already one step ahead of you, because I didn't wear any panties today."

"I figured as much freaky girl, I just wanted to hear it out yo mouth."

"What difference does it make hearing it from my mouth if you already knew?" Lisa asked as she slipped out of her baby blue Victoria's Secret laced boy shorts and put 'em in her Fendi purse.

"It makes my dick harder to hear my freak talk freaky shit."

Lisa felt her pussy juices drip down her inner thigh as her clit twitched some more and started to throb. She gathered the paperwork on the case she was working, put it away, and headed downstairs.

"So all I gotta' do is tell you I don't have on any panties and my best friend in the whole world will stand up for me?"

Black reached down and grabbed his hard dick. He hadn't fucked Lisa in a while and had been thinking how good that pussy was all day and now that he had her on the phone he wanted to nail her ass even more.

"Yeah, that'll make him stand up, but you have to keep him that way, and it's gon' take more than small talk for that."

Lisa was walking through the lobby of the firm.

"More than small talk huh?"

Everyone in the office building knew and respected Lisa so as they saw her they gave her friendly smiles and waves. She responded, while also thinking 'Not now; I got a dick to suck' as she stepped along.

"Yeah."

"Well, I got a couple of nice wet and warm spots to put him in. Will that keep him standing up for me?"

"It depends."

"On what?"

"Do you swallow?"

"For you, I'll do any damn thing."

"Then yeah, we can work somethin' out."

Black was looking out his driver's side mirror for any suspicious activity, a habit he had acquired from years of getting it in the streets - so he didn't even notice Lisa had walked out the front door of the firm.

"So let me ask you this?"

"What's that baby girl?"

"How long will it take for you to get it in my mouth?"

"As long as it takes you to get downstairs and hop in the car."

Lisa tapped the passenger window, Black turned his head and Lisa said.

"Pull it out."

She had a look on her gorgeous face like a little kid at Christmas. Her green eyes sparkled as her hair blew in the wind. Black thought 'Damn! This bitch is bad!'

She had on a baby-blue silk Fendi blouse with a skirt to match and matching three inch Fendi heels.

Black hit the locks and she got in. She bit down on her lip as she took in her man wearing his Tru Religion jeans and shirt, red and white Bulls hat and all black Air Max's.

As soon as Lisa got in the car she leaned over like she was gonna' kiss him, but instead slipped her right hand in his pants, grabbed his dick, pulled it out, reached back with her left hand, pulled her skirt up over her waist exposing her beautiful ass and said.

"Told you I wasn't wearing any."

And wrapped her mouth around Black's dick. Black turned his hat back and to the right as he looked to see if any cars were coming, there wasn't, he put the car in drive and rolled off.

As Lisa walked out the door of the firm bubbling over with a radiant smile on her face, Derrick, who had been routinely watching her since their phone conversation, sat across the street waiting for Lisa to leave on her lunch break. It had been a month and a half and he was beginning to think he was wrong until he saw the look on Lisa's face as she looked around for Black's car.

Derrick noticed the 300C when it pulled up and made a mental note to check it out because if dude was getting' money, Derrick might be able to use him on his team, but that thought was over when Lisa bent over and tapped the window.

Derrick smiled. "Looky, looky here. I seeeeee you ."

Derrick could see in the car well enough to tell Lisa and Black had more than a business relationship. Then when he saw her head disappear into Blacks lap, he knew he was on the right track.

'Yeah, so that's whose dick you suckin'. Right on Derrick, now we getting' somewhere."

He whispered as he U-turned and fell a few cars behind them.

Black drove casually through downtown enjoying the loving effort Lisa was putting into sucking and caressing his dick. Lisa was savoring the moment licking, rubbing, holding, looking, and storing a mental picture of the dick she had missed so much.

She slowly stroked and kissed it before she plunged it down her throat taking it all in before slow and expectedly bringing it back out.

She whispered and talked to it while Anthony Hamilton played low in the background and Black just laid back in his already slightly reclined seat with his left hand on the steering wheel and right hand massaging Lisa's ass, occasionally slipping a finger in her hot little pussy as he jumped on the I-290 west headed to Oak Park.

Once they got on the 290, Derrick watched them easier, because Black was in the far right lane and Derrick was in the far left a half of car length behind.

Black was so caught up in the wicked knockdown his lawyer bitch was giving him; he wasn't paying too much attention to surrounding cars.

He didn't give a fuck who passed by and saw him getting his dick sucked, he wasn't dirty so he wasn't worried about the police, plus he had the coldest lawyer in Chicago literally on his dick so he just sat back and enjoyed the ride.

The more Lisa got into sucking Black's dick and the feel of his fingers sliding in and out of her the higher her ass went up in the air. Before long she had her left knee in the seat with her naked ass in plain view of the window sucking deep, long, and fast ready to taste Black shoot off in her mouth.

Derrick watched as Lisa's ass rose in the air and her head bobbed up and down with a smile on his face.

"There you go baby. Good to see that mouth is good for a whole lot more than talkin'. Yeah, that's my man because you suckin' his dick like it was the last dick on earth, and guess what? I see you. Yeah, I see your little hot ass. It seems a shame to kill you, but hey – you out there baby."

A moment later, Black shot off and Lisa swallowed it all down and finally came up for air. The look on her face and her smile as she touched her finger to Black's lips and kissed him on the cheek before resting her head in his arms confirmed to Derrick this wasn't a new relationship - She had feelings for this nigga', feelings that he could tell developed over time.

He took down Black's plates as they were getting often at Harlem Ave. They waited for the light to turn green then pulled off behind the cars in front of them, made a right on Harlem and headed to Lisa's condo.

Once they pulled up, Derrick parked a few cars back on the other side. Lisa got out adjusted her skirt, let her blouse hang, and stepped quick and jubilantly to the door with her keys out.

The diamonds on Black's neck, wrist, and ears caught the sunlight from every angle letting off blinding sparkles as he slid up behind her and put his hand under her skirt gripping her ass.

Derrick checked him out real good, nodded his head and said.

"Yeah, that's my man. Pop yo ass nigga' and yo hoe too."

Derrick watched as they stepped in and closed the door behind them.

Lisa got to her condo door, which was one of four in this particular building and stuck the key in. As she did, Black was lifting her skirt and pushing her against the door.

Lisa submitted to his power and pressed her cheek against the door. A second later Black kicked her legs apart, pulled his dick out and plunged it inside her. Lisa gasped as he went inside her in the hallway.

She moaned aggressively. "Yeah!" As he went deeper, she turned the door knob, the door flew open, and they stumbled inside laughing. Black had her by the back of her long silky hair and waist, still inside her.

He kicked the door closed as Lisa bent over with her palms on the thick plush carpet and legs straight. Black held her by the sides of her waist sticking her hard and long. Each time he went in, Lisa head and body jerked as her hair bounced.

"Oh my God daddy."

Her words jutted out as the satisfaction of the dick she was receiving flooded her whole body. Black pushed forward and Lisa followed his lead until she reached the couch. She pulled herself up over the arm of the couch, put her knees on the arm, and buried her face in the cushions. Her ass was high and just right for Black to drill her. He smacked her ass hard. The sting of his hand sent sensations through Lisa's body and she came hard and frantically.

Suddenly she rose up.

"Yes! Hell fuckin' yes! Fuck me nigga'! Fuck me!"

She yelled at what could have been the top of her lungs. She was pushing her ass back against his dick wanting to feel the pure power of him driving into her. Black grabbed her hair and pulled it hard and tight. The pain was stimulating to Lisa.

"You like that shit don't you hoe!"

Lisa grunted out a "Yeah, yeah, Yes! I-I-Loovvvee it-it-it."

"I know you do!"

"Who gon' fuck you like this?"

"No-no-nobody, only you!"

Lisa came again and flipped out screaming.

"Fuck! Fuck! Fuck! Damn! Fuck its good! That's right give it to me!"

Black went in on her and a few seconds later pulled out.

"Turn around."

Lisa spun around immediately and Black started jaggin' his dick off in her face. She opened her mouth and grabbed his dick from him and caught as much as she could until he finished cumin'.

Once he finished she calmed down slightly and just rubbed and rolled his dick in her hands then stood up.

"Come on."

They went to her bedroom and she came out of everything but her heels. Black came out his clothes, she sucked his dick until it got hard again, and it was back on.

About two and a half hours later Black and Lisa made their way out of Lisa's pent house. Lisa was bouncy, giddy, and vibrant with a smile on her face from ear to ear.

She had changed outfits and now was wearing all red and her hair was still wet from her shower. She had the look of a woman happily in love, not of one who was still grieving the tragic violent death of the man she had once loved.

The more Derrick saw, the more convinced he became. The run on Black's plates came back to a Latrice Lang who lived on the east side on 81st and Eberh0eart. He ran Latrice's name and it came back as a Cook County Jail Correctional officer.

"Oh so, you getting' money huh baby girl. Well pop yo ass too."

Derrick was on something and he wasn't gon' be satisfied until he nailed everyone that was involved with his missing dope.

He followed Black and Lisa back downtown and watched as they both got out the car. Black threw Lisa the keys, she walked back in the firm building and he trotted across the street and jumped in her Benz SL and drove off. If Derrick didn't know before, he knew now, and now it was only a matter of time.

Derrick followed Black all the way to Lakeshore Drive. Black dropped the top, flipped in and out of lanes, finally got into an open one and punched it. Derrick lost him.

"That's cool my man, real cool. I'm at yo ass and I know both yo bitches - So I'll catch up with you."

Derrick got off on 31st, turned left, and got back on the highway headed north. He drove back by Lisa's job, the 300C was gone. It was 4:43 p.m., May 25, 2012

CHAPTER 13

June 1, 2012

Black walked into the barn, headed to the third stall, pulled the latch and went down into the underground lab.

Latrice and Dee were in the kitchen with the surgical mask on standing over two big black pots. Normally the pots would have had two or three pounds of mustard greens cooking in them, but today's menu consisted of thousands of dollars being served up one kilo of cocaine at a time.

A large wholesale box of baking soda holding five hundred individual store bought boxes sat in the far right hand corner alongside the stainless steel counter. On top of the counter were ten individual boxes of baking soda, a box of plastic surgical gloves, two - two foot long stainless steel stirrers, and two large stainless steel salad bowls.

Black walked in with a smile on his face.

"What's good?"

"Hey baby."

Latrice replied joyfully as she stepped away from the stove, pulled her mask down and gave her husband a kiss.

"Are the kids alright?"

"Yeah they good." He answered and added. "Look at y'all in here lookin' like some regular ole mad scientist."

Walking over to the stove Black could smell cocaine in the air even though the vents were quickly sucking the vapors safely outside. He looked in the pot and saw that the baking soda and cocaine mixture was gradually becoming yellow oil, which when the ice water hit it, would magically transform the thirty-six ounces of powder cocaine into seventy-five to eighty one ounces of crack.

"How many y'all cooked so far?"

"This the second batch." Dee answered.

"What it look like?"

"Man this shit so fire its jumpin' and flippin' back like a Jesse White tumbler."

"He ain't lying baby. I don't think you ever had no cocaine this good."

"Aiight then, that's what's up, I like to hear that. Y'all make sure y'all don't beat it up too bad."

"You ain't gon' have to worry about that both of them last shits came back to eighty-six ounces." "What!? Get the fuck outta' here."

"Straight up nigga', and I gave one of the smokers what I cooked last time and ole girl said she smoked all night off that ball, and it didn't leave nothing bogus in her pipe."

Dee chuckled and went on.

"Baby girl said the cocaine was so good she had to call her girl over to help her get down."

Black clapped his hands together, and sang.

"Music to my ears let's get this money man, this money man, this money man. Let's get this money man, this money man, that dollar, dollar bill."

He came up behind Latrice, put his arms around the back of her waist, held her lower stomach, and continued his song while he kiss her gently on her neck as she stuck her ass out against his dick.

"Aye nigga'! I don't know what the fuck you on in there, but its eighty-six ounces in here with you name on 'em, so let's get it." Shy yelled from the other room.

My oldest boy know he be missing his daddy." Black joked.

"G' here I come, I'm checkin' out the mad scientist and his sidekick."

"Did you bring the blunts?"

"Hell naw I didn't bring you no fuckin' blunts! I told you that shit over wit'! Yo hype ass!'

Black tapped Dee on his shoulder and whispered, "Watch this."

"Man who the fuck you think you is nigga'?!" Shy yelled as he stormed into the kitchen. "I've been gettin' money for years..."

"Nigga' shut up!" Black said as he threw Shy a box of blunts.

"Aiight then." Shy replied with a smile, then pointed at Black and said.

"Nigga' you gon' make me fuck yo ass up. You think you can whoop me, but I'll beat yo black ass."

"And what I suppose to be doing while you whoop my husband?"

Black smiled at Shy.

"Yeah nigga', what wifey 'posed to be doin' while you whoopin' me?"

"Shiit, she can get it too, or better yet, I'll just get the nigga' while you're not around."

"Then let me ask you this" Latrice said while still stirring the cocaine in the pot.

"What 'Trice?"

"Then where yo little ugly ass gon' live at, and better yet, where yo bitch gon' work at because I'm fuckin' her ass up on the spot as soon as it go down?"

"Right! Stop playin' Nia a do that to yo ass."

"Okay, don't get yo bitch whooped for no reason. You know just like I know - she can't handle nowhere near the type of smoke I got for her ass."

Black jumped in. "Come on man let's get this shit." He kissed Latrice on the cheek. "Okay baby, we should be done wit' these in a minute, how many you want us to cook?"

"That's on y'all, get down how you live."

"Okay."

"You straight Dee?" Black asked.

"Yeah I'm good."

"Oh yeah, you and Solid aiight out there in Schaumburg?"

"Fo sho', fo sho'. It's decent out there, a lot of niggaz hustlin' and we gon' kill 'em in Elgin and Aurora when it's all said and done. I'm talkin' about its plenty of niggaz out there buyin' ten and fifteen of 'em at a time. We ain't been out there two months and I know seven niggaz and Solid know about five or six and all of 'em coppin' four or better and three of the niggaz touchin' fifteen every two weeks."

"Damn, y'all niggaz a do fifty of 'em in the door then." Black said.

"Yeah if them niggaz still out there when we get ready."

"That's aiight, because if they're not somebody else gon' step up."

"True dat, true dat."

"So I'm sayin'," Black continued,

"Them niggaz just puttin' they business out there like that?"

"Man you know how shit go. We got that custom rim, detail, and paint shop, so don't nothin' but heavies really rotate in there and since game recognize game, hustlas holla at hustlas. They just think me and Solid retired from the game, but niggaz know how that goes."

"Yeah, I feel you - So how wifey doin'?"

"She cool, up there workin' for Humana Hospital. The kids goin' to Schaumburg High School, everything lookin' good. You know I'm low key and spotless anyway. As long as Solid keep his head, I ain't worried. I been doin' what the crooks do for damn near twenty years and it's a reason why I ain't never been popped."

Dee was the oldest of all them, being thirty-nine. He'd been married for fourteen years, with his wife for seventeen years, had a sixteen year old son, and a fourteen year old daughter. He was already established. Dee and his wife had property in Chicago, which he borrowed money against to establish a state-of-the-art rims, detail, and custom paint shop. Solid gave him a hundred thousand dollars of his three hundred and fifty thousand and they signed as full partners. Solid needed Dee, because although Solid was a down hustla', he didn't always think things out, not to mention he was loud, flashy and flamboyant, which was the downfall of most niggaz.

So what Dee offered him was a chance to stay involved with the game and its players, while at the same time developing a low-key professional status. Dee explained to Solid the importance of only dealing with customers on a business level in a work environment. If any of them were being watched they could in no way be associated with them other than them being a customer in the shop.

The police would no doubt check Dee and Solid out, but everything would come back clean. The police would still watch for a while, but after a year or so they would see the only thing they were involved in was car business.

"Aiight then man, y'all gon' ahead and finish doin' what you do. Me and Shy gon' handle ours." Black went into the other room where a box of plastic surgical gloves sat on a table, along with two large digital scales, a butcher knife, large box of razor blades, and five boxes of plastic baggies.

"Once again it's on." Black happily said to Shy.

"Yeah I feel you G'. How long we been comin' to the table together?" Shy asked.

"For years, and remember I told you way back. One day we was gon' be at this muthafucka' baggin' up more shit than most niggaz' will ever see in they life."

"Yeah, no doubt, I remember that."

"I know you do, and this is something else to remember. Between the six of us, six months from the time we start movin' this shit we gon' be pushin' a thousand bricks a month not countin' the blows. A year and a half later shit gon' triple. Within four years we gon' be the main supplier for every city and small town from St. Louis to Chicago. We finna' give 'killin' the game' new meaning. With slow and steady calculated steps. Remember that G', slow and steady wins the race."

Shy listened to Black and thought to himself that it was at least forty to seventy small cities and towns between St. Louis and Chicago. He knew off top, him and Black could lockdown at least fifteen of 'em just in the Central part, Dee and Solid had twenty to twenty-five or 'em up north and Flinno and Moe had about the same down south.

Once they got on, it would be easy to move five hundred bricks apiece, that wasn't a question, but Shy did have one question.

"I feel you, we gon' be movin' a lot of shit, but let me ask you this?"

"What's that?"

"Where the fuck is we gon' get all this dope from?"

"Don't even trip, trust me, it's a muthafucka' out there right now who lookin' for niggaz like us who they can sell three, five, and ten thousand bricks at a time. Niggaz feel more secure when they don't have to scatter they shots. The more people they fuck wit' the greater the risk. By the time we man up on the paper - that connect gonna' be den surfaced, and once we get in bed together, we fuckin' all day every day."

Shy looked at Black and wondered where this nigga mind is at sometimes. They had known each other for years and Black never ceased to have a plan about gettin' money that didn't come together just like he said it would.

It was like the nigga' had a magic chess board, and he only played the game against himself. And since he played all day every day, he no longer thought one more in advance; he thought four, five and sometimes six moves ahead. He saw shit that other players didn't see until it was too late and by then, they couldn't do anything about the attack coming.

It was scary sometimes how thorough the nigga' was. A lot of cats are either good
thinkers, or good gangstas, but not Black, he was both. And that's what made him so dangerous.

See, simple street 101 tells you that it takes both, brawn and brains to survive, shine, and excel in the game. One without the other is a body bag or a prison sentence waiting to happen.

Black was good though. A born hustler' who could out think the best of 'em, plus he didn't have no problem popping' a nigga' in the head, murkin' his mama, and then turning around and banging the nigga' bitch.

The man was a force to be reckoned with and Shy was just glad to be with him and not against him. Shy looked up to Black and always did, because he knew fuckin' wit' Black meant, he would either get rich or die trying. And he didn't give a fuck about the dying part because he was gon' live life to the fullest until death came around the corner.

Black looked at Shy while Shy rolled the loud and said.

"Man nigga', have I ever fucked up when that paper was involved?"

"Naw, and I didn't say you did. I just be trying to figure out where yo mind is sometimes."

"My mind on that money - and that money on my mind."

Black said laughin' as he put a chunk of cocaine on the scale and watched the red digital numbers shoot to twenty-eight and stop.

"You see that nigga'." Black pointed to the scale. "That's where my eye at."

Shy looked over at the scale, nodded his head and Black spit a freestyle while he was wrappin' the ounce in the plastic baggie.

"I got ambition muthafucka', all I see is the dough - And I'm addicted to the game so I'm bound to blow - So bet I make these streets feel me like they feel. Jay flow-cause I keep it tight like that pussy on a thick ass hoe."

CHAPTER 14

July 7, 2012

Everyone had come to Chicago for the 4th. Afterwards the ladies and Dee went back to their newly founded suburban and southern homes while Black and Shy spent a few days in the Chi.

Black spent his days with Lisa and now at 8:15 p.m. he was waiting for Shy to pick him up at her house. Suburban life was relaxed, but since Black was back in the town the comfort of not carrying a gun was over. His Glock 17 sat on the bedside table.

"Yeah, my man should be pullin' up in a minute."

Lisa rolled her naked body on top of Black, pushed her upper body up so her beautiful breasts dangled in front of him, put on a sad face and playfully protested.

"I'm not ready for you to leave."

Black cuffed her ass and kissed her titties looking up at her.

"Don't trip, I'ma' bend back on you before I shake it out the city, but I got business to take care of and I can't get it done with my dick in you all day and night."

A chill shot through Lisa as she was immediately reminded of how Black had been working her out for the last two nights. She shook it off with a vibrant smile.

"Whew! Don't say THAT ...Like THAT. It gives me flashbacks."

She kissed him and hopped out the bed.

"I know baby, I got things I gotta' handle too. I'm sure it's somebody out there blowin' up my phone needing me to save 'em." She said as she walked into the bathroom and started the shower.

"I hope I don't ever need you."

"Well if you do baby, you know it won't be anything in the world to stop me from saving your fine ass. Even if I gotta' taint the jury, fuck the judge, and suck the state's dick."

"What if it's a woman?"

Lisa stepped in the doorway of the bathroom smiling.

"I eat pussy good too."

Black laughed as he sat up in the bed. He had already taken a shower and had on some Levi jeans, a white wife beater. He reached under the bed, grabbed his peanut butter Air Force Ones, put 'em on, then put on his Cleveland Browns fitted cap and tilted it slightly to the right.

He put his watch and chain on then walked to the kitchen, poured himself a glass of milk, grabbed the box of cupcakes and walked back in the room.

"So when am I gonna' see you again?" Lisa yelled from the shower.

"I'll see you for a minute before I leave, but after that I won't be back this way for a couple weeks."

Black answered as he bit half of cupcake and washed it down with some milk.

"I'm tryin' to get this car lot together."

"Oh, I understand, I know you got things to do." Lisa turned off the water.

"Baby will you get me a towel."

Black got up, went to the linen closet, grabbed Lisa a towel, handed it to her, and sat back down, his phone rang and Shy's name popped up on the screen.

"What up nigga'?" "You ready?"

"Yeah, give me five or ten minutes."

"Cool I'm out front."

Black put the phone down and opened another cupcake as Lisa walked into the room.

"That was Shy, I'm finna' get outta' here in a minute."

Lisa had the towel wrapped around her and walked up on Black. "Give me a bite." He put a piece of the cupcake in her mouth. "Thanks."

Outside Shy was blazing a blunt when an old school black Cutlass on spokes rode pass slowly bumpin' Marvin Gaye 'Let's get it on.'

Shy looked over at him and he eyed Shy as he rolled pass.

"That muthafucka' clean." Shy whispered to himself. pulled up alongside the Cutlass. They talked for a minute or so, then the Cutlass pulled off.

"Who the fuck is these niggaz?"

Shy pulled his Glock 18 from his waistline and sat it on his lap. Less than a minute later three of the niggaz got out the car and walked towards Lisa's condo. Shy called Black as they walked across the street.

Black picked up on the second ring.

"I'm on my way out."

"Aye G', it's some niggaz comin' up to the crib. I don't know if they goin' there, but it's three of 'em and shit look shady."

"Aiight."

Black grabbed his Glock and cocked it back. Lisa was standing in the mirror combing out her hair. When she heard the gun slide back, she turned to Black.

"What's the matter?"

"Stay right here."

Lisa backed away to the bed and sat down nervously with her towel wrapped around her. Black stepped out the bedroom door, took a couple steps, looked around and suddenly the door was kicked open. Black started dumping in the doorway.

'Bak-ka! Bak-ka! Bak-ka! Bak-ka! Bak-ka! Bak-ka!'

He hit the first person coming in and the other two cats started busting with their arms around the wall shooting blindly. Bullets sailed through the air ripping through the walls of Lisa's condo. She screamed as Black hit the floor and yelled to her.

"Get on the floor! Get under the bed!"

Lisa dropped and got under the bed as her heart pounded and tears ran down her face. One of the bullets hit the fish tank in the wall and gallons of water rushed out soaking her under the bed.

One of the other niggaz rushed through the door but didn't see Black on the floor. Black let the Glock ride.

'Bak-ka! Bak-ka! Bak-ka! Bak-ka! Bak-ka!'

The nigga' yelled out as the bullets ripped through his body sending him stumbling backwards hitting the wall. Blood soaked his clothes and stained the wall.

Black jumped up and realized he knew the nigga'. He was a vice lord from Leclair Courts. The third cat broke out running.

"Lisa you straight!"

"Yeah!"

Black shot off after him. The dude hit the door hard and it flew open. Shy watched the door slam against the wall and the nigga' shoot out toward the Chevy. A couple seconds later Black shot out with his arm extended busting at the car. Bullets shattered the back side window and riddled the door.

The driver took off with a screech, hit a parked car and kept going. Black was in the middle of the street popping at the niggaz as they sped off. Shy pulled up and Black jumped in the passenger seat.

"Get them niggaz! Right the fuck now! I'm killin' all them bitches!"

Shy skeeted off behind 'em down Harlem. The Chevy turned on Madison flying down the street dipping in and out of traffic. Shy was four or five cars behind 'em.

"Catch them niggaz G'! Don't let them muthafuckas get away! I mean that shit!"

"I'm on 'em!" Shy yelled

The Chevy went through lights and Shy was gaining. Horns blared from other cars as they were giving instinctive warnings of potential accidents, cars pulled over to the curbs on both sides of the streets, and people walking watched as cars sped down Madison like a movie scene.

Once they got in range, Black leaned out the window bustin'. He hit their back window and it shattered. The Chevy turned up Central and while making the hard right, it slid into a minivan that was waiting at the light.

!BOOM! Glass from the Chevy and minivan shattered and fell into the street. Black was steady dumping' at the car. The Chevy kept going, but now Shy was right behind 'em.

They came up on Jackson, and cars were lined up waiting on the light and since traffic was heavy, the Chevy was forced to stop with no place to go.

Shy stopped and him and Black bailed out and immediately rushed the car dumping' inside. They both let off about fifteen shots apiece leaving both men a bloody mess.

People on the block and in cars ducked down as the shots rang out sounding the alarm of another gangland murder on Chicago's Westside. Sirens wailed in the background as police closed in. Black and Shy jumped back in the whip, skidded off around the cars and across the now clear Jackson.

They jumped on the E-way, headed south and twenty-five minutes later came up on the 63rd street exit.

They got off, made a left, headed toward King Drive, made a right on King Drive, took it to 79th, made a left, went to Eberhart, made a right, drove to Black's old house, pulled in the garage, and closed the door.

Black's phone was ringing, it was his cousin. He answered.

"Cuz!"

The music was loud in the background and people were laughing and talking.

"What's up Cuzo?" "Where you at?"

"Fuckin' around with the Moe's in Moe-Town with Moe and Solid."

"Y'all niggaz meet me on the block right now, some niggaz just tried to hit me!"

"What?!"

"Yeah nigga, right now! Me and Shy on the block in the garage."

"On Eberhart?"

"Yeah."

"We on our way!"

When Black hung up, he called Lisa. She had been blowin' his phone up since five minutes after he left. She picked up immediately.

"Hello!"

"Yeah."

"Oh my God, are you alright?"

"Yeah I'm good."

Relief flooded Lisa. Police were all over her house so she stepped in the bathroom of her room and closed the door.

"What the hell is going on?"

"Shiit I don't know, I was there wit' you."

"Who were they and how did they know you were here?"

"I don't know how the fuck they knew I was there, but that nigga' in your living room is a Vice Lord from Leclarie Courts. What's going on there, I hear police radios?"

"Yeah, they're everywhere, but I'll handle all of this here. You just get your ass the hell out of Chicago."

"You better get yo ass the fuck out the city too because these niggaz know where you live and that I fucks wit' you, so they might be back."

Lisa was silent for a couple seconds then replied.

"You're right, I didn't even think about that."

"Well yo ass better start thinkin'."

"I'm sorry, I will."

"Don't trip, but look I'ma' hit you later, and you get yo ass up outta' there, you understand me?"

"Yeah baby, I'm gone."

"Aiight."

"Okay - you be careful."

"I'm good, you be careful"

"I will."

Lisa hung up the phone shaking her head, but just couldn't help thinking - this was one of the reasons she loved

Black, but bullshit wasn't nothing, this was a little too fuckin' close to the streets than she cared to be. Without a second thought Lisa said.

"Time for a real long fucking vacation." It was 9:27 p.m.

Black, Shy, Moe, Solid, and Flinno sat in the garage at 10:36 p.m. loading up AK's, SK's, and techs. Black decided, 'Fuck that', he wasn't leaving until after they lit up Leclarie Courts.

At 10:45 p.m. they jumped in two stolen cars with hats and hoods on headed back out west. Twenty minutes after eleven they were pulling up in Leclare Courts.

Leclare Courts was a series of row houses off Cicero Avenue. There were one-ways that led deep into the project complex where the strip came alive to get money twenty-four seven.

Niggaz and females walked about blowing' loud and drinking every kind of liquor while they talked shit, sold rocks, blows, weed, shot dice, and listened to the sounds beat in cars. And like every project and block in the Chi while all that took place, there were at least twenty firearms on the niggaz and females, or in stash spots. Shit kicked off at the drop of a dime and what the Leclarie Courts didn't know, was the dime was about to drop.

Black and his guys pulled up behind one of the row houses where no one was in front, got out with their hoods on and guns in their hands. They crept through the shadow alongside the row house like A.T.F. agents on a raid.

From where they were they could see a crowd of niggaz and not too many females. Ready for war, they stepped out and started dumping in the crowd. Shots were being let off by all five guns and in seconds Leclarie Courts turned into CHI-RAQ. Screams filled the air as the sound of the guns echoed and fire from the muzzles spit off into the night. People were running trying to make it to cover as bullets tore through them, dropping them to the ground leaving them to feel the heat of bullet wounds as blood poured from their bodies with the same intensity as the screams coming from their mouths.

"Get down!"
"Where they at?"
"Ahh!"
"Help me!"
"Move! Move!"
"Where they at?!"
"Where they at?!"
"Aahhh! I'm hit! I'm shot! I'm shot!"
"Aahhh!"

People dropped to the ground and scrambled for cover as bricks were knocked off the sides of walls and glass shattered.

"They over there! They on the side of the building!" A female voice screamed.

Niggaz began shooting' back. Before long, niggaz converged from different parts of the Courts unloading with their own heavy artillery as the call to arms rang through the concrete desert of the projects.

Niggaz had family and people they loved and were willing to get out on the front line for the cause of the land.

The Courts literally sounded like a war zone as flashes of light lit up the night. It was on now and Black knew they were out gunned and out manned, but he accomplished what he came to do. So after multiple people lay dead and wounded they all bailed back in the cars and sped off.

Police raced to the area a minute and a half after they had made it out. They shot back out south, dumped the cars and guns in an alley in Killer Ward off Ashland where Shy's truck was parked, and headed back over east. Once over east, Flinno and Moe got in their car, Solid got in his, and everybody hit it out of Chicago.

12:00 in the afternoon, July 8, 2012.

"This is Chicago's very own W.G.N. news at noon with Micah Matere, Alison Payne, Tom Skilling on weather, and Robert Jordan. Hello, I'm Alison Payne and our top story comes from west suburban Oak Park where a vicious shootout left two people dead at the home of one of Chicago's most prominent criminal lawyers, Lisa Peterson. Details are sketchy at this point and Ms. Peterson declined to give a statement, but it is known that her apparent involvement was limited to the assailants chasing another unknown man into her home yesterday evening around 8:30 p.m."

"Apparently the unknown assailants somehow gained entry to Ms. Peterson's home where the shootout took place. After shooting and killing two men, a third suspect fled from the scene according to neighbors in the residence. The unknown assailant who is described as tall, dark skin, with a medium build pursued the man out of the condo doors shooting at a car that was apparently waiting outside. After multiple shots were fired, the assailant was picked up in a vehicle and they pursued the other vehicle in a high-speed chase eastbound on Madison Avenue which ended on Central and Jackson. Where two men jumped out of a blue Caprice Classic, ran up to the car firing multiple shots inside the vehicle, killing the two passengers, and then fled on the expressway southbound."

"Alison, are there any leads on the vehicle or description of the other individual?" Micah Matere questioned.

"Not at this time. All the police have as a description is two black males." "Thank you. To follow up this story of the deadly shootout," Micah Matere continued, "We have another shooting that occurred in Leclarie Courts at approximately 11:15 last night. The shootout left seven dead including a pregnant woman who was the mother of three, and five others hospitalized with gunshot wounds. Police say the shooters were armed with high-powered automatic weapons, military issued and let off more than a hundred rounds before fleeing the scene in two unknown vehicles. No one got a look at any of the assailants and is not sure as to how many were involved in the actual shooting; we have one of our reporters live."

The news switched to a picture of Leclarie Courts where people crowded the area with hurt, angry, sad faces crying over the dead and injured.

"Juan." Micah Matere introduced.

"Thank you Micah. Just a short time earlier, this was the scene of a vicious gun battle when two cars pulled up right here in this very spot and an unknown number of individuals armed with high-powered automatic weapons, began shooting multiple shots into a crowd of people that were gathered to my right. As you can see from the shell casings, there were a number of shots fired; corners of homes were literally knocked off as bullets barreled through the concrete."

"No one knows or is saying what provoked the violent incident, but gangs and drugs are suspected to be the root of the cause."

Micah Matere interjected.

"Was there a description of the vehicles?"

"No not at this time. Everyone understandably took cover except those who were struck by the initial gunfire. As further details surface I will report them to the station. This is Juan Vogul for W.G.N. news at Leclarie Courts, back to you Micah. Thank you."

"Our next story is about a drug raid on Chicago's Southside where twelve kilos of cocaine and nine firearms were seized from a home on 67th and Paulina."

CHAPTER 15

12:10 p.m., July 8, 2012

    Derrick sat in front of his TV watching the coverage on the W.G.N. news. As soon as the two shooting stories ended he turned it off and sat on his couch silently thinking.

After a few minutes he said. "Who the fuck this nigga' think he is, Double O'Seven super gangsta'?"

He was silent again for a moment, then spoke.

    "Damn, how the fuck did these niggaz miss the hit? Better yet, how the fuck did this nigga' kill all of 'em?"

He got up and walked to his window.

    "And I bet that bullshit in Leclarie Courts was him too. Who the fuck is this nigga'? Well, it don't really matter because whoever the fuck he is, he better have a squad of Gangsta niggaz ready to die for him because it's on and poppin. And that bitch. Oh she definitely is dying with him."

For the first time since Derrick had become a dirty cop he felt challenged. He was used to niggaz either being too scared to go to jail or too stupid to put him out there. So he did what most crooked authorities did, he played on the fact that he kept an ace in the hole, his badge, but this was different.

Black wasn't goin' at gunpoint, and he was handling the business on the spot. Derrick realized that comfortability wasn't a luxury that Black considered. He stayed on his toes and remained focused and obviously he thought things out and had the nuts to pull it anytime, anyplace.

This nigga' was gon' be a problem and Derrick knew it. While he thought, Derrick remembered riding pass Shy, and Shy looking at him.

    "Damn, I wonder if that was one of his guys. Because if it was that muthafucka' got a look at me and my car. So it won't be long, if not already, that Lisa figures out that I was involved."

Now that was a problem for real, because Lisa knew too much, and with her being the best at what she did, she could easily bury Derrick under the prison. Derrick quickly found himself getting deeper in a hole that he was already struggling to get out of.

"Aiight D'man, get yourself together. This is just another street nigga' and street niggaz always fuck up."

He told himself, but so far, Black had managed not to fuck up, and he had a lot going in his favor. Money, heart, and a good bitch with more connections with officials than Derrick had.

When Derrick looked at all of that, he had to admit that shit could go the wrong way for him in a heartbeat. Then a thought came to his mind. 'Maybe I can get this nigga' on the team and once I got him, then I can wipe his ass down.'

But he quickly dismissed that because the only way to do it was through Lisa, and that would mean her finding out he sent them niggaz to her crib, plus he realized Black was a leader, not a follower. Whatever he was into he was calling the shots and whoever he was fuckin' with were trusted niggaz who knew he wasn't about no games. "I wonder who the fuck Latrice is to him. Maybe I can play on that. Yeah let me see if I can catch up with this bitch, cause I gotta' find out who this nigga' is, I need some information." Derrick said to himself.

Shortly there after he got on his police computer, punched in Latrice Lang, and her Cook County Correctional officer information came up. He checked it out thoroughly and found out her name had been changed from Marks to Lang. So he went a little deeper into his police computer and gained access to City Hall marriage license applications.

After searching for a while he found Latrice Marks and Darren Lang. He punched in Darren Lang's name and he had a record on file, along with a photo. The photo was old, but Derrick knew at first glance it was his man. 'Yeah nigga'. So you the one out here causing me all these problems? Well let's see if I can cause a few of my own.' 12:10 p.m., July 8, 2012

Latrice sat at home in Bloomington staring at the 56 inch flat screen on the wall as Alyson Payne described the events of yesterday's shootings. Latrice knew where Lisa lived and was more than familiar with her lawyer expertise. That was the main reason she never put up any fuss in regards to her and Blacks relationship.

As she watched the news she could just see Black doing exactly what was being reported. She shook her head and said.

"This boy gon' either get himself killed, or a million years."

Black didn't make it home until almost 2:30 in the morning and was still sleeping, so he hadn't spoken to Latrice yet, but he didn't have to say a word, she knew.

Latrice wondered what Black and Lisa wondered though; who they were, and how they knew he was there?'

Latrice was from the block, so she didn't need Black to remind her that these niggaz could be at her too, she knew. Especially because if they knew Lisa, they had to know about her. They had been together for what seemed like forever, so anybody who knew Black well enough to know Lisa - had to know her.

She just didn't know if they knew they had moved to Bloomington. She looked around at her nice rented home, thought about the neighborhood, schools, the peacefulness in comparison to Chicago and how happy she was to be there, but none of it mattered if she had to have it without Black.

She went and ran herself a hot bubble bath, grabbed her portable CD player boom box with her 'Who is Jill Scott' CD and soaked herself while she tried to forget just how deep not only things were, but also how deep they could and would get knowing her husband. She didn't even want to think about it - She closed her eyes and let Jill Scott take her to another place.

After Derrick got all the information he could get on Black and Latrice he printed off a copy of both their pictures. As the pictures came out his printer, he grabbed, looked at 'em, and smiled.

"Pussy. Ah yeah, a niggaz biggest downfall."

He said to himself and tossed the pictures on his desk. He walked to the kitchen, poured himself a cup of milk and grabbed a box of cupcakes off the refrigerator. He sat down on the couch, grabbed the remote for the stereo, pressed play on the CD player and Juelz Santana sounded through the speakers.

"And this is for you Dame and it came from the heart - This ain't shame, if it was it wouldn't have come from the heart."

Derrick opened a cupcake, took a bite and washed it down with a swallow of milk. As he listened to ' The Blue Print' he picked up his phone and dialed Lisa's number. The phone just rang.

At O'Hare Airport, Lisa looked at her cell phone, and saw Derrick's number come across the screen.

"Nope. Don't feel like talking to you right now."

After six rings Lisa's voicemail picked up. "You've reached Lisa Peterson; sorry I'm unavailable, but if this is in regards of retaining me for counsel, please leave a brief message and I will contact you at my earliest convenience. Beep."

"Lisa, this is Derrick. I just wanted to know if you were alright. Give me a call when you get a chance."

Derrick hung up and couldn't help thinking if Lisa had dodged his call because she already knew he was involved.

He thought about that for a moment then said.

"Well it ain't really shit I can do if she does know, so I'll cross that bridge when I get to it."

Then he called C.G. the phone picked up on the first ring. "What's up?"

"I need to holla' at you."

"Well holla'."

"No, I need to do it in person. I got something for you. Meet me at the Rock-n-Roll McDonalds in a half hour; I'll be parked in the back."

"I'm on my way." Derrick smiled.

Derrick opened another cupcake, bit half of it, washed it down, and did the same to the other half, he put the glass on the table, grabbed the pictures of Black and Latrice, his department issue nine millimeter and headed out the door. It was 1:05 p.m.

12:31 p.m., July 8, 2012

Lisa dialed Black's cell phone but the voicemail picked up. "Holla'! Beep..."

"Hey baby, I was hoping I would have caught you. I'm gonna' be gone for two or three weeks. I'm at the airport on my way to Cancun. I wish you were going with me. You know you can still reach my cell phone, so call me tomorrow, by then I'll be settled in. If I don't hear from you I'll give you a call back. Be safe, I love you."

Black was leaning against the bathroom sink talking to Latrice when Lisa called. He looked at the number and thought, 'I'll call you back.' Latrice was calmly soaking while Black explained what happened.

After he was done, Latrice with her eyes still closed, head resting on the back of the tub and water up to her neck, said in a nonchalant tone.

"And you're sure this Vice Lord nigga' is behind all of this?"

"Baby all I'm sayin' is I know the nigga', and the nigga' know I get money."

"So did he think the money was at Lisa's house or something?"

"I don't know, but to tell you the truth, them niggaz didn't seem like they was at me for the paper. They kicked the door in on some killa' shit. It just so happen that Shy saw 'em and gave me the heads up, so I had the burner in my hand. If I wouldn't have started bustin' then they would have - So I don't think they came for money."

"Have you been into it with this nigga' before or somethin'?" Latrice asked with her eyes still closed and head resting on the back of the tub.

"Nope."

"So why the fuck would he be trying to kill you?"

"Man baby, I don't know."

"Well you need to be tryin' to find out."

Latrice sat up and the bubbles covered spots of her chest looking like patches of snow resting on fine crude oil. She looked at Black with hard eyes and a serious face, then sternly pointed her index finger at him and said.

"Because understand this. If these niggaz know about Lisa, then they know about me, and if they know about me, then they know about our babies' gotdamn it. So whatever the fuck you doin', you ain't doin' the shit right - So you better clean that shit the fuck up, and I mean right muthafuckin' now - Not tomorrow, not next week, right the fuck now Darren! Do you under fuckin' stand me?"

She stared for a moment then leaned back in the tub and closed her eyes. Black shook his head and walked out the bathroom.

C.G. pulled in the back of the Rock-n-Roll McDonalds, got out his two door Tahoe, and jumped in the car with Derrick.

"What up D'man?"

Derrick didn't reply. Instead he handed C.G. the pictures. "You know anyone of them?"

C. G. looked at the pictures for a few seconds then tapped his finger on Latrice's a couple of times.

"Ole girl look familiar, I know her from some place, I just can't place it."

"She used to work at Cook County."

C.G. nodded his head.

"Yeah, Ms. Lang bad ass. Now I remember her. My cousin stay around her area over East."

"You sure?"

"Positive."

"What about the nigga'?"

"I've never seen him, but I know for a fact cuz know where she live. Why what's up?"

"That nigga' got something of mine and that's his bitch. So since I can't touch him, I'ma' touch his hoe and then bury his ass."

"So what you talkin' 'bout?"

Derrick went in his pocket and pulled out fifteen hundred dollars and gave it to C.G.

"Take this, find the hoe, and don't kill her just trunk the bitch. Once you trunk her get at me and I got another thirty-five hundred for you. If you fuck around and come across the nigga', air his ass out and then air out the broad. You take care of this here and I got somethin' for you that's gon' put you on and I'ma' make sure you stay on."

"How long I got to take care of this shit?"

"You got the money in your hand right?"

C.G. knew that meant starting right now until the business was handled. He hopped on his cell phone and called his cousin Maine.

"Hello."

"What up cuz?"

"What's up?"

"Where you at?"

"Finna' get cut up on Cottage Grove."

"How long before you go in the chair?"

"About twenty, twenty-five minutes, why what's up?"

"I'ma' holla' at you when I get there. I'm at the building so don't leave, I'm on my way right now."

"What you on nigga'?"

"I'm on this paper vic, so don't worry about nothin' else."

"Aiight G', in a minute."

C. G. hung up and turned to Derrick.

"So these flicks mine then right?"

"Yeah."

"Aiight big man I'm on it. I'm finna' holla' at cuz and track this hoe down. Now look, it might take a few days, but once we find the hoe I got you, so don't' be blowin' my shit up - just know I'm on top of shit, aiight?"

"Yeah, just make sure as soon as you snatch the bitch you get at me - immediately."

"Man this hoe don't mean shit to me unless I get her to you - So she gon' be on the first thing smokin' right at you my man."

"Well I'm out, get at me."

"Fo'sho."

C.G. got out the car and Derrick took off. C.G. got in his truck, fired up the blunt in the ashtray and rolled off.

CHAPTER 16

August 6, 2012

Black was at the empty lot he and Latrice had rented for the used car business. It was on the south end of Bloomington in between the Layfette Club, a rim shop, and across the street from Taco Johns.

It is a nice location because traffic was good up and down Main Street daily. Plus it was close to the west, Bloomington's highest drug traffic area - So all the young hustlas would eventually come to recognize "D's" as the place to get their first whip.

Black sat behind the desk in an eighteen by eighteen foot room that was now the office of the owner of D's used automobiles. The walls were flat white and nothing hung from them yet. In the back of the desk was a five by four foot window overlooking the back of the lot.

In the front of the desk was an eight by five foot window that looked out into the reception area, which had all glass windows overlooking the front of D's.

There was another desk in the reception area with a computer on it that hadn't yet been set up, to the right of that desk a Hinckley and Smith water dispenser sat against the wall. There was red carpet throughout the establishment and four chairs that would eventually be occupied by potential customers.

In his office, Black sat across from Shy talking on the telephone to auctioneers who he knew through his own contacts and those of whom he had met through Lisa and Latrice.

After he got off the phone with his last contact he said to Shy.

"Yeah lil bro, in about another two months it's gon' be on and poppin'."

"It's all good?"

"Yes sir. I'ma' put some good shit out here; start with about fifty or sixty cars and maybe ten trucks, but I ain't gon' have no bullshit, nothin' under a '05 and all of 'em gon' be in good condition."

"No doubt. Yeah this shit comin' together."

"I told you that nigga' and watch when shit really start unfoldin'. Nia should be opening her spot in what, two or three days?"

"Yeah, the shop about ready now. She got all her workers, equipment, OSHA been out there to inspect and everything is up to code, everybody has their licenses and the clientele is just waiting for the grand-opening."

"That's what wifey was tellin' me. She said Nia cuffed a lot of clientele from these other joints when she grabbed up their barbers and stylist."

"Yeah G', she fucked some shit up for some other joints." Shy added laughing.

"What's funny?"

"Naw, I'm just trippin' because she came down here on some Gangsta' beauty shop shit." Black laughed at that.

Shy pulled a blunt out.

"Hell no nigga'! Not in here!"

"What?!"

"I told you man, I don't want that shit around me. I'm tryin' to make sure these people don't have a reason to fuck wit' me."

Shy looked at him crazy, got up, walked around to where Black was sitting, pulled out the drawer in front of Black and a chrome .45 laid there. Then he said.

"Stand up."

"Stand up? For what nigga'?"

"Just stand yo goofy ass up."

Black stood up and Shy lifted Black's shirt and there securely tucked in his waistline was Black's baby.

"You trippin' bout a blunt, but you got .45's and Glocks and shit on you. I got news for you nigga'! You not the police, F.B.I. or Secret Service. You a G.D. from out south, so you know what that mean? Them Shits is illegal so stop fuckin' with me 'bout my blunt. "

Shy said and went and sat back down.

Black shook his head.

"You a hype."

He pointed his finger at Shy.

"And I got my eye on your cluck ass, and the first time one muthafuckin' bag come up missin', I'ma' smoke yo little ass out."

"Yeah nigga' I heard it before."

Shy said as he fired up his blunt.

Just as he was blowing out the smoke from the first pull, Nia and Latrice came through the front door.

"Yeah this is nice girl, I like it." Nia commented.

"Thank you. It's gon' be a whole lot better, we still ain't put nothin' in here yet, but by the time we get ready to open it'll be right."

"Yeah girl, you know I know how that goes. I just finished my shit."

"And it looks good too girl."

"Thank you baby."

Latrice put on a playful excited face as she patted her hair.

"And I was the first one to get my shit laid." Then held out her hand, Nia slapped her five.

Latrice walked in the office with Nia behind her.

"Hey baby." And as she walked pass Shy she said,

"What's up Smokey? Neck respect."

And slapped him on the back of his neck.

Shy hollered.

"Okay now Latrice you gon' fuck around and make me smack the shit out yo black ass!"

"Shut up boy, she was just playin' wit' you." Nia said.

"Why you always takin' her side like she fuckin' you or something?"

Nia ran up on Latrice, grabbed her by the waist and playfully grinded her while saying.

"Because she is, you didn't know nigga', you on the outs. All I want you for is yo money."

"Look, baby-mama's get it too."

"Nigga' we a get down on yo little ass in here."

Latrice cut in as she jumped at and put her face right in Shy's face.

"What punk? What?"

Shy sat in the chair seemingly unbothered and blew smoke in her face.

"Beat it bust downs, y'all blowin' me."

Black laughed at the show that was taking place because it was what they had all grown to love.

They were a family outside their family. Shy was Black's little brother, Nia was Black's and Latrice's sister, and of course Shy was Latrice's little brother. Years of coming up in the streets had given them a love for one another that could never be compromised or broken. They would all be together in a marriage until death do them part.

"Let me hit the blunt baby."

Nia asked as she sat on Shy's lap.

"Damn 'Trice, yo nigga' gettin' all this money you would think his cheap ass would of bought some fuckin' chairs for this joint."

"That's how the rich stay rich; they get the shit they need, not what other people want 'em to have." Black answered.

"Yeah, well you're going to want people to come in here and buy cars." "And?" "And what nigga'? They gon' want to have a place to sit down goofball!"

Black laughed and Nia added, "It's not funny Black, start getting' tight if you want to and I'ma' stop fuckin' wit' yo ass."

"Then what I suppose to do? Cry you a river or something?"

Nia was hitting the blunt and didn't respond, Black continued. "I ain't yo man. You stop fuckin' wit' me, I ain't gon' have to worry about not gettin my dick sucked."

Nia blew out the smoke.

"Nigga' fallout wit' me for real and I bet you 'Tricey don't be suckin' that little shriveled up ass dick no mo'."

"Check yo hoe G' before I gotta' put her out my joint."

"Fuck her, remember she only fuck wit' me for my money anyway."

Shy closed his eyes and went on in a white snobbish manner.

"Have her removed from the premises."

They all laughed.

"So baby, did you talk to the people about the cars?"

"Yeah."

Back sighed and then rubbed his eyes with his index finger and thumb.

"All day it seems like."

"Yeah that shit ain't like baggin' dope, you gotta' put some work into it." Latrice acknowledged.

"True dat, true dat, but it's all good though. Within two months we should have fifty or sixty cars and about ten trucks, all of 'em '05 and up. I didn't want nothin' too old or nothing too new either, but they all gon' be in good runnin' condition - no traps."

"Well that's good, it's all working out."

How much dope you still got left to cook and bag?"

Nia asked. Black looked at Latrice.

"What, twenty-three, twenty-four more keys?"

"Yeah something like that. Hoe you need to have yo ass out there workin' too."

Latrice said to Nia.

"If I come, I want a brick of that shit off top."

"What you gon' do wit' it?"

Black mused in a 'yeah right' sort of tone.

"What you think I'ma' do wit' it?"

Nia stood up with the blunt in her hand, reached in Shy's waistband, grabbed his pistol, stepped back, leaned against the wall, hit the blunt and said.

"Post up and flood the block nigga'."

Black laughed. "You goofy den a muthafucka'."

"There you go girl." Latrice said clapping her hands and laughin'. Nia pimped back to Shy and said, "Hold this down shorty." And handed Shy his gun back. Shy just shook his head.

"But look baby, we gon' get on up outta' here because Londa gon' get to panicking if we ain't there right at seven."

"Yeah I know. Tell cuz I wish I could be there but..."

"Yeah yeah nigga' I know, but niggaz wanna' kill you."

Black drew back with a crazy look on his face.

"Damn! Where that come from? I was gon' say, but I got business to handle."

"Business my ass, that's why you walkin' around Bloomington with the pipe on you."

"Trust me baby, these niggaz don't want it."

Latrice leaned over and sweetly said.

"I know baby."

And kissed him on the lips softly.

"But look, I'll call you tonight and probably won't be back until tomorrow."

"Y'all have fun and tell my lil cuz happy birthday for me."

"I will."

Nia kissed Shy and they walked out. It was 4:47 p.m. Friday evening.

At 7:15 p.m. Nia and Latrice were parking over east on 72nd and Kimbark. Niggaz were on the corners getting money and blowing blunts ganged up. Cars and trucks were stopped in streets talkin' to niggaz and females on the block, while hypes and dope fiends bought bags and hurried off to their get high spots. Music vibrated the concrete and car windows while trunks rattled bass lines from Kanye West and inner city underground producers.

"We not in Kansas no mo' Dorothy."

Nia commented in reference to them being back in the Chi from Bloomington.

"I know that's right girl."

Latrice stepped out the truck wearing Prada head to toe. An all-white body dress that accentuated her every curve and if it were possible, made her beautiful deep dark complexion seem even darker.

She had on a diamond ankle bracelet, a diamond toe ring, Black's blue diamond earrings, and her diamond, gold, and platinum chain with diamond charm that read 'Wifey.'

Nia wore a white Gucci tight fitting pullover quarter-sleeve shirt, a matching Gucci skirt, white Gucci heels, a diamond ankle bracelet, Gucci watch, diamond crescent earrings, her gold hoop eyebrow ring, and a gold chain with a diamond and gold charm that read 'Nia.'

Before they could get to the door, Yolanda, Latrice's first cousin, who was more like a sister, was standing in the doorway holding her phone out.

"Yeah. Two more minutes and I was finna' start blowin' your shit up."

"Hey girl, Happy Birthday." Latrice said smiling as she hugged her.

"Happy Birthday little cuz." Nia added handing her an Armani bag.

Yolanda took the bag and rushed into the house letting out an excited scream. She sat on her black leather couch and went into the bag. Nia bought her a red Armani dress with matching heels, some jeans and a matching Armani blouse.

"Oohh, thank you big cuz." Yolanda got up and hugged Nia. Latrice handed Yolanda two boxes.

"This is from me and Black and he said Happy Birthday."

One of the boxes had a platinum and diamond eighteen inch tennis necklace in it, the other, two karat diamond and platinum earrings.

"Dammmmn Cuz." Yolanda whispered still staring at the gift. "Y'all snapped."

Then she let out a loud scream and began to stomp her feet. Her seven year old daughter and five year old son came running out the room.

"What mama? What?" "Look at what you auntie bought me!"

They both looked at the chain and earrings and said.

"Man that's tight." "Auntie Latrice you a baller." Netta said. "I'll be glad when my birthday come."

"I bet you will." Latrice replied.

"So I'm sayin', I know you got somethin' to drink and smoke before we go out?" Nia asked.

"And you know this man."

Yolonda looked at her kids,

"Bye!"

They both pouted, turned and walked out. Yolonda reached in the side of the couch, pulled out an ounce of Loud and tossed it to Nia.

"I hope you can roll, because I can't."

"Come on girl, you know I got this."

"Cool the blunts on the stereo."

"You got a razor blade?"

"It's up there too."

Yolonda answered while walking into the kitchen. She came back with a fifth of Remy and a half gallon of cranberry juice, then walked back and got three glasses filled with ice. She poured all three of them a big drink and toasted to her birthday.

"Netta! Jayvon!" Yolonda called. The kids shot out their room.

"Huh mama?"

"Y'all ready?"

"Yes."

"Okay, y'all can go over to Sherry's house."

That was music to the kid's ears. Netta ran for the door and Jayvon yelled,

"Wait for me!"

"Little girl, wait for your brother, and hold his hand goin' across the street."

"Okay mama."

Yolonda stood at the door, watched them cross the street, and run up to Sherry's door. They knocked and Sherry opened the door a few seconds later.

"Thanks girl!" Yolonda yelled as she waved happily.

"No problem you just have a nice time. Sherry replied waving back.

"We will, I love you."

"Love you too."

"Sherry watching the kids huh?"

"Yes girl, and I almost thought I wasn't gon' be able to get nobody."

"Shiit, I would of been callin' Mike Mike's ass and makin' him come get his babies." Latrice replied.

"I didn't even feel like wrestling with that punk. He still hot cause I won't fuck him no more. That nigga' is a trip girl. He know's I have a man and he still just expect me to give him the pussy like it's still his."

"Yeah, niggaz think once them babies come out you, with their face - that they own yo ass." Nia added.

"Don't they girl. Now I can't lie. I give the nigga' some pussy every now and then, but he can't just expect it all the time."

Nia fired up the Loud and by the time they had smoked the whole blunt, and had two drinks, they were ready to ride. They stepped out the door looking like models.

Yolonda favored Christina Milian except she had chinky eyes and a sexy gap in her teeth, light brown micro braids and a thicker than life body. She was bad and a ghetto buck ass female.

They headed downtown to Club 212, blew a blunt on the way and walked through the door fucked up and ready to kick it. The club was packed, the music moved through their bodies as they danced in perfect harmony like the latest girl group.

Niggaz drove on them recklessly and they shot 'em down like fish in a barrel. They all had guys and neither of them would get down on 'em. Yolonda fucked with Mike Mike on some once in a blue moon shit and the moon hadn't been blue for months, but not enough drinks and weed in the world could make them get out there with a nigga' in the streets. They were out just having fun as girls.

Latrice had one double shot of Remy and cranberry juice the whole night, but Yolonda and Nia got bombed. By the time the night was over they were both loud and obnoxious.

On the way home they stopped at J & J Fish on Stony Island to get some perch dinners before they went in. Latrice was the closest one to being sober so she went in and ordered the food - Ten minutes later Yolonda and Nia came stumbling in on bullshit.

"Damn girl, what the fuck they doin', catchin' the fish?!" Nia said.

"You know how slow these muthafuckas is." Yolonda replied.

"Y'all just drunk, they ain't been no long time."

Latrice said smiling at her drunk ass girls.

While they were waiting for their order Maine and C.G. pulled up in a brown four door 2009 short body Caddy and parked next to the Black's '2012 Denali the girls were in.

Maine looked in the window and said.

"Damn G', there that bitch go, right there."

"Who?"

"Ole girl from the County."

"Latrice?!" C.G. replied.

"Yeah nigga'!"

C.G. looked in the window.

"That is that hoe. What's up G', you got your burner right?"

"Fo sho'."

"Aiight we finna' snatch this bitch up."

"And we robbin' these hoes, look at them bitches, they laced." Maine added.

A couple minutes after they pulled in, the ladies order came up and the girls strolled out, got in the truck, backed out, and pulled off. The whole while talking and laughing enjoying the remainder of their night, not even realizing they were being followed.

Latrice jumped on Stony Island, took it to 71st, made a left, and another left on Dorchester, she came back up to 72nd, made a left, took it to Kimbark and made a right. She parked and they all got out.

"Girl I'm fucked up." Yolonda said.

"Well Happy Birthday baby." Just as Latrice got the words out her mouth, Maine and C.G. pulled up and bailed out.

The girls had their backs to the street so all they heard was.

"If anyone of you bitches turn around I'ma blow yo muthafuckin' brains out right here in the middle of this block."

Neither of them were strangers to the stick up game and all of 'em had been schooled on what to do and that was to just give that shit up. They all stopped and didn't move. Yolonda and Latrice were thinking the same thing. 'I know the folks on the corner got bangers,' but neither of them were willing to risk being shot trying to call 'em.

"Lay the fuck down on yo stomach!"

Maine commanded. The voice sounded familiar to Londa but she was drunk and too scared to quite place it. They all laid down and as they did their short dresses rode up exposing three different color shades of blackness in the form of beautiful well rounded asses.

C.G. went around unfastening chains, bracelets, watches, and snatching out earrings. Once he was done, he grabbed Latrice by the top of her hair.

"Get yo muthafuckin' ass up bitch!"

"Aahhh!" Latrice let out a short scream.

"Bitch you better shut the fuck up before I blow yo muthafuckin' face off."

Maine started falling back and as C.G. was pulling Latrice toward the car Latrice heard him say.

"Hurry up, pop the trunk."

And immediately she blanked and start pulling away, swinging her arms, yelling and screaming.

"You not putting me in no got damn trunk nigga'!"

"You want me to pop her G'?" Maine said agressively.

"Naw, D'man want her alive."

Londa heard that and jumped up, Nia was right behind her. Nia was closest to C.G. so she ran up and clawed him in the face as Latrice struggled to get free. Londa ran over and as she did, she saw Maine. Shocked and surprised she screemed out his name.

"Maine!?"

In the midst of the struggle Latrice heard the name and instinctively glanced over at him as Londa was yelling.

"Nigga' what the fuck wrong wit' you?! What the fuck you on!? Bitch yo ass gon' die..."

And in an instant Maine pulled the trigger twice.

The first shot hit Londa in the head, blood flew on Latrice splattering her face and dress. She closed her eyes as she felt the warmth of her cousin's blood. The second shot hit Londa in the stomach. Her body twisted as she was knocked off her feet to the ground. Yolonda was dead.

Nia yelled.

"You muthafucka'!"

And Maine shot again. He hit Nia in her upper right shoulder spinning her around and dropping her to the ground. After the third shot and the screams, lights came on, on the whole block.

Niggaz ran from the corner with guns out.

"We gone G'."

C.G. ran for the car, Maine was already jumping in. Niggaz came running from their cribs with pistols out.

"Get them niggaz! Get they ass! They just killed Londa and Nia! Get 'em! Get 'em!"

Latrice screamed hysterically as she went from body to blood soaked body.

The four niggaz on the corner hit the street and rocked the brown caddy trying to pull off. Three of the niggaz had nines, the other a forty-five.

"Pop! Pop! Pop! Pop! Pop! Pop! Pop! Pop! Pop! Pop!"

Maine swerved as bullets tore through C.G.

Driving with his head down steady swerving through the street, Maine hit a parked car. As soon as he hit it, he jumped out and started running down 72nd while niggaz licked off shots at him that missed, but C.G. wasn't that lucky. They hit him eight times in the face and body killing him on the spot.

"Call the ambulance! Please somebody call the ambulance! Please somebody help me!" Latrice screamed not knowing that somebody had already called the ambulance and police. Sirens already echoed through the night and gradually got louder.

The niggaz who gunned down C.G. disappeared. Then from across the street Sherry's door opened and Netta saw her auntie crying. She broke off the porch followed by her little brother. When they got across the street they saw their mother with half her face knocked off laying twisted in a pool of blood while their auntie held her in her arms crying and screaming.

When the police got there they went to Nia first, and she moved. They quickly called in a rush on the ambulance, then went to Yolonda. In extreme shock, Latrice snapped.

"Get away from her! Just stay the fuck away from her!"

She held Londa in her arms rocking her back and forth.

"I'm sorry baby, I'm sorry – I'm so so sorry baby."

Her tears fell onto her cousin's deceased body. It was 3:08 a.m., August 7, 2012.

Chapter 17

At 5:33 a.m., Black and Shy were running into Jackson Park Hospital on 75th and Stony Island. Nia had already been operated on. The bullet went in the corner of her upper chest between her shoulder and breast, then out the back of her armpit. The .45 caliber slug left a big wound and caused a lot of bleeding, but she was alive.

Yolanda died on the spot, and with her, a part of Latrice, Black, Shy, and Nia died also.

Latrice and Yolanda had been raised practically as sisters, and Black, Shy, and Nia knew Yolanda for as long as Black and Latrice had been married, which was five years now. So there was a lot of pain and hurt moving through the hospital.

Latrice blanked out on the police and refused to let the kids go with anyone but her, so Netta and Jayvon were both sleeping in the same hospital room as their auntie. Emotionally drained and traumatized, the kids could only fall asleep with the hopes that when they woke up it would all have been a bad dream.

When Black and Shy reached the individual rooms, both Nia and Latrice were recouping; Nia from her gunshot wound, and Latrice, who was still sedated from the medication it took to calm her down was recouping from shock.

Shy walked in Nia's room, saw her, and shook his head with anger and sadness in his eyes. While watching his woman lying there with her eyes closed, tears rolled down his face. She looked dead and that was a picture Shy wasn't prepared to see. He held her hand.

Shy couldn't believe it, because not even fourteen hours ago they were just laughing and joking and now Nia lay there almost outta' reach to him forever.

"Don't go baby, I need you girl."

Tears trickled into his mouth as he squeezed her hand tighter, while gently rubbing it saying. "Please God, don't take her from me. I love her too much."

She was alright, but it just felt too close. Looking at her brought the reality of death to his doorstep. And like for everyone, no matter what we say about our belief, when death is at our door step we call upon God - We call upon him; and ask to be delivered.

Shy touched Nia's face. It had never felt so warm, or so soft to him, she never looked so beautiful or vulnerable to him, and he never loved her as much as he did at that moment. He saw his daughter all over her face and he knew at that moment he never wanted to let her hand go, and he wouldn't - Not at least until she woke up and smiled at him.

Black walked into Latrice's room and saw Netta and Jayvon sleeping in the chairs with blankets over them. Netta looked just like Londa and just looking at her caused tears to well up in his eyes.

He walked over and stood a couple feet from Latrice's bed. She was all cleaned up, just medicated and sleeping soundly. On the side of the bed was a sterile plastic bag that held all of her clothes. Black could see the blood smeared on the inside of the plastic.

He picked up the bag, sat down and held it in both of his hands staring at it. Memories flashed through his mind of all the times he, Latrice, and Yolonda had spent together. He thought of the first time he met Londa.

"This my first cousin, slash sister, slash best friend in the whole world, and this is Black."

"Black! Hell naw, what's the nigga real name just in case I gotta' get at his ass for fuckin' wit' you."

Londa was feisty and pretty, she had that ghetto attitude and style about her that was attractive to street niggaz and intimidating to white men.

When Black first met her, she was wearing a pink halter top, low cut blue jean shorts, flip-flops with her hair wrapped in a scarf. She looked at Black with the eyes of an apprehensive father meeting his daughter's boyfriend for the first time. He thought about that as his memory casually moved forward a few months to a time when they were all playing spades.

"Pop y'all ass nigga'! I told you this little lame ass nigga' you brought over here couldn't play no cards. I should make his ass strip."

Londa was talkin' about Shy; they were all drunk off Remy, high blowing Loud. He flashed another few months ahead.

"Man Darren, my sister really love you and I really love you too. For real I'm so glad y'all got married. I never had a real brother, but I know this, if I did - I couldn't love him no more than I love you."

They were in Black's car at Rainbow Beach smoking a blunt and that was the first time he ever saw Londa cry. He flashed a few months further.

"Black them Stones from Terror town comin' down here right now, they lookin' for you!"

Londa's mouth was busted, her shirt was ripped and her hair was all over her head.

"Man what the fuck happened to you?"

"I just got through whoopin' two of those bitches because they was talkin' 'bout tryin' to set you up. They didn't know you was my brother - So I checked one of 'em and they must of thought it was sweet cause they tried me and got they ass banged. But them niggaz drivin' around lookin' for you."

No sooner did she say that, the back window shattered. The Stones shot it out. Black hit the gas and skeeted off. A year further.

"Get the fuck off me nigga'! You watch muthafucka' – I'm finna' have yo ass kilt!"

Londa swung her door open and Black and Shy were standing at the door just getting ready to walk in. Londa's eye and mouth was bleeding. She saw Black and pointed behind her.

"This nigga' just beat my ass like I was a man for no damn reason!" Black and Shy rushed Londa's baby daddy and beat his ass until she got tired, and then his last memory.

"What's up big bro?"

"What's happenin' lil sis, that birthday comin' up huh?"

"Yeah and we gon' kick it, so y'all gots to bring your bougie asses back to the block. I swear niggaz start getting' a little money and the first thing they do is leave the hood. Fuck that, not me, I'm a hood sick, hood bitch, can't switch, wont flip - If I gotta' leave the land wit' my dollars then it don't make sense."

"Oh, so you a rapper now huh?"

"Jack of all trades nigga'."

"Yeah I feel you."

"But for real, y'all gotta' be here, you comin'?"

"I'ma' try, but I got a lot of shit happenin' right now."

"Yeah Tricey told me what happened and I saw that shit on the news, but you cool though right"

"Yeah, but I'ma' give the city a little air for a minute."

"Yeah I feel you on that, but Latrice comin' right?"

"Let me see, hold on. Aye baby Londa on the phone line." Latrice picked up another phone in the house.

"Hey birthday girl."

"Hey birthday girls big sister."

"You silly and stupid."

"Black just said he wasn't comin'."

"I didn't say that, I just said..."

"Nigga' you ain't comin'." Londa blurted out and then went on to say.

"But just because his ass ain't comin' you bet not pull no bullshit and say you ain't comin'."

"Girl I will be there, don't worry about that. Me and Nia comin'."

"Good, be here at seven and don't make me blow yo phone up. Boy put that shit down before I beat yo little ass!" Londa yelled at Jayvon.

"Girl let me call you back. I'm finna' beat yo little nephew's ass."

"You ain't gon' do shit." Black said as he laughed.

"I know, but he don't know that, bye."

By the time Black had strolled down memory lane his face was full of tears and his heart was broken. He looked over at his nephew and niece, then at the bloody clothes in the bag.

"Damn Londa, how the fuck this shit happen?"

For the first time Black was thrown off losing Londa was really close to home and it made him realize how much he truly loved Latrice. He didn't even want to imagine how she must be feeling.

A few seconds after that thought ran through his mind he heard a soft whisper. "Baby." He glanced up and Latrice was looking over at him. She looked drained on every level mentally, physically, emotionally, and spiritually.

Black slid the bag under his seat, not wanting Latrice to see it, then got up and walked over to her. He grabbed her left hand with his and stroked her hair from her face with his right.

Latrice's eyes were lost and hurt, so sad that they made his heart sink into his stomach.

"Londa dead. That nigga' killed Londa. He shot her right in the face. He killed my sister."

Tears streamed from her eyes.

"I know baby, I know."

"He shot Nia too and she might be dead."

"Naw she's cool, Shy in there with her right now."

"We takin' the babies back with us and I'ma' get custody of 'em. Mike Mike ain't on shit and I want 'em outta' Chicago."

"Okay baby." Black agreed.

Latrice closed her eyes and fearfully said,

"Baby, they were after me. They tried to put me in the trunk."

"What?"

Black immediately became focused.

"What you mean they tried to put you in the trunk?"

"They tried to put me in the trunk. That's when Londa and Nia got up and while me and Nia was fighting one of them niggaz, Maine shot Londa in her face and then shot Nia."

"Maine?"

"Yeah it was Maine baby. I saw his ass and so did Londa. She even said 'What the fuck is you doin' Maine?"

Latrice was right back on Kimbark again listening to Londa.

"Nigga' what tha fuck is you on? Yo ass gon' die!"

Then Latrice heard the shots again. She closed her eyes tight, but tears still managed to escape from them. A moment later she went on with her eyes closed as if she was still watching it in her mind.

"He knew who she was; he just didn't give a fuck. He just killed her and he was probably gon' kill me too."

"You talkin' 'bout Maine who stay on St. Lawrence?"

Latrice opened her eyes.

"Yeah baby Maine. He got a sister name Jasmine and his brother be working the block on 69th. I know exactly who it is and so do you. That's why I didn't tell the police shit. I want that muthafucka' dead, and I mean it, that muthafucka' better die Darren."

Black was confused. He thought to himself 'What the fuck is Maine on? Why is this nigga' at me? He one of the folks and I ain't ever fell out wit' this nigga'."

"He had another nigga'wit' him. He said don't shoot me, I wasn't no good to him dead, D-man want me alive. Baby what is goin' on?"

Black shook his head slowly as he stared over the top of Latrice's head still thinking. Then adamantly said.

"I don't know, but you can believe this. Every nigga' who involved in this shit dying. That nigga' Maine just killed his mama, his brother, his sista' and her shorties. I don't know who D'man is, but as soon as I find out. I'm killin' him and then I'ma find his mama and shoot her in her fucking face.."

It was 6:11 a.m., August 7, 2012.

After Nia was released from the hospital Black and Shy trailed her, Latrice, and the kids to the I-80 West which was the expressway that led out of Chicago and connected to I-55 South to Bloomington.

"Okay baby, y'all good from here?" Black said into his cell phone.

"Yeah, we'll be alright. How long y'all gon' be down here?"

"Not too long. We just gon' handle this little lightweight business and I'll be home before my side of the bed gets cold."

"It's already cold."

"Well put little Darren in my spot until I get there."

"It won't be the same."

"But it will be somethin'."

Latrice had a flash of Londa's head jerking back and her body flipping over as her cousin's blood sprayed her across the face, it sent a chill through her body.

"Baby be careful!"

"I stay careful."

Latrice sighed. "For real baby, be careful."

"Look baby girl, you know me – I'm built for this shit, this right up my alley. Bring it hard and sharp and keep it gangsta. Trust me. I'm on my square, you just hold me down from where you at and let daddy take care of this business."

Latrice loved the hell out of Black and that was one of the main reasons, because he wasn't 'bout no games. Business was business and everything else was bullshit. And one thing he did not do; was mix bullshit with business.

"Okay baby, but you call me."

"How could I not, you my favorite lady with both my babies and if don't nobody else know, you know, without you I'd go crazy."

Latrice smiled and replied.

"I love you so much."

"I know you do and that's why you on yo way back home and I'm down here makin' sure it's safe for you to be there. But look, let me get off this phone."

"Okay."

"I'ma hit you later."

"You better."

"I will."

"Okay, I love you, bye."

"I love you too baby, bye."

While Black spoke to Latrice, Shy spoke to Nia. They ended their phone calls seconds apart. Shy had already turned around and was now headed back into the city. As the highway exit numbers decreased from 131st to 127th, to 119th, to 111th, to 99th, to 75th, they rode silently while 50 cent hummed low through the speakers.

"Many men - wish death upon me - Blood in my eyes dog and I can't see – I'm tryin' to be what I'm destined to be - And nigga'z tryin' to take my life away. Many men."

It was 2:40 in the afternoon. Chicago was alive and people were out all over the place. Shy and Black rode through taking in the same sights they had seen for years, but the feelings in their hearts were so cold at the moment that they really weren't at all moved with the city life that had made them what they were today.

Shy stopped at the Amoco gas station on 75th, grabbed a box of blunts, then rode to 57th and Shields and spent a hundred on loud.

Black didn't even say anything because he knew his man was feeling it right now. Black had called Flinno from the hospital about 7:30 that morning and Flinno left right out the door from Centralia.

Flinno had been in Chicago for a hour moving around getting at the couple pistols he kept on the land so he didn't have to ride the E-way five hours with burners on him. He met Shy and Black at Shy's sister's house, and for the next six hours they laid low getting shit together.

Flinno brought two .45 automatics with him, Black and Shy had brand new Glocks with extended clips, filled to the tip.

At 8:40 p.m. they stepped out into the warm night air. The first place they went was 65th and St. Lawrence. They passed by Maine's mama house. She was sitting outside enjoying the gentle breeze as they passed.

"Look at her big fat ass. I should dome that big bitch right now."

Black said. Shy just kept rolling at a normal speed.

"Cuz you sure this bitch Jasmine want to fuck wit' you?"

"Yeah cuzo, the bitch been at me for a minute."

"Aiight, cause I know we gon' see her ass, so you know what's up?"

"Fo sho'."

They rode up 69th and saw Maine's little brother with a couple of his guys out there checkin'.

"Yeah nigga', yo brother did this to you."

Black whispered as they drove pass.

About a half hour later they were riding up 63rd and made a left on King Drive. Flinno flew some Trays at the B.D.'s posted up as they turned. Then, just as they were passing McDonalds Flinno said.

"There she go cuz! Let me out right here!"

Shy pulled over in front of Parkway Gardens and Flinno bailed out.

Jasmine was coming out of McDonalds with a bag under her arm while eating a. strawberry sundae.

"What's up lil mama?"

"Hey, what's up Flinno?" Jasmine replied with an interested smile.

"What you on?" Flinno asked.

"Shit, just up here getting' my babies somethin' to eat."

"You got something in there for me?"

"I don't have anything in here but some cheeseburgers and fries."

"I eat cheeseburgers." "You got money to buy your own too."

"So what - I might wanna' eat yours.'

"They ain't mine, they my babies."
"I eat sundaes too and that looks like it's yours."
"You want some?"
"Depends on what comes wit' it."
"Boy what you talkin' 'bout?"

She knew what he meant and she was ready to set it out right then too. Flinno could have talked her into the bathroom, nailed her, and got the cheeseburgers too, if he wanted.

"I'm talkin' bout you. What you on? Come smoke something' with me."

"Oohh, I want too, but gotta' take my babies their food."

"Don't trip, I'll take you. Then cuz can drop me at my whip and me and you can get on somethin' from there."

"Aiight, we can do that because I sho' didn't feel like walkin'."

"That walkin' is what got that ass sittin' out there like that." Flinno patted her on the butt.

"Boy you stupid."
"Yeah ok."

Flinno said while thinking

'Bitch if you really knew.'

They crossed the street and got in the car. Shy was just putting fire to the blunt. He hit it, passed it back to Flinno and pulled off.

"Damn, y'all smokin' good, that's that 'loud I can smell it."

"Aye Flinno." Shy said.

"I gotta' stop somewhere first aiight?"

"Yeah, but lil mama gotta' get this food to her shorties."

"Don't trip, I got you baby girl." Shy told her.

"It's cool, I was walkin' anyway."

Flinno passed her the blunt while Shy drove up to 75th and made a left.

"Jasmine?"

"Huh?"

"So what's up wit' yo brother?"

"Who, Maine?"

"Yeah, where that nigga' at?" Black asked.

"I haven't seen him since yesterday. He been up north in the Greens wit' our cousin."

"You can't get at him, I got something for him?"

"Nope, he just got a new number and I don't have it yet, but I'll see him sooner or later. You want me to tell him you tryin' to holla' at him?"

Black nodded while biting his lower lip.

"Yeah, something like that."

Shy hit it up 75th until he got to Rainbow Beach. There were only three other cars there. Shy pulled off in the cut and parked. Jasmine was feeling the 'Loud and this scene to her looked oh too familiar. She was a runner and niggaz had ran her ass on a regular basis up until a year ago, but as she looked around at the three niggaz in the car, she'd already decided whatever they wanted to get on she was up with it.

Shy turned down the music and Black spoke up.

"Aye Jasmine?"

"Yeah, what's up boo?"

"Look man, yo brother fucked up, and he fucked up real bad."

Those weren't the words she ever imagined she would be hearing. Instantly her heart sank into her stomach and fear reached out and wrapped itself around her entire body.

"What you talkin' about Black?"

"Just what I said baby girl. For real, shit fucked up and it's fucked up in a way that can't be fixed."

"What you mean? I don't know what my brother did. I told you I ain't seen him since yesterday."

Black grabbed his pistol and cracked it back. The sound of the gun made Jasmine jump and brought tears to her eyes. She looked at Flinno; he just shook his head and hit the blunt while staring out the side window as if he was looking at the rocks.

Jasmine began to tremble as fear swelled deeper within' her. She thought about her four and five year old babies at home hungry waiting on her to come back.

"Please don't do this. Please don't do this. Please, please don't do this."

Her face was streaming with tears and her voice as cracking.

"Bitch shut the fuck up!" Black snapped and turned around with the pistol in his hand. "Yo dumb ass is already dead."

Flinno's words came rushing back to her thoughts, 'Naw girl, you stupid,' and that's just how she felt. Chasing some dick and a high had cost her life.

"Bitch take them muthafuckin clothes off." Black said with eyes of hatred. Jasmine was so caught up in his last words to really hear what he said after that; so she just looked at him with sorrowful eyes and a face full of tears.

"Bitch you think I'm playin' wit' you?!"

Black said a little louder and then smacked her across the top of her left eye with the gun. Instantly blood began to flow from her eye. She screamed, "Aaahh!" as she fell to the right hitting her head on the window.

"Oh my God please! Please don't do this!"

Blood covered the left side of her face and ran down her shirt and pants as she quickly unbuttoned her blouse. She raced out of her shirt kicking her shoes off at the same time. She unsnapped her bra and her nice round titties slightly hung and rocked back and forth as she unbuttoned and pulled her pants and panties off.

Once she was naked, she sat there bleeding, sweating, and crying.

"Please don't kill me. Please don't." Jasmine whimpered with sad eyes.

Black looked at her and the memories of the bloody clothes in the plastic bag at the hospital filled his mind and that made him smack her in the head again.

This time blood poured out from the top of her head. She screamed hysterically.

"Aaahhh! Oh my God! Oh my God! Oh my God!" Black grabbed her by the hair and put the gun right on her forehead. "Shut - the - fuck - up!"

Meanwhile Flinno passed the blunt back to Shy who hadn't turned around once, and then looked back out the window.

Black opened the car door, got out and then opened Jasmine's. No one could remotely see anything even if they had been looking, which they weren't, because in all three cars people were fucking or doing they thing.

Black grabbed Jasmine by the hair and put the pistol between her titties. Flinna gathered her clothes and shoes and got out the car just as Shy was opening the glove box to popped the trunk.

"Bitch I'ma' tell you this one time and one time only. If I hear one word out yo ass I'ma' have my man pull this car over and I'ma' empty this whole fuckin' clip in yo ass – you understand me?!"

Jasmine nodded with her lips pressed shut.

"Get yo ass in there."

She crawled in the trunk naked except for some white ankle socks, and balled up in a fetal position. The last thing she saw as the trunk closed was Black's angry face.

They rolled down St. Lawrence on 65th and saw Maine's mother and brother on the front porch. Shy pulled over and parked just as they passed the block. The house was the forth one from the corner. No one was on their porches and the shorties were at the end of the block serving.

Cars lined the dark street along with the trees that grew close to each house. Black and Flinno got out and walked casually up St. Lawrence with their hats low and hands in the pockets of their hoodies.

Normally they would have been stopped a half of block in advance and commanded to take their hands out their pockets, but security was on the other end of the block where they were getting money at.

They approached the house and stepped as if they were going to walk pass, then Black said.

"Aye fammo', ain't you Maine's brother?"

"Yeah."

"He in the crib?"

"Naw."

"Well this one time you gon' wish his ass would have been."

Flinno and Black pulled out their guns.

"Mama get down!"

Maine's little brother jumped in front of his mother but there was no place to hide. Black and Flinno unloaded into both of them. Their bodies jumped and jerked as they were being filled with bullets. Black walked up on the porch and put two bullets in both of their heads and then they ran back around the corner and burnt out.

They hit it up 65th to Cottage Grove, made a left and headed to the low end. Jasmine was bleeding even worse in the trunk, her head pounded and when she heard the gunshots she peed on herself.

Seven or eight minutes later, Shy pulled into an alley on 43rd under the L' station. Shy got out, Black popped the trunk, and Jasmine looked up at Shy like an abused child fearful of her parent.

Shy shot her three times in the face and closed the trunk. He jumped back in the car, hit it down the alley made a left on 45th, went back to Cottage Grove, made a right, went to 47th, made a left and came up to Shy's sister house.

Shy and Flinno wiped down their guns, dropped 'em in the car, got in Flinno's car, Black then drove the guns and the body down 47th to a vacant lot behind the liquor store, popped the trunk, grabbed the gas can, tossed his pistol in the trunk, doused the car and Jasmines body, and tossed a match.

The car went up instantly as he ran and jumped in the car with Shy and Flinno. Flinno jumped on Lake Shore Drive and they headed out of the Chi. Once they were on I-55 Black called Latrice. She picked right up.

"Hello?"

"What's up pretty lady, you alright?"

"Yeah, I was just laying here with the kids thinkin' about you."

"Oh yeah, what was you thinkin' about?"

"That I need you home."

"Well I'm on my way back right now. Did you cook somethin'?"

"Naw, I just ordered the kids pizza."

"Will you cook me somethin'?"

"Yeah, what you want?"

"Some fried chicken, biscuits, and rice."

"How long before you get here?"

"I guess about a little over a hour."

"Alright, is everything cool?"

"I told you it would be didn't I?"

"Yeah."

"Well don't ask me no more." Black said in a smooth playful manner, but meaning every word.

"Okay baby, I'm sorry."

Black made it to the crib at 2:08 a.m. Latrice had his food waiting for him in the oven. While he ate he explained what happened and although it wasn't Maine, Maine would feel it.

Netta and Jayvon had'nt spoken a word since they left the hospital and it would probably be a while before they got back to their normal selves. But auntie Latrice and uncle Darren would make sure they did all they could to help them move on and recover from the loss they were experiencing.

Latrice was truly hurting inside and Black could see and feel the pain all over her. So once he ate, he took a shower and made slow gentle love to his wife.

Latrice needed the closeness, the loving touch, the attention, and Black gave it to her. When they were done, Latrice laid in Black's arms and he held her securely all night and for that moment, Latrice forgot about what was going on. It was August 9, 2012.

CHAPTER 18

March 10, 2013.

"So this is it huh?"

"Yeah, it's just a little somethin', what you think?"

Lisa looked around at the many cars on the lot nodding her head in approval.

"It's nice; I have to admit that you did a really great job."

She looked onto Main Street and saw the traffic in a constant flow north and south and noticed the many faces that turned to see the vehicles that were strategically parked in view of the street.

"You have a real nice location here too."

Lisa commented as she turned and walked toward the entrance. She looked at the name on the window and amusingly said.

"D's used cars."

She twisted her lip and shook her head as she said,

"My, my, my, how we've grown."

Black had a contract with a local detail shop and a mechanic to keep the cars clean, shined, and in good running condition. It was March of 2013 and D's had been open for five months and business was booming. Profits were minimal, but at the rate the cars were moving, the first year's profit margin would exceed expectations. Black had built a wonderful report with the auctioneers and quickly became a valued client, so his choice of cars were always the best of what they had to offer.

The once bare wall reception area and office now had pictures of Black and Latrice from their wedding, children's school and baby pictures, ribbon cutting ceremony from the grand-opening, a glass plaque that held the first dollar they made, pictures of some of the first customers, and a few local charities, businesses, and youth sport teams that he sponsored.

He had accomplished what he desired as far as painting a picture of himself as a business tax paying citizen with a loving family who carried no criminal ties.

Because Latrice now worked for McLean County Jail as a Sergeant, she not only added to his clean image, but also referred many police and correctional officers to her husband with a guarantee of a nice deal.

Their only association was with Shy and Nia, who had also quickly become the talk of the town. 'Nia swooped up almost every piece of hair and nail business in town. Her prices were in most cases lower, the service was better, the establishment was more comfortable, the hours were later, and she paid the workers better and with them mostly being from the town, they directed all their clientele to Nia's.

Nia and Shy were squeaky clean and got to know a lot of people in professional capacities who took a liking to their accomplishments in the cosmetology field, and them as well.

Just as Black predicted, things were going great for the four of them. They had already become familiar with the hustlers, from the ones copping weight, all the way down to the ones selling bags on the block.

Latrice used her position to weed out those who were already police informants and she also kept a close eye of who got caught by police, when they got caught, what they got caught with, and bonds and who made them - So she would always be aware of who was making deals with the police. The ones who stayed on their square became casual acquaintances who were unknowingly being solicited for future drug sales.

They were done cooking and bagging all the cocaine and ended up with a hundred and twenty-two keys of hard crack from fifty keys of powder.

Just as things were going well for Black and Shy in Bloomington, things were also going well for Flinno and Moe in Centralia, and Solid and Dee in Schaumburg.

Between all of them they could clear out the barn right now, and have all the cocaine sold in three days, open blow spots and move the heroin over the next year.

Black knew that and felt good about it, but his dilemma was that no one had touched basis with a solid connect. He conceivably saw that they would be able to cop five hundred bricks of pure cocaine and ninety to a hundred bricks of heroin. That wasn't no baby shit, so not only did they need a connect who could cover it, but also someone they could be secure in fuckin' with.

Black knew anybody who was getting down on that scale had more than enough money and power to touch all of them if any bullshit surfaced, he didn't have any plans of pulling any stunts, but he didn't want any pulled on him either.

They were stepping into a level of the game they hadn't been before, so his thoughts were centered around how he was gonna' protect his money and get somebody to trust him well enough to even fuck with him on that scale.

They still had another year before moving the dope, so he figured if anyone found the connect they still had enough time to develop a semi-reasonable relationship, maybe not good enough for what he wanted, but gradually it would build. But like most things he had no control over, he didn't let it bother him.

Everybody had cooled off about Londa's murder, but were still a little heated it happened in the first place. But Londa was gone, nothing could change that, and that was accepted.

The kids were good though. They'd actually moved on well and adapted to the change of environment and parental figures nicely. Maine was still out there though, and no doubt D'man was still pulling strings.

Black already put a few things together concerning D'man. He figured whoever D'man was, was also the one who sent the niggaz to Lisa's house. So he figured D'man was close to the niggaz they killed and robbed in some way. Either that or they were somehow connected on the get money side.

Black also knew the nigga' had juice on the northwest side, because the Vice Lords he sent were from out west and the nigga' who called out his name was a G.D. from the Greens up north.

So the nigga' had to be on because he was fucking with the folks and Vice Lords enough to send hits out. Which made sense because a nigga' who had that much heroin alone was a heavy, but regardless of how much money he was getting, he lost millions on that one lick, not including the money, and that's what bothered Black, because that wasn't the type of bread you just chalk up. So he knew everyday he had to be the main focus of D'man's thoughts. Even if he didn't want the cash, Black knew D'man most definitely wanted that ass.

Black honored the game though and everything about it - So he could respect that, but just because he could respect it didn't mean he was gonna' honor this nigga' stalking him down like some type of animal. Hell Naw!

So just like Black was on his mind, he was on Black's. The only problem was this nigga' had the advantage because he knew Black and Black didn't have a clue of who he was, but he did have a clue on who might know. So like always, Black was on the business.

"Damn baby girl, every time I see you, you just keep getting' finer and finer."

Lisa blushed and smiled inside and out. Her three week vacation turned into three months. She was granted the leave from the partners of the firm because they too were fearful for her life. It was too much of a coincidence with her being a high profile lawyer and such a vicious act occurring at her home.

So she rerouted court dates, juggled clients, and prepared defenses while she went from Cancun, to the Bahamas, to the Virgin Islands, and capped things off in Aruba.

She talked to Black throughout her travels, but Black wasn't a phone man period, especially when it concerned illegal business, so no conversation had taken place concerning D'man.

Once Lisa made it back, she was swamped with court dates and meetings with her
Superiors, as well as clients. Once the holidays hit, she spent that time with her parents and then was right back to

grinding cases. By the middle of February she was caught up and finally had some down time.

Black had already talked to Latrice about everything and she also thought it was best that he find out all he could, so Lisa was invited to Bloomington.

Lisa and Latrice had lunch together before Lisa even made it to Black. Latrice made a point to introduce Lisa to everyone at her job and enlighten those who weren't familiar with her to Lisa's phenomenal career. Lisa met co-workers, police officers and detectives, and even through she was a criminal lawyer her expertise was recognized, admired, and respected amongst law officials and that added to Latrice and Black's clean image.

After lunch, Lisa dropped Latrice back off at the County Jail and headed to 'D's in her Benz. As always, she was stunning. She wore a purple Cashmere sweater, designer Prada jeans, and black Gucci boots with three inch heels. She only wore her diamond earrings and Gucci watch as jewelry accessories, but her look altogether said she was worth millions.

With a smile as bright as sunshine she looked at the man she just couldn't get out her system. Lisa brought him, Latrice, and the kids all sorts of gifts back and now she was receiving the only gift she needed or wanted - Some time with Black.

"You talk about I just keep getting finer and finer, look at you. Come here so I can check you out."

Black was doing the grown man thing now. Business on a professional level was his main objective, so he mainly wore suits, silk shirts, slacks, dress shoes, and conventional business attire. He'd taken the rims off the cars him and Latrice owned, put his real flashy jewelry away, and only wore less noticeable, but still expensive pieces.

Today he was wearing his diamond earrings, a tan silk Armani shirt, with black Armani slacks and square toe black Gators, his diamond encrusted wedding band and a Bulgari watch with a gator strap.

Him and Shy were working out regularly, so he gained a few pounds in muscle since Lisa last saw him and like always he was well trimmed. Lisa took him all in as well as his intoxicating seductive cologne.

Things had changed dramatically though, and since Black didn't want any unnecessary talk, he introduced Lisa as a friend of the family and kept things friendly, even in the office.

Lisa was trying to be as patient as possible, knowing that later on they were going to dinner and eventually she would end up in a hotel room with her legs kicked back behind her head getting the best dick sex had to offer her.

"Whew! I see you trying to pump it up around here huh?"

Lisa commented as she reached out to feel his chest.

"Yeah, a little bit."

"More than a little bit."

Lisa replied shaking her head, truly feeling over whelmed at what was before her.

"I don't know if I can handle you now."

Black laughed modestly as he pulled his slacks at the front and sat on his desk. Lisa smiled as she studied her man, liking the way his loose but well fitted long-sleeve silk shirt hung as he sat slightly sideways with one foot on the floor, the other hanging exposing his Armani dress socks.

"I leave for a few months, come back and you all Mr. G.Q. on me."

Black looked at her with the sexy smile she loved and answered.

"G.Q. or not, you know me. I'm the same ole G', shit don't change." "Well I hope not, because that same ole G' is what keeps me wet."

Black laughed.

"Well it's good to hear you the same ole freak."

"Only for you baby, and believe that."

Black sat all the way back on the desk.

"So what's up? It seems like a month of Sundays since I talked to you?"

"Boy you just talked to me a couple days ago."
"Well let me rephrase that."
"I think you better."
Lisa smiled.
"It seems like a month of Sundays since I saw you and talked to you."
"Now, that's better. You gotta remember, I'ma' a lawyer, so words mean everything, but to answer your question. Not too much has been going on." "How you like the new place?" "It's nice, really nice. When you gonna make it down there?"
Black sighed and shook his head.
"Awe shit, I've seen that look before. What's the matter?" Lisa asked.
"Man, I just been tryin' to piece some things together, that's all."
"Like what?"
"Well, first of all Latrice's cousin got killed a few months back, and Shy girl, Nia got shot."
"Oh my God, is she alright?"
"Yeah she cool."
"Why didn't you tell me about that? I like Nia."
"You know how I am with the phones and this is the first time we've seen one another, but the thing is, they weren't after Londa or Nia - they were after Latrice."
"Latrice?! What do you mean they were after her?"
Lisa sat down and her lawyer mind went into effect'
"Some niggaz from out south tried to trunk her. Well not just from out south, one of the niggaz was from up north." "Up north where?" "The Greens I think, but I'm not a hundred percent sure." "What makes you think he is?"
"The nigga' who killed Londa and shot Nia, Latrice knew him, and I had a little talk with his sister trying to find him. She told me he'd been up north with his cousin in the Greens, his name Maine and he got away."
"Where did this happen?"
"72nd and Kimbark."
"I heard about that. I had no idea you all were involved."

"Yeah, right at the forefront, but anyways, while they were tryin' to put Latrice in the trunk, Maine said to the other cat, 'Do you want me to pop her?' and the dude said, 'No she ain't no good to me dead. D'man want's her alive."

When Black said D'man, Lisa got an instant flash of being at home with Tuko listening to the many conversations Tuko was having with Derrick on the phone or in person. Tuko and his brother always referred to Derrick as D'man. That was the only time she had ever heard that nickname, but she was sure that Derrick wasn't the only one who went by it.

But even though Black mentioning D'man caught Lisa off guard, it still didn't make enough sense to her to put two and two together, because why would Derrick be after Latrice she thought.

Black asked.

"You don't know anybody by the name of D'man do you?"

For the first time since her and Black had been together Lisa lied.

"No, not that I can really recall. Why?"

"Because whoever this D'man is, I think he sent them niggaz to your house too."

That fucked Lisa up because that brought sense to the question she had been asking herself. 'How did anybody know Black and her were involved, especially enough to know where she lived and when he'd be there?' Then Derrick's words popped in her head, 'and everybody involved, you know what I'm saying?'

Lisa remembered, Derrick's words had implication that was directed towards her, but she didn't know why. But even with this information she still didn't know how, not only she, but now Black, was playing a part in what Derrick was involved in. From what she knew, Derrick only dealt on the north side, he wouldn't have any reason to even know Black, let alone consider him to be involved in anything.

'What the hell is going on?' Lisa thought.

"Yeah it's crazy, but that's what I've been dealin' with." Black said.

"That is crazy baby. I don't know, but I'll see what I can do. I come across so much information just representing these guys and one thing is for sure and that's all the big time guys know of or have some type of interaction with the others. You'd be surprised at how many big time dope dealers are moving hundreds and hundreds of kilos in Chicago alone. Not to mention in low-key suburbs. My name is first on their list of lawyers and one thing they love is client lawyer confidentiality. So you'd also be surprised at how much they trust me with their personal business."

Black damn near fell off his desk at her words. 'How the fuck did I miss that?' He thought.

"But you can believe this baby, I'm on top of it and if it's anything to find out, I'll find it."

"Yeah, that's good because I don't know what the fuck is goin' on. I can't even go back to the Chi because if I catch a murder I'm really out there, and if a nigga' try to get at you, Latrice, or me, you already know how it's goin' down."

Lisa took Black's words just the way he wanted her to. Latrice's name didn't even
register to her, all that registered was, "If anybody tries to get at you or me, you know it's goin' down."

It was confirmation to her. Confirmation that Black would kill for her, and if he would kill for her, then he had to love her, and that was all she had ever wanted to hear him say, and for Lisa that was close enough.

She bubbled over inside and her pussy was soaked and even more anxious to have Black inside her than it had ever been. She crossed her legs trying to push back the feeling.

"Shit been fucked up since then, because I can't get money the right way. I need a new connect. Somebody I can trust and who is gon' trust me enough to sell me a lot of shit."

"How much?"

"Man baby, your boy been makin' major moves over the last couple years, plus the dough from investments. I'm tryin' to turn it on. I need somebody who is gonna' be able to do three hundred bricks, but I'm lookin' for five hundred."

Lisa was shocked and turned on even more. She never imagined that Black was anywhere near that level. Everything she had ever dreamed of in a man who was in the game had just unfolded with those words. She knew without a doubt that she would always play a tremendous part in Black's life from that point on. Because he would always need her, because heavies needed lawyers, and she was the best of the best and everyone knew it. But now she would solidify it even further.

"Baby, if you're doin' it like that, let me find someone for you. That way you don't get involved with the feds or anyone shady."

"Can you do it?"

"Just trust me baby, I can do more than you could imagine."

CHAPTER 19

June 13, 2013

Solid was rolling down Madison in a platinum May Bach with custom Lamborghini doors, cream Gucci seats, eight inch plasma screens in the headrest, Kenwood seven inch fold-away plasma screen built-in CD player, with an eight disc CD and DVD changer, his name was customized in the middle of the steering wheel, and he had a stash spot that held two .45 automatics, sitting on 22" Giovanni's.

He was wearing a cream Gucci suit, with cream eel skin Gucci square toes matching the interior of the Maybach, a twenty-five thousand dollar platinum Jacob watch, yellow two karat diamond earrings, and a 20" platinum chain diamonded out.

Solid was on his way to the Cotton Club, but was sliding through the land stuntin'. He most definitely had the attention of everybody he passed in traffic as he banged some Chi-Town underground G- Black.

"I hit the block on the grind - Nine on my waistline - Gotta have it I must shine - I
hustle! I got fetish fo finer things – chasin' these big dreams - So niggaz best believe that I- will - hustle!"

He could feel the world watching him as he pulled on the loud pack stuffed in a Black Jack. He was feeling and loving the whole scene. Solid had that chop and knew he was killing the game. Him and Dee had already reached a hundred thousand in profits from the custom shop and he was enjoying it.

Solid was still up a hundred and ninety thousand after the car, jewelry, clothes, and crib. He was comfortably tucked away in the little suburb of Schaumburg and had a hot ringing name of a baller who owned the hottest custom shop around. He wasn't moving any dope and the business was not only legit through bank financing, but was profiting at an alarming rate which accounted for everything he owned, so police could dig and pick all they wanted, because it was all clean.

Dee was a true hustler and had been for years. Before niggaz was thinking about hiding dough in property and business he had already been doing it.

He had property that dated back almost fifteen years, and his wife worked as a nurse for all of those fifteen years. They paid taxes, made investments, bought, sold, and juggled property for quick and long-term profits.

He had no criminal record, wasn't associated or affiliated with any organizations and they had a long standing relationship with one bank. Him and his wife's name was solid as a rock, and clean as the board of health, and now that Solid was a full partner, he too had become clean as them on paper.

For Solid that was the American dream. He had money and didn't have to worry about being able to spend it. He was comfortably away from the cut - throat Chi-Town inner city dope game heavies, so he didn't have to worry about niggaz shutting him down because he was getting too much paper.

He didn't have to worry about the triple cross that your best friend and hood rat hoe you fuckin' on the side laying down because he wasn't moving dope. Yet he was getting legit money and that always tended to shine a different light on shady cut - throat moves. So since he was a stunner by nature, he was doin' his thing and loving every minute of it. It did"t get no better than this for Solid. If heaven had a ghetto he was flipping through it right now as superstar.

The custom Lamborghini doors were custom for real. The front doors went up, but instead of the back door sliding or coming out, it flipped up the opposite way. The first of its kind, his own design, and when niggaz saw it which they would tonight, he would let 'em know,

"You gotta' pay to do what playa's do."

With eight thousand dollars cash in his pocket, a hundred thousand on his body, and riding in a hundred and seventy thousand dollar whip, he felt like the million dollar man with a bulletproof ego.

He called his man Stan, who was getting money out west.

"Yeah, Yeah." Stan said into his I-phone. All kinds of music and voices sounded out in the background and Solid could tell that the hustlers were parking lot pimping.

"What up nigga'?"

"Who dis?"

"Solid."

"What up hustla'? How you livin' these days?"

"I'm good, I just hit the land, where you at?"

"I'm already on location at the Cotton Club. You know the playa's gotta' give the people what they want daddy-o."

"Right, I'm feelin' you. Well check it out, save me one of them VIP slots cause yo boy finna' teach 'em how to stunt in rare form."

"Where you at?"

"Getting' on Laramie, I'ma pull up on you in less than twenty minutes."

"Aiight, then, I got you playa'."

"All well."

Solid hung up the phone geeked to get to the Cotton Club. He hit it on the E-way, flipping in and out of traffic and the closer he got to downtown the more he felt like the city was his. Downtown was lit up and looked like a city in itself. A city for ballers to rotate in and out and around the towering buildings and five-star restaurants.

This was the life, the only life, and Solid thought; since you only get one, he was glad his turned out like this. Fifteen minutes after he got off the phone with Stan, he was pulling into the parking of the Cotton Club.

It looked like a hustlers reunion, all the true to life playa's were out with the coldest of the cold first round draft pick hoes either at their side or solo stuntin' themselves waiting to be drafted for at least one night.

Navigators, Denalis, Cadillacs, drop top Caddies, a couple Bentleys, 'Vets, and Porshes painted in all shades filled the lot owned by niggaz and females in tailored

Armani, Gucci, Louis Vuitton, Burberry, Stacy Adams, and custom cut suits with matching exotic skin shoes. Females fashioned the latest Prada, London Fog, in their three and four inch heels lighting up the night like stars in the sky.

It was enough diamonds, platinum, and gold in the lot alone to be cashed in and feed a small country. Solid was just where he wanted to be. He rolled up next to Stan's two tone purple Benz 600 and let the window down.

"What up playa'?"

The blended Loud smoke spilled out into the air.

"Damn nigga', I see you playa!" Stan said with surprised enthusiasm. All the niggaz and females in that area checked out the new kid who had hit the block.

"Yeah, that nigga' shit right." With a hint of jealousy and envy stirring inside of them, and the ladies thought. 'Damn who the fuck is this nigga'? And how can I get him to get at me?' Even the ones who were with recognized ballers felt Solid when he made his appearance.

Solid felt the vibe, but he knew in a minute it would go up ten or twenty more notches.

"Yeah big man, real niggaz do real things." Solid said as he got out the car letting the Lamborghini doors flip up. "Hell naw girl, look - at - this – nigga' right here." A few hoes said as the doors went up.

Loud smoke continued to file out the car like a stage prop for a play. Solid stepped out and as the smoke cleared everyone immediately saw that cream Gucci interior matched Solid's Gucci suit and shoes, his Jacob matched the ride, and Solid matched the true definition of a baller.

"I'll teach you how to stunt." Solid said eyes low feelin' good from the Loud "Check it Stan and don't let nobody tell you this ain't the first place you saw this."

Solid flipped up the backdoors the opposite way and Stan shook his head, but being a playa' and hustler for years, he couldn't let Solid know how impressed he was because as a part of the hustlers code 'Dick Riding, was strickly prohibited.

"Yeah nigga', yeah nigga', you right. That shit on point."

Solid pulled on his blunt and stood there like he was in a class by himself in the prestigious college for hustlers.

"Look, bring yo baby to my shop and I'll bless you."

It was a statement that wasn't meant to be offensive, but Stan couldn't see it any other way. The thing for him wasn't the fact that Solid was on, but how did he get on, and get on so hard. Stan knew Solid for years and knew the nigga' wasn't getting down anywhere near this status.

Stan had been checking seriously for years, so he knew what it took to flip that car and jewelry Solid was rocking and still be able to stay on. He knew every major heroin spot in the city and Solid wasn't associated with any of them. And yeah cocaine was good money, but it wasn't no paper like that herion paper.

Stan knew Solid wasn't selling bricks, or at least thought he knew, and he most definitely knew that, yeah money was good in suburbs, but not like the city - So how the fuck did this nigga' come up, he thought.

"You doing big things nigga'." Stan stated.

"Naw, I'm just starting to do big thangs, I ain't even turnt it on yet. This here."

Solid pointed to his car, flicked his earlobes, pulled at his chain, tapped his watch, jacked his slacks, and reached in his pocket and pulled out his knot.

"Is just the opening act. Wait until I headline on center stage. You think niggaz hate to see me out here now. Check they faces in a few months."

Stan knew just what Solid was sayin' because he was one of the niggaz who was hating to see his face, and every word, gesture, and slick smile Solid gave off burned deeper and deeper inside of Stan.

"But I don't give a fuck because the more they hate the more they motivate."

That really pissed Stan off because those were his own words coming back to bite him in the ass.

"Come on big pimpin', it's on me, I'm buyin' out the bar in this muthafucka."

Once in the club, Solid bought bottles and bottles of Moet. That was his shit and he made it known to the whole VIP section. One of the baddest females in the club was Adrena, light-skinned, five foot five, hazel eyes, juicy lips, long silky brown hair, a big banging upside down heart shaped ass and a nic nice chest. She was jazzy as fuck and a super duper snake.

Her and Stan were jammed, they came up in the game together, and together they were responsible for a lot of niggaz demise. Stan tried to sic her on Solid, but Solid was so caught up in himself he wasn't thinking about Adrena. But it didn't matter though, because the drunker Solid got, the more he fucked up and slowly, Stan got what he wanted anyway.

"Stan, let me holla' at you fo a minute Big Tymer."

Stan had seen it a million times, so like the spider, he just waited for the fly to land in his web. Solid and Stan stepped over to a booth away from the crowd. Solid had an open bottle of Moet and a closed one. He poured them both a glass and said.

"Look playa', you been my man for a long time, so this just from me to you. Whatever you want - I got it. I got white and that Mexican mud, however you want it, grams, ounces, or
whole thangs, plus as much as that hard shit you want."

"Yeah it's like that huh?" Stan replied. "Just like that."
"What the numbers lookin' like?"

"Playa' prices for all the playa's. I come up on a little stain and it put a nigga' all the way right so just between me and you I'm tryin' to shake this shit."

Stan thought to himself. 'I knew it was something.' And then his mind got to movin'.

"Damn, it sounds like more than a little stain the way you talkin' bout havin' it."

"It was decent, you can believe that."

"It had to be if you workin' white, brown, and yay."

"Yeah, well let's just say a few niggaz won't be takin' no trips to Belize no time soon."

"Belize huh?"

"Yeah Cha-lee, some up north ass niggaz. I been sittin' on it for a minute though."

Then clear as a bell, Stan knew the deal. This was one of the niggaz who had D'man's shit. It all came to him in a flash as he remembered his and Derrick's conversation.

"What you know 'bout anybody who den hit some good licks?"

"I don't know shit 'bout no licks man."

"Well keep yo ear to the streets for anybody trying to move bricks of cocaine, China white, and brown. You come up for me and I'ma' throw you a brick of white, brown, and of yay, you feel me." "All the way around the board playa', all the way around."

Now Stan sat in the Cotton Club more than a year later listening to Solid's dumb ass, thinking to himself, 'Two birds wit' one stone.' He could get this goofy ass nigga' out his way and come up at the same time.

"So I'm sayin' big Solid, I fucks wit' you - So let a nigga' know what I gotta to do to get down wit' you."

"Don't trip my man, I got you. We gon' rotate, but for right now, let's do what playa's do."

And Solid sat back, put the bottle of Moet to his lips, and turned it up. It was May 17, 2013.

May 18, 2013

"This is Chicago's very own W.G.N. news at noon with Micah Matere, Alison Payne, Tom Skilling on weather, and Robert Jordan. Hello, I'm Alison Payne and our top story headlines a major drug bust on Chicago's Northside. Head Narcotics detective, Derrick Trumball, was at the forefront of a major drug and gun seizure where more than two thousand five hundred kilos of cocaine was confiscated.

The raid took place on Belmont Avenue. Fifteen men were arrested in the raid including three individuals from Turkey. All the men are being detained downtown in the M.C.C. Federal Building. Bonds have not been set and for the three Turkish men and it doesn't appear that any bond will be set."

Micah Matere interjected. "Alison, are bonds not being set for the three Turkish men for fear of them fleeing back to Turkey?" "That would be the best guess at this point, but authorities also have reason to believe that those three men are actually at the head of a sophisticated drug ring that has been saturating major cities with cocaine and heroin."

"Is there any word of how long of an investigation it was that lead to this tremendous bust and arrest." "No, not at this time, but our news team will be at the federal building as the story unfolds."

"Okay, thanks a lot, in other news..."

CHAPTER 20

The next morning after the news aired, Lisa was in a meeting with the president, vice president, and partners of Brickman and Edwards.

"As we are all aware of at this time there has been a large take down of drugs and guns that resulted in the arrest of fifteen individuals. Our firm has been chosen for the representation of individuals by an out of country financer. The financer has agreed to pay the full cost of every individual arrested upfront with one request, the three individuals from Turkey see no federal time. We have explained in detail that those are guarantees that we are not at liberty to make, but as a policy we are obligated to go above and beyond to ensure that we do all we can to secure the freedom of all clients

"He is aware that bonds are more than likely to be denied due to the nature of the case, and regional dwellings in which they are rooted. His desire is to have these three individual back in Turkey. We will appoint a team of lawyers for the twelve, but the three individuals from Turkey; we will all work personally and diligently on their cases. Lisa, you will be the head lawyer at the forefront of all litigations, plans of attack, and public relations. We will be in the background aiding you in every possible way and in any and all case law.

"This will be a tremendous asset to our firm's notoriety, prestige, and standings if we can secure a victory. So we don't have to stress to you Lisa, the importance of your success. If you secure this victory it is all of our deep rooted desire that you be made partner with the firm. We don't want that to pressure you because we understand how much of a value you are to us – So regardless, you will be a respected member of our team, but a victory of this magnitude is deserving of partnership, and we are all in agreement on that."

Brickman ended his speech and Lisa was overwhelmed not only in the confidence that was placed in her, but also in the opportunity that had been presented. She lived for cases like this and while watching the news she knew she would be selected. Lisa just never imagined that a partnership would be a part of the deal.

"Thank you Mr. Brickman, Mr. Edwards, and all the partners of the firm. As always I will pursue a victory in this and that has nothing to do with becoming a partner. I have an obligation to the firm and to the client, but above all to myself to perform far and above the ability of my adversary. So I will diligently fight for a victory in this case as I have in every other case I have won."

"All the cases you have won. You have an impeccable record, and we the utmost faith in." Mr. Brickman interjected.

"Thank you, I'll try not to let you down."

"We won't be let down no matter what the outcome is, because we know if you lose, it was only because the case could not have been won."

"Once again, thank you. Now who will I be working with?"

"Your clients will be Valdamir Trayvinc, Ivan Doushic, and Moury Shalavin, and you are to report on a regular basis to Stons Terkle, he is the financial provider for all fifteen men and it is of grave importance that he remains abreast on all things."

Lisa scribbled the names down in her planner and circled Stons Terkle's name to emphasize the importance.

"Okay gentlemen, I'm on top of it. I'm going over to the federal building to meet with these three men now and I'll call Mr. Terkle when I'm done."

It was 1:09 p.m., May 18, 2013, Derrick sat at the foot of his bed looking at himself in the mirror. His black police issue millimeter sat on his dresser next to his detective shield. He straightened his back and admired his broad chest and shoulders with a smile and hint of conceit.

He nodded his head up and down and said.

"You did good nigga', you did real muthafuckin good."

He stood up and his long navy blue shorts hung loosely to his knees as he walked to the corner of his room where three large duffle bags sat.

He squatted down, unzipped each one of them, and the already loud smell of cocaine became even more evident in the air. Derrick had seventy-five kilos in each bag that he'd skimmed off the top from yesterday's bust.

Dollar signs danced in his head and a surreal feeling of euphoria came over him. He thought to himself.

'Just a few more years and it's all over wit'.

No more Chicago, no more police work, and no more dope. All that will be left is sunshine and exotic behinds.

His cell phone rang, he looked at the face of it and Stan's name was spelled across it.

"Stan my man, what's good?"

"You tha' man, it's yo world."

"I know that, talk to me 'bout somethin' I don't know."

Derrick walked from his bedroom to the kitchen with his phone to his ear.

"A little more than a year ago you lost a little somethin' somethin'."

Derrick had a box of cupcakes in his hand, he sat it down next to the glass he was 'bout to pour milk into.

"Yeah a lil somethin' somethin'. I remember somethin' like that."

"Do you remember what you said a lil information concerning it was worth?"

Derrick reached in the refrigerator, grabbed the milk, poured a glass, and put the milk back.

"I remember what I said the information was worth if in fact the information was legit."

"Well how long will it take you to get to our favorite lunch spot?"

"Half hour."

"Aiight, lunch is on me, see you in a minute."

Derrick put his phone on the counter, opened the cupcakes, took a bite, washed it down with some milk and smiled.

"What's done in the dark always comes to the light, and this little light of mine –I'm sho' finna' let it shine. Pop yo ass Darren, you and those hoes."

It was 1:32 p.m. Lisa went to the federal building and put in a formal appearance stating she would be lead council representing the three Turks who had been taken into custody as a result of last night's drug bust. Just as she and the firm thought, bail was denied.

She spoke to the Turks collectively and individually so she could feel them all out for weaknesses. For Lisa there was nothing worse than a weak man, especially one who played the game, reaping the benefits the game had to offer, and the moment he got caught became a Kodak moment, and let his true colors come shining through, and with those colors the real bitch behind the man reared its ugly head.

Lisa had no sympathy for soft niggaz. That had been instilled in her since her relationship with Dewitt, then reinforced as a criminal lawyer, and cemented with Black.

Any turncoat witness, Lisa made a point to devour and shred any possibility of credibility of any statement made as result of any offer or negotiated deal with any authority figure.

She took it to the point of exposing any and all information concerning the turncoat witness or snitch, bitch nigga', pancake, pussy, hoe, or coward ass muthafucka who couldn't stand up and be the man it took to take the time for his crime to all sources allowed by the law that would put his or her name out as an informant.

She had even in a couple cases publicized the information to the media during press releases. As a result the two turncoat witnesses who were being held in Cook County Jail refused to cooperate for fear that their lives were in danger.

Lisa was a bad bitch, and every prosecutor - State or Federal had an underlying fear of facing off with her in the courtroom. Because just as soft, sensual, stunning, alluring, and sexual as she was as a woman - She was a hundred times the aggressor in the courtroom.

She was smart, notoriously blood-thirsty with more strategies and checks than a chessboard. She had a die-hard reputation for trials, no agreements. Lisa had an uncanny ability to pick a jury and paint a picture like Picasso in their mind that displayed entrapment, bias investigations, tainted evidence, disregard of penal statutes, coercion, and total disrespect of the law that all law officials were obligated to follow, and with every minor infringement she had multiple case laws that ruled in favor of the defense that got statements and evidence thrown out before trials began causing the prosecutors case to collapse before their eyes.

Lisa was sharp. And because she was, prosecutors knew they had to be better than one hundred percent when they faced the drop dead gorgeous adversary in the courtroom.

So as Lisa used all her womanly charms while interviewing her new clients, she found no bitch in any of them. They were rock solid, born into the Turkish Mob and had years of dedicated loyalty to their family. She saw in each man that they would die before they participated in anything with the authorities and she quickly grasped the understanding that cooperation with the authorities held a deeper and more monumental consequence than their own death, and that was a consequence they were not willing to accept.

Once she'd gotten a feel of the men that satisfied her, she began to let them know a little bit about herself so they could be more comfortable in being open in any and all information that might help in their defense, but as she started she was cut off by Valdamir.

"Ms. Peterson, there is no need for you to explain your credentials to us. It is not by accident that our people have selected your law firm. We have followed your continued success for a number of years. Many people who we deal with in Chicago you have already represented and by doing so, you have allowed for our business relationships to stay intact.

"Our family has long since recognized your excellence in performing to the highest degree of representation. You've been discussed many a time at our dinner table back home. We admire your tenacious aggression and unwillingness to even entertain with informants. We know that you are rock solid and we are completely comfortable in your representing us."

Lisa was thrown aback at the magnitude of her reputation. She knew she was good in fact better than good but she had no idea that her name was spoken of in other states, let alone other countries.

The case had just become personal, and any case she took personal, Lisa took on like good sex - She sweated and grinded through it all night until she could do nothing but collapse. Because she knew, just like with a night of long good sex, the sweat and grind made her sharper and more determined to prove her loyalty to the one she sweated for.

She had a good vibe and she would ride it until the case was won. She finished talking to her clients and left the M.C.C. building. It was 3:11 p.m.

Derrick pulled up next to a low-key grey Honda Prelude parked in the lot of a hole in the wall restaurant off Roosevelt and Lafayette. Stan was in the car eating a chili dog and a paper basket full of cheese fries.

Derrick opened the passenger door, grabbed a greasy brown paper bag off the seat and sat down.

"What's happening D'man?"

Stan said with that slick west side smile. His tapered baby fro with razor lining, and Gerald Levert beard fit his plump light-skinned face and thick eyebrows.

"I hope mines look like yours."

"Open the bag and see."

Derrick opened the bag, pulled out the red and white paper basket with wax paper covering the cheese fries, and put it on his lap on top of the brown paper bag. He unraveled the wax paper around the chili dog and said.

"My nigga'."

"I told you lunch was on me. I know what you like big fella'."

Derrick let out a chuckle as he situated his lunch in his lap.

"If you know what I like then where's my..."

"Pink lemonade." Stan finished his sentence.

"Right in the backseat. I didn't want you to kick it over when you got in. This my daughters ride and she worse than her mama and I really ain't trying to hear her mouth."

Derrick grabbed his drink, put it on the dash, took a bite of his chili cheese dog and before he finished chewing said.

"So I lost a little somethin' somethin'. What you know about it?"

Stan took a sip from his straw, put his paper basket back in the bag, balled it up and tossed it out the window in the garbage can next to the car.

"Last night I bumped heads with this little nigga' high-sidin' his ass off. Doin' it real big, Maybach, jewelry, the whole hustla' kit."

Derrick bit into his chili cheese dog, ate a couple fires, and sipped his pink lemonade nonchalantly as he listened.

"So the nigga' cut into me like' I got that shit, whatever you want and as much as you need on the white, brown, and yay."

Derrick nodded his head as he chewed.

"But the whole time I'm tryin' to figure out how the nigga' got on because I know the nigga'."

"You know the nigga'?"

Derrick asked without turning to Stan.

"Yeah I know the nigga'."

"Who is he? What's his real name? Where does he live? Where does he hang out? Who does he get money wit'? Who's his bitch? Who does he fuck on the side? What is he?"

Derrick never seemed this anxious about anything, but Black had hit a spot in him that he never felt before. Derrick wasn't really tripping if he got his product back, if he did, cool, but what he really wanted was Black and everyone close to him.

"Come on man, I don't know all that about the nigga'."
Derrick looked at him with a frustrated smile and said.

"Well you don't know him then and beside that, fuck what this nigga' said about him havin' whatever you need, a lot of niggaz got whatever you need, but that don't mean they got my dope. You feelin' me Stan?"

Stan felt unbalanced because he knew Derrick had the ability to shut down everything he was on overnight, send him to jail, or have him hit, and bullshit wasn't nothing because he knew Derrick would do the shit, because he'd seen it with his own eyes several times.

"Come on D'man, how long we been fuckin' wit' each other?"

Derrick leaned on the car door, faced Stan and took a sip of his pink lemonade.

"Five years, two months, one week. Your mama stay in Maywood, your daughter stay on Lavernge, your son go to Austin, you and yo wife stay on Jackson, you got a joint on Karlov, Kildare, and Kilpatrick and the bitch you creep with on a regular basis stay off Chicago Avenue. "

That was some scary shit, and Stan knew Derrick meant for it to be just that.

"So I'ma' say this again, I know you didn't call me down here for this bullshit ass story and lunch?"

Derrick paused, chuckled, and continued.

"You know what I could be doin' right now Stan my man?"

Derrick put his hands in front of this face with his thumbs almost touching resemblance of a picture frame and said.

"Picture this. No better yet, picture me. Picture me getting my dick sucked Stan, by possibly the baddest Asian bitch that exist."

Derrick nodded his head.

"Can you picture me Stan? Can you picture me?"
Stan nodded.

"Good. Now while you picture me Stan, picture me watchin' the thickest white hoe you can imagine suckin' the pussy of the sexiest caramel skin sista' you have ever seen. This sound like good shit don't it Stan?" Derrick said still smiling with his hands up. Stan nodded "But you know what I did instead Stan?" Stan just sat there not saying a word.

"Go ahead Stan, take a guess."

"You came down here."

Derrick pointed his right index finger at Stan and said.

"Bingo. Right on the money Stan. Instead of getting on some freak shit, I elected to be down here with you, and why? Because you my man Stan - So please - Stan please."

Derrick closed his eyes as he shook his head.

"Don't disappoint me. Sing to me Stan, move my muthafuckin soul."

Every thought Stan had of having the upper hand on Derrick diminished.

"The nigga' name Solid and he moved out to the suburbs somewhere, I don't know where yet, but I got a number."

"You got a number?"

"Yeah."

"That's good, yeah that's real good, numbers are always good. Aiight gon' finish."

"The nigga' said he had been sittin' on the shit for a little over a year. Said he hit a lick on some up north ass niggaz who wouldn't be goin' back to Belize any time soon."

That was what Derrick wanted to hear. His smile broadened.

"I knew you had it in you, Stan my man. So when you gonna' make this phone call?"

"I don't kn..."

"Right now."

Derrick said without a hint of room for compromise. Stan pulled out his phone, went through his list of numbers until he found "Solid" and touched the screen. After two rings Solid picked up.

"What up big man?"

"Oh it ain't me, you the true for real playa'. What's happenin' with you big Tymer?" Stan replied.

"Awe man, I'm just on some laid back shit at the shop."

"So I'm sayin', can I still get that playa price on them doors? I wanna' fly out the lot just like you."

"Fo sho' nigga', if I said it I meant it."

"Yeah, you said a lot of shit."

"And I meant all of it."

"So when can we make this happen?"

"Let me get at my people."

"Now see, there you go. You made it seem like you were the man, now I see what's up, you just makin' moves for another nigga."

"Look pimpin', I told you I got you and I got you playa', just slow down. We on some low-key shit right now, but its finna' go down. So let me get back at you, but just know you first on the list, and because I got you on hold so to speak, I'ma' bless you fo' real."

"So when can I see this shop?"

"As soon as you make it to Schaumburg."

"Schaumburg? You pulled a move for real didn't you?"

"Yeah man, I told you I'm on some other shit, but look we right off Higgins road, you can't miss us. It's a big neon sign that says 'Custom Profiles'."

"Aiight I'ma' get at you and then we can talk about that other business."

"When you talkin' about?"

"I don't know, I'ma' hit you within the next couple days. Let me get my paper right."

"Aiight nigga' you got the number, use it."

"No doubt." Stan pressed end call.

"The nigga' said he gotta' holla' at his guys because they ain't makin' no moves yet – So they must be still sittin' on the shit."

That made Derrick feel even better. He could knock these niggaz off and get all his dope back. It couldn't have gone down any sweeter.

"This nigga' in Schaumburg. He say he got a business name 'Custom Profiles' off Higgins Road and I know if he runnin' a business then somebody else is behind the scene because the nigga' ain't that sharp."

Derrick's first thought was 'Darren is'.

"So maybe the niggaz he hit wit' all together and they getting it on out there."

"Yeah, yeah I can see that. Well look, give me a little time to think about this and I'll get back at you."

"So we cool then D'?"

"All the time Stan. Here throw this out."

Derrick handed him his garbage. When Stan turned to throw the garbage out, Derrick pulled out a key of the cocaine he got last night, put it on the seat, and got out the car.

Stan turned around when he heard the car door open.

"That's you." Derrick pointed to the seat.

"Once I holla' at these niggaz you got the rest comin'."

Stan was payin' attention to what Derrick was saying and the key was just sittin' there. Derrick pointed to the key and said.

"You know cocaine is illegal right?"

"Yeah." "Well put that shit up then nigga'. You never know who the police might be."

And walked to his car, got in, and drove off.

CHAPTER 21

September 21, 2013

The buzz in police stations, courtrooms, and the federal building was the same story splattered across the front page of every newspaper throughout Chicago.

'LISA PETERSON PULLS OFF STUNNING VICTORY FOR TURKS.'

While in Turkey, Stons Turkle watched the news on a closed circuit channel.

Federal prosecutors were stumped as Lisa Peterson pushed tenaciously in demanding of trial for her three clients who never waived their rights to a speedy trial. Prosecutors were forced to fold their hands as the demand for a speedy trial had already been accepted months earlier.

Federal prosecutors, who apparently were relying upon the testimonies of three federal informants to link and therefore prove the defendants violated the 'Racketeer Influenced and Corrupt Organizations Act,' better known as the RICO Act, came up short so to speak. The RICO Act, targets individuals who profit from criminal organizations but somehow manage to avoid illegal activities. Federal prosecutors did not charge the three Turkish citizens with guns or drug trafficking because the RICO Act, which is designed to combat organized crime syndicates would have assured a life sentence in federal prison if the three were found guilty.

But that meant prosecutors proving the three who were not personally involved in the sell of any narcotics, profited from the sales. That required exhaustive investigations and indictments that read like an organizational flow chart. Prosecutors rely on evidence obtained through wire taps, listening devices, and informants to prove these cases.

According to reports, the three informants that could tie everything together were executed only four days prior to this court date. One was killed in a bombing in Washington, D.C., another in Streamwood, Illinois where he was being held in protective custody and the third here in Chicago. Prosecutors are fully aware that these murders directly involve this trial, but have no evidence substantiating their claims. Lisa Peterson stepped in court today with motions to dismiss all direct and indirect evidence gathered as a result of the informant's testimonies or cooperation.

Which meant all written, oral, and video recorded statements. Lisa Peterson stated to Federal Judge, Scott Patrone, that it was quote - unquote, 'Not her job to secure the safety of federal witnesses, but it was her job to secure the rights and freedoms of her clients. If the witnesses are not alive I cannot challenge their statements, so they become nothing more but words on a piece of paper and idle chatter.'

Lisa Peterson who was already prepared to challenge the testimonies pushed that not only her motion be honored, but also her previous motion for speedy trial. Federal Judge Scott Patrone had no choice but to grant the trial proceedings and Federal prosecutors were left with the choice of proceeding with a trial with no evidence or withdrawing their case.

Stan had been keeping in close contact with Solid by phone trying to get as much information as possible. Derrick didn't want any more fuck ups, he had missed Black twice, mainly due to underestimating him, and that wasn't going to happen again.

Derrick realized Black was not only a thinker, but a real good and patient one..And Black's decision not to move the dope was evidence of that.

Derrick admired Black, but also knew admiration couldn't interfere with self-preservation. So Derrick took his time. He'd been out to Schaumburg several times watching and learning all he could. He did background checks on Dee and Solid based on the names associated with their business. They were clean.

Derrick learned that Dee was a family man, but also knew he was no more than a smart drug dealer who had managed to avoid the pitfalls of the game. Solid on the other hand was an ass, and like Stan said, Solid didn't have the brains to orchestrate a business or keep it running so he knew Dee had to be one of the guys he hit the lick with.

Whatever they were doing though, it was evident, they weren't moving any dope, nor was Black around period. If Black was there he was so low-key that he didn't even associate himself with his business partners.

Derrick spent four months moving the dope he got from the Turkish bust, so he could be fully focused on Solid He didn't want any more mishaps, and this time he needed results, which meant he personally had to handle the business.

When he heard the verdict from the Federal Building, Derrick couldn't do anything but shake his head. Lisa was a piece of work and he knew without a doubt when he got Black he had to get her too, but since the hit on Black at her house, Lisa had been too hard to pinpoint, once he set his mind to it he would get at her. She still had her number listed for potential clients, but Derrick just didn't feel the need to rock the boat. He didn't want to get her lawyer mind to turning and wind up turning over some rocks that would have been better left unturned.

Derrick pulled into 'Custom Profiles' parking lot at five minutes to ten in a police issue Caprice Classic, and him and Mike got out the car with their badges hanging around their necks.

Dee was inside talking to Black on the phone when Derrick knocked on the door.

"Damn big man, the police at the door."
"The Police?"

"Yeah, and it ain't Schaumburg, they in a city car. Hold fast let me see what's up."

Dee held his cell phone in his hand while he unlocked the door.

"Can I help you?" Dee asked staring at Mike and Derrick's badges and guns that were holstered in side harnesses.

Derrick looked at him sternly and said.

"Yeah, you can help me and you can start by getting' yo ass the fuck from in front of the door so me and my partner can come in." And pushed his way pass.

Once inside, Derrick walked around staring at the rim displays, color charts, pictures of cars that had been painted and customized at the shop, customers in before and after pictures of their cars, and the many impulse items that were strategically placed so customers would pick them up as last minute purchases.

"Man this is nice; you got a nice little spot here Devon."

"Thanks." Dee replied showing no sign of suspicion.

"Where's Michael?"

"He's in the back; can I ask what business you have here?"

Black could hear the whole conversation clearly on the other end of the phone. Derrick casually walked to the back and Dee instinctive followed and Mike followed behind Dee. Stan came in a moment later and the bell that alerted the opening of the door jingled. Dee looked out and Stan was locking the door.

Dee knew bullshit was in the air, but he didn't have a gun at hand for one and two, this was the police so he had to just be cool and ride it out.

"What's up Michael? Or should I say Solid?"

Derrick said with a smile and Dee looked at Solid. Solid looked at Derrick with obvious confusion and asked.

"Do I know you?"

"Naw, but you gon' wish you would had."

"I'm gon' wish I had, what makes you say that?"

"Because I have a funny feelin' if you would have known who I was you wouldn't have ran in my people joint up north and hit 'em. Well my bad, hit me for my fifty bricks of yay and thirty bricks of heroin."

Solid's face showed apparent surprise and Derrick mimicked with an over exaggerated surprised open mouth face with dramatized comedy added and said.

"Wow! Funny how runnin' yo "You a playa' Devon?"

Dee didn't say a word.

"Come on man, you can tell me. We all playa's in here, ain't we Mike?"

"Last time I checked I was a playa and I know you and Stan playa's - And from the looks of this shop they look like they on some playa' shit - So yeah D', we all playa's in here."

"See what I'm sayin' Devon, we all playa's."mouth a tear yo ass."

Black listened closer now. Stan walked around the corner with a big ass smile.

"What's up big Tymer?"

Solid looked at him and instant hatred boiled inside him.

"Oh don't get up." Stan said sarcastically.

"Damn big pimpin' you was right, this muthafuckin' shop is the business. I see why you spoke so highly of it. I would have been down here sooner, but I was on my business, you know a hustlas work is never done."

Solid wished he could have shot Stan in the face right then.

"So I'm sayin', can I still get that playa price we talked about?"

Solid didn't say a word as Dee stared at him thinking 'This stupid muthafucka.'

"Oh, my bad. I see you got yo man right here and you might not want him to know you givin' out plays. That's on me - my fault playa'."

Derrick pulled his .45 automatic from the small off his back, walked up on Dee and tapped him under the chin with the barrel as he smiled.

Dee still didn't say a word.

"Now come on man, don't tell me the cat got yo tongue."

Derrick went on with the barrel still pointed at Dee.

"Now shit gon' get real fucked up in a second because we can't get nowhere like this. Y'all gon' make me think y'all don't recognize a 'P' or something." Stan and Mike laughed.

"Come on now Solid, I know you got somethin' to say as much as you was talkin' at the Cotton Club. Don't be shy my man, D'man good people. He the type of nigga' you need in yo corner."

Black heard D'man and thought, 'What the fuck?'

"See you still a shorty in the game. You ain't made it to that level where you understand that the police ain't always your enemy."

Black thought, 'Damn, this nigga' the police for real.

"But don't trip because if it's one thing I know, it's never too late to learn."

Derrick cut in.

"Aiight, aiight, aiight. This shit is getting old real fast. Now some muthafucka finna' start talkin'. First, where's my... Naw better yet, first where is this nigga'Darren?"

Black's heart dropped at the mention of his name.

"Darren? Who the fuck is Darren?" Dee replied.

"Oh, so you talkin' now. That's good." Derrick said as he laughed. "But the shit ain't good what's comin' out yo mouth."

He looked Dee right in the eyes and put the barrel of the .45 right on his chin.

"Now come on Devon, do we really gotta' play this shit all the way out like this? Darren, Latrice's husband, the one who fuckin' the lawyer bitch, Tuko's ex-girl and we all know Tuko is the Belizean y'all ran in on, he was my man and that was his bitch and apparently Darren's too. This shit is simple, I'm here, I'm the police, y'all robbed a nigga' fo my shit and I want it back. I know this nigga' Darren kicked this shit off - So I'ma' ask you one mo' time muthafucka, where-the- fuck-is-Darren?"

Anger fixed itself on Derrick's face like a man who had just walked in on his wife sucking his best friend's dick.

"Now act like you don't know if you want to nigga', but I bet I get that ass when I pull this trigga'."

Black whispered, "Damn" to himself. Dee stood there looking at Derrick's angry eyes and said.

"Man Playa', like I said. I don't know who the fuck you talkin' bout."

"Wrong answer nigga'."

Derrick jagged the .45 back and before Dee knew it, Derrick put the barrel on his forehead and pulled trigger. "FAWOUH!!!"

Black pulled the phone quickly away from his ear as the sound of the gunshot banged against his eardrum.

The .45 kicked back in Derrick's hand as the bullet tore through Dee's skull knocking his head back and Dee's body with it sending his brains splattering on the wall behind him. Dee fell to the floor with a thud and his cell phone slid in the midst of Derrick, Mike, and Stan.

Derrick turned to Solid.

"Now, don't make me make another example playa', cause to tell you the truth, I don't even give a fuck about the dope. I get that shit like free government cheese, so what you got right now is a choice to make. Choice number one. You can think I'm playin' and find out like yo boy that I ain't bout no games."

Solid looked at Dee laying there twisted, blood running from his head onto the white tile.

"Or choice number two. You can act like you wanna' save yo ass and still get some money nigga'."

It was a no brainer for Solid.

"Man dawg, Black ain't down here. That nigga' tucked away down south somewhere. I ain't never been to his crib, but I know he got the dope down in Clinton or somethin'. I swear to God, I only been there one time and on my mama I don't know how to get down there, but all I gotta' do is holla' at the nigga' and I'm there. All that shit 'bout the lawyer bitch, I don't know nothin' about. All I know is we was 'pose to go in the joint, kill everybody, grab the dope, and get little. Shy and Black got the money from upstairs. From my understandin' it was' pose to be a nigga' and a bitch upstairs and they was gon' kill both of 'em. If that's the lawyer broad then look, she was 'pose to get it too. I didn't know shit bout yo people dawg, if I did, I wouldn't have been up wit' none of that shit."

Black listened on the other end. "You bitch ass nigga'." Solid could have said anything at that point and saved his ass, but for the first time in his life, this hoe decides to tell the truth, the whole truth, and nothing but the truth.

They say a chain is only as strong as its weakest link and Solid was by far Black's weakest link.

Derrick couldn't help but laugh because he even recognized the bitch in Solid. He wasn't surprised though because he'd seen enough paper gangsters to know just how they look and sound when they fold.

"You wouldn't have been up wit' it huh? You hear that Stan?"

Stan let out a chuckle,

"Man, you'd be surprised at what niggaz would or wouldn't have done had they just known."

Derrick turned to Stan smiling and said.

"You know what Stan my man, you right."

Derrick had the gun in his hand moving it as he spoke using hand gestures and all Solid could do is watch the gun.

"That reminds me of this cartoon I use to watch when I was little. That old G.I. Joe cartoon. You know the one I'm talkin' 'bout Mike?"

"Yeah, the one where they always say at the end 'Now you know and knowing is half the battle."

"Right, right, that's exactly it. You a good nigga' Mike. Good fuckin' memory too. I like that shit."

Derrick said laughing, and then turned back to Solid

"Now you know, and knowing is half the battle. You know what else you know now Solid?"

"What' that."

"That I ain't bout no bullshit. You just saved yo ass Mr. Thompson, and just because I'ma' fair man - better yet, since I'm a playa' and we all playa's in here right?"

Solid nodded his head wit' scared eyes.

"Yeah D'man, we all playa's and playa's stay on playa' shit."

"Right, you so right. So this what I'ma' do. I'm finna' give you a playa' play. I'ma' let you ball nigga', but you know what you gon' do? You gon' ball for me and you gon' hit yo man Black and find out where he at. When you do, you gon' let me know, and if you don't."

Derrick shook his head as he walked over to Dee and pointed at him with the gun.

"This be yo mama, yo daddy, sistas, brothas, cousins, babies, nieces, nephews, and anybody you fuck wit' who look like you, you feelin' me playa'?"

"No doubt, I'm feelin' you like some bomb head on a bad bitch."

Derrick laughed and went on.

"I like that, I like that forreal." He smiled and pointed at Solid.

"You know what Solid, you is a playa'. So in the words of Goldie the pimp, we can do this like playa's, or get on some gangsta' shit. And if that happen."

Derrick shook his head, blew out a long breath, bit down on his lip, put the gun barrel to Solid's head, and looking at him in his eyes said.

'We gon' make every muthafuckin day, a training day, but you can believe this here playa'. I ain't gon' die at the end like Denzel."

He slid the mag back.

"But you can bet a whole lot of other muthafuckas are."

He put the pistol back in his waistline.

"Come on; let's get the fuck outta' here. I expect to hear from you, Stan got my number." The three walked out.

CHAPTER 22

7:30 a.m., September 22, 2013

Stons Terkle called Lisa the morning after she won the case for his Turkish Mafia Family. Lisa looked at her phone as she rolled over on her pink Victoria's Secret silk sheets, and saw the international number. She tapped her screen and sat up letting her beautiful full breast dangle.

"Hello."

The deep Turkish accent of the older man's familiar voice sounded through the phone.

"Lisa."

"Yes."

"Hello, this is Stons."

"Good morning Mr. Terkle."

"Please, call me Stons. We have been dealing with one another long enough not to have to feel so impersonal."

"I'm sorry Mr. - I mean Stons."

Stons chuckled on the other end of the phone.

"Don't worry my dear I know with your professional personality it may seem awkward, but you'll get use to it. I wanted to congratulate you on your victory. It would seem more appropriate to do so in person, but I'm afraid that I do not have the luxury of traveling as I would like at times."

"I understand and trust me; it's appreciated all the same."

"I want you to know that I never doubted for one moment that you would win."

"Well, I appreciate that, but I can't take all the credit with the sudden de..."

Lisa paused being aware of the dangers of speaking over the phone.

"Speak freely my dear; this is a secure line both ways I assure you."

Lisa thought for a second about what Stons said then continued.

"Well, considering the sudden deaths of the witnesses, the prosecutors had little to
fight with."

"Yes, those deaths were indeed unfortunate."

Lisa found Stons words amusing knowing full well he had or orchestrated the deaths, but like all her clients personal business - She kept it to herself.

"But you clearly forced their hand by putting them in a position months earlier to have to be prepared for trial. Had you not done that this case could have been drawn out for years?"

"Well maybe not years."

"When you're behind bars you'd be surprised at how time has the tendency to feel like years, even if it isn't."

Lisa had to admit, she never thought of it that way.

"You are quite a remarkable young lady and you have the respect of the entire family, so I'll be blunt.

Lisa got up and walked to the bathroom, her naked body magnificently flawless in every aspect. She sat on the toilet, relieved herself, and drip dried as Stons spoke.

"I want you on my team."

Lisa didn't quite understand what he meant, so she interjected.

"I'm sorry."

Stons went on.

"My team and I would like you to be the personal lawyer of the family."

Not only did Lisa not know how to respond, she didn't know how to take it as well. She'd never thought of being anything other than a lawyer for a firm and also knew very well becoming a lawyer for a Mob family would definitely shine another light on her in regards to prosecutors. Stons continued.

"I know this may be a bit much, but as you are well aware, we have followed your career for quite some time now, and we have found in you what is hard to come by, which is trust. As you can probably imagine, we do business with many U.S. States. Our people are major suppliers of both heroin and cocaine. So we have many who are in need of top notch representation at a moment's notice. However, where representation is easy to come by, lawyers who have such a deep rooted despise for informants and also respected in the courts for their professionalism is very hard to come by.

"I'm prepared to offer you a five million dollar retainer and pay you by the hour per case, plus traveling expenses for any and all clients. Because of your extreme expertise, anything less than seven hundred dollars an hour for you time would be unthinkable. At that hourly wage I understand a five million dollar retainer will soon dwindle, but I assure you we are more than able to cover any bill that is acquired during the course of your service.

Stons had Lisa's attention, but it wasn't the money part, it was the major supplier of heroin and cocaine that grabbed her.

"What you must understand though is this. If in fact you accept my offer your obligation would be to the family. At any given moment we may need you in any of the fifty states in America, and I need to know that the families business will take precedence over other clients."

Lisa knew she could juggle clients, but she also knew taking on such a position would automatically remove her from the firm and she had just made partner. The money she would make at seven hundred dollars an hour would far outweigh any amount the partners would offer, but did she really want to leave the firm?

She quickly weighed the situation. First, she recognized, she'd still be doing the same thing, only for more money, not to mention there'd be less people hording over her, but ultimately the firm didn't matter or the money. But what did was Black.

Lisa figured if she could secure this connect for him in such a way that it would basically come straight to him, Black would have no choice but to love her the way she needed him too. So she took a deep breath, thought to herself, I'm going for it,' and said.

"That's a very generous offer, but what if I were to say that I'd be willing to become your personal lawyer under these conditions only. First of all let me say this. You have established the fact that you can trust me - Not that you can trust me, but you do trust me. Which is good because you can and always will be able to. I'm a very different kind of woman Mr. Ter... I mean, Stons. I became a lawyer because of a very special man in my life. He received a lot of time and then was murdered in prison.

"My life was changed because of this man and that's why I fight so hard to secure victories in all my drug cases. I have a special spot in my heart for individuals in your line of work and I have a very special man who is extremely near and dear to me in my life now. He is an exceptional man in my eyes and I would do anything for him. Right now he is in need of assistance that your family can provide. He needs someone who can effectively supply quality material in large amounts."

"And when you say large?" Stons asked.

"I mean for starters five hundred kilos of cocaine and at least ninety kilos of heroin."

"Yeah that's a nice starter, but I wouldn't say that was large."

"Well, like I said, for starters."

"Yes I see, is that all?"

"No, it has to come to him. Meaning, make it to the states in a fashion that he can easily get it."

"That is not a problem; we have our people at customs."

Lisa was getting more and more excited.

"Now, just to keep things all above board, the two of you will deal through me. That way there will be no misunderstanding. I'll handle the money on his end and the supply on your end, but you will be responsible for getting the money out of the country."

"Lisa I am starting to like you very much."

"Thank you, but please let me finish."

"Go on my dear."

"I only deal for him. I will never accept a single gram for anyone else in the family or carry one single dollar for them. I owe you my loyalty as a lawyer; that is all. Anything outside of that compromises my ability to work effectively. If I am found to be having any other interactions with your family other than lawyer/client, it could launch an investigation that could jeopardize us all."

"So I need you to ensure me that nothing of the sort will ever even come up as a matter of conversation. And it's important that I deal with one individual in the family who does not deal with anyone else in the family. This is for all of our safety as well, I prefer them to be a woman, but it's not as important as it is for them to be clean."

Stons took in all Lisa had said and was highly impressed at her thoroughness. He understood that he propositioned her and she countered with a well thought out proposal of her own at a second's notice. He knew she was special, but her words made him want her more.

"So do I have a lawyer?"

"Yes you do, if my man has a supplier?"

"Yes he does."

Lisa was ecstatic.

"Well thank you Stons, I never imagined that my day would begin on such a good note."

"I had an idea you'd be coming aboard, but never that it would be under such desirable terms."

Lisa laughed.

"I told you I was a special kind of woman."

"Indeed you are. Yes you are indeed."

"Thank you Stons. I will submit my resignation to the firm Monday morning and oh, before I forget, the five million dollars."

"Yes."

"Make that the payment for the first shipment."

Ston was even more impressed with her loyalty to the one she spoke of.

"You are indeed a very special woman and I'm sure the gentleman you are backing is very much in love with you, and if he isn't, then he will be eventually."

"Oh is he." Lisa said confidently.

"I can believe that. Okay my dear, I'll be in touch with you. I'll call always from a secure line - So just wait on me my dear."

"Okay Stons."

"Thank you once again."

"No. Thank you Stons."

"Yeah so I called in the hit on him as soon as I hung up the phone." Latrice and Shy were in Black's office listening to him explain what happened last night.

"So that pussy ass nigga folded huh." Shy remarked.

"Yeah G', but he didn't do shit but kill his self."

"And his family." Latrice added to Black's statement.

"Fo sho' baby girl, the chump would have been better off takin' one for the team. At least then his people would be alright."

"Damn that's fucked up."

Latrice put her hand on her forehead as she shook her head.

"Damn Dee, I know Felicia is messed up."

"Yeah baby, I don't even know how to go about that one."

"About what?" Shy said.

"About her losing her guy."

"Man shiit, she knew what he was on and what could come behind it. We all facin' the same shit. Niggaz tried to hit you, Latrice, shot Nia and killed Londa, so it ain't like we haven't all felt it."

"Yeah Shy, but I'ma'woman and her and Dee have been married for a long time. When you've been married for that long your whole world is centered around the person you're with and the children you've made with one another."

"And." Shy said with discontent.

"What you mean? And?"

"I'm just sayin'. What if Black would have got hit, or they got you in that trunk, or Nia would have got killed. Does that make her loss any less hurtful than ours would have been?"

"Well first of all, it wasn't a matter of whose loss was more or less painful to me. All I was sayin' is that I know Felicia is shook."

"Well I'm shook too. You shook, Black shook, and Nia shook, but bottom line is we can't let that throw us off. When Black put this shit together everybody knew the consequences were jail or death. Not just us, but all our women. Everybody was good wit' it, and ate good off of it. So we can't just be good when it's all good and not when it's all bad. We gotta' be good wit' it even when it's all bad - So all I'm sayin' is that we can't just fall back and cry and shit."

"So what, you ain't cry when Nia got shot?"

"Yeah, but I'm not crying now, and I ain't tryin' to make it sound like I ain't feelin' her pain, but at the same time, she gon' have to do what everybody else did - get over it and keep it movin just like Netta and Jayvon doin'."

"Well, I'ma' make sure that I help her." Latrice replied.

"That's yo job." Shy countered. "You do yo job and let me and Black do ours."

Latrice left it alone and changed the subject.

"So what you gon' do about Solid baby?"

"Kill his ass." Black said bluntly.

"I know that, but what about this police nigga'?"

"Oh don't even trip, I got his ass too. This pussy muthafucka think he can play both sides of the streets, but I ain't goin' at gunpoint! He may think I am, but that's because the nigga' don't know me. But that nigga' Solid."

Black paused as anger built inside.

"I been thinking all night on how I'ma' do his ass. He gon' wish he would have gon' took his like Dee, because it ain't finna' be nothin' nice fo his pussy ass!"

Black didn't say anything about Lisa, he decided he would deal with that situation his self. He really didn't want to believe she was up with any of the bullshit that was goin' on. So he wanted to talk to her face to face so he could look in her eyes. He'd be able to tell if she was on any bullshit and if she was, then she just had to get what she had coming.

"So how long before his people get hit?" Latrice asked.

"Two days. In two days they all will have gotten touched and you'll have pictures."

"Who was all on his list?"

"Shiid, everybody; Moms, grandma, his girl, her shorties, his sista', and his two brothas'."

"Damn that's a stupid ass nigga'. What was he thinkin', he know how you are and that you don't say shit you don't mean, especially this serious. He must just didn't give a fuck about his people."

"I don't know."

Black shook his head and just then his phone rang. He looked at the screen and said.

"Speakin' of the devil, here go fuck boy right here."

Black pressed the send button and said.

"What's good nigga'?"

"You big playa', how you feel?"

"Awe man, just tryin' to stay alive."

"Yeah I hear you - Me too. Look check it out, I gotta' hit it down the Lou to check some shit out fo' the shop, so I was gon' bend on you on the way through."

"When is that?"

"I'm getting' on the road now."

"Oh yeah, you makin' moves huh?"

"All the time playa'."

"Yeah I heard that, well look, check it out. It's about 11:30. So what I'll do is meet you at t

Mobil gas station right off the Pontiac exit at 1:30. Where my man at?"

"Who, Dee?"

"Yeah who else?"

"I just hollered at him, he had to get on somethin' wit' the wife and kids."

Black just shook his head and thought 'Snake ass nigga', then said.

"Aiight then playboy. I'll see you in a couple hours."

"Fo sho'."

Black hung up and placed his phone on his desk. Meanwhile Solid was calling Derrick.

"I'm finna' get up wit' Black right now."

"Yeah, when?"

"1:30, I'm meetin' him around his way."

"That's real good. Now make sure you find out where he lives and how to get at my merch, hear me?"

"Yeah I hear you; I'm on top of it."

"Okay now, you take care of this and you good wit' me, and Stan ah tell you I take care of my guys. I ain't 'bout no games, you handle yours and I'll handle mine, you feel me?"

"Yeah I'm feelin' you."

"Okay then, hit me when you know somethin'."

"Aiight I got you."

Solid hung up the phone and headed to the E-way while Black was back at his office saying to Shy.

"Look, check it out. I want you to go to the farm and put all the pits in the kennel, bring two baseball bats, some extension cords, a few bottles of rubbing alcohol, and some vice grips. I'm finna' go meet this punk."

"What if he got somebody wit' 'em?"

"If he do they ain't gon' pull it right there and you ah see us comin' up on the farm. If somebody is on my heels just lay for 'em and air they ass when they get to the farm house. If somebody in the car wit' 'em, I'll call you and let you know. Put one of the baseball bats at the barn door because we fuckin' this nigga' up."

"Aiight G' I'm on it."

Black looked at Latrice.

"Baby you think you can get some of them adrenaline shots from your girl?"

"I don't see why not."

"Does she have somethin' to shoot 'em wit'?"

"Yeah she has those tranquilizer guns."

"Aiight, get on top of that and I'll see y'all a little later."

Shy and Latrice got up and walked out. About fifteen minutes afterwards Lisa called. Black took a few seconds to think about if he wanted to talk to her and then answered the phone.

"Hello."

Black said with an obvious bad tone. Lisa hadn't heard that tone since Black stopped fuckin' wit' her for trying to bump Latrice's spot. She recognized it immediately and worry knocked the joyful excitement right out of her body.

"What's the matter?" She asked.

"I don't know, you tell me what's the matter?"

"What do you mean?" Black fell silent. After a few seconds Lisa spoke.

"Darren... Darren..."

He still didn't say anything.

"Oh, so you're not talkin' to me huh?" Black sighed in the phone.

"Well can I at least know why?"

Then in a calm and disappointed manner Black spoke up.

"Damn baby, I thought you was my girl?"

"What does that mean?"

"Just what I said, I thought you was my girl."

"I am your girl and you know that Darren, so I don't understand why you would even be saying that." "If you my girl then why you lie to me?"

"Lie to you! Boy I ain't never lied to you a day in my life."

"D'man." Black said as if he was making a profound statement.

Lisa was silent as the name shot through her like a lightning bolt and she immediately saw herself sitting in Black's office saying.

"No, I don't know a D'man."

Black questioned her silence.

"So I'm sayin', what? You ain't talkin' to me?"

Lisa still didn't say anything for a second as she tried to figure out how Black knew.

"Naw baby, I'm talking to you. And yeah baby, I lied."

Black sat down as the hurt of hearing Lisa say the words set in on him. When he finally spoke his tone was different. It was sad and confused.

"Why would you lie to me especially when I told you this nigga' was tryin' to kill me?"

"Because baby, I didn't know."

Lisa answered in a heartfelt sincere apologetic tone.

"I know one person name D'man and there was nothing in the world I could think of that could help me understand why he would be after you, especially trying to kill you. So I just figured the name was coincidental and it wasn't him. I would never have kept anything like that from you. Especially that baby I love you more than I love myself and you know there is nothing in this world I wouldn't do for you. So you gotta' know if somebody was trying to kill you I would have not only told you, but did everything I could to stop that person."

"Man that shit sound good."

"Baby please don't do this to me. Don't disrespect the love I have for you by even implying what I feel for you could be anything other than love."

Black didn't say anything. Seconds went by like minutes to Lisa. Finally she spoke up.

"Baby please talk to me. Don't shut me out like this again. The last time you did this my world fell apart and now I love you even more, so I know I won't be able to stand it."

Before Lisa could finish her words tears were streaming down her face. Her voice cracked, her heart cried, and her mind raced.

"I love you Darren." She said softly. "And you know I do."

Black still didn't say a word. Lisa couldn't stand it any longer, she snapped.

"Don't do this to me! Don't you fuckin' do this shit to me goddamn it!"

"Man calm the fuck down and stop crying."

Lisa hung on to his words as hope shot through her. She took a series of short breaths trying to calm down.

"I know you love me and that's why I can't understand why you would have held any information back from me, especially somethin' concerning my livelihood."

"I'm sorry. I was wrong and I'll fix it."

"Naw, I'ma' fix it. I don't want you even talkin' to this nigga' at all. If he calls you don't even answer your phone. When I get ready for you to holla' at dude I'll have you get at him, you understand me?"

"Yes."

Lisa said like a child who was being scolded. Although her heart was recouping, the authority of Black's voice and words stimulated her. She loved that about Black, he was strong and aggressive, she felt meek, docile and fragile in his presence and his dominion over her was arousing.

Lisa dealt with men all day long. Men whom she dictated to because she held their lives in her hands, so they were weak and submissive to her. She dominated and overpowered men in courtrooms - used men for stepping-stones in her career, for Lisa men were mere pawns in her chess game who were to simply speak when spoken to and until then, just shut the fuck up while she did her thang, but Black was different, extremely different.

He was a man's man and when that nigga' spoke she listened and got her ass incompliance with whatever the fuck was goin' on, and not in one minute, or thirty seconds, or even a tenth of a second - She got on it that very second.

Lisa was gone in the head over Black, but the thing was, she knew it and not only loved every minute of it, but wouldn't have it no other way.

"I'ma' get that nigga'. But right now I got somethin' else to do so just hold fast, let me put some thought to it."

"Okay." She replied.

"So what's up wit' you?"

"I'm good. Damn you threw me off by being mad at me. I called you to let you know not to worry about your little problem anymore."

"What little problem?"

"The one you were having with finding someone to trust who could trust you."

Black understood.

"So I ain't gotta' worry about it anymore?"

"Nope, not at all." Lisa said with reassured happiness.

"Why is that?"

"Because I love you."

Black chuckled as he spoke.

"You been lovin' me. But that ain't stop me from havin' the problem in the first place."

"Well, let's just say you're five million dollars to the good on your goods."

Lisa's words took a second to register in Black's head. He knew what he heard, but couldn't believe he had heard it.

On the other end of the phone Lisa was smiling in the mirror as she put on her diamond drop lip gloss.

She was on her way to see Black. She'd gotten her hair done the other day and it was flowing the way he liked it, and now she stood at the mirror wearing only her fire engine red laced bra and thong, and Luciano Padovan crystal butterfly red fuck me pumps. Her matching red dress and scarf was on the bed ready to be slipped on after she rubbed herself down with Armani Code body oil and sprayed her Armani Code perfume.

"Five million to the good huh?"

"Yeah baby, it's all taken care of. You don't even have to travel, it's coming to you."

Now that was some for real too good to be true shit, Black couldn't even find the words.

"I know it's a lot to take in right now, so let it digest and we'll talk about it tonight when you take me out for dinner."

"Yeah aiight, let's do th...'

Black caught his self.

"Damn, tonight?"

Lisa stopped in mid-motion of rubbing her ass with body oil and with her hand still on her ass said,

"What?"

"I'm just sayin', I'm on somethin' right now and I gotta' take care of this."

Disappointment fell on top of Lisa and she suddenly felt weighted down. Black could feel it through the phone and knew he couldn't just let her down like that.

"You know what though baby, fuck it. It's still early; I can just take care of this and leave some for later, that's better anyway. Meet me at the car lot at 8:00 p.m., we'll have a late dinner and spend the night together."

Lisa was instantly relieved.

"Boy I thought I was finna' have to smack your butt. You better make room for me, especially after I just spent five million dollars on your ass."

"Right, right, I feel you."

"And I'm lookin' good in your favorite color."

"Cool don't trip 8:00 p.m., but let me get outta' here so I can handle my business."

"Okay sweetie, I'll be there, bye."

"Aiight bye."

Black had been parked across the street from a Mobil gas station since 1:00 p.m. low-key in a beige 2005 Ford Taurus waiting to see who, if anyone showed up with Solid.

At 1:25 p.m. Solid pulled up in his platinum Benz. Ten minutes later he called Black.

"Yeah what's up where you at?"

Black said as if he was rushing.

"I'm where I suppose to be."

"Bet. Don't move, I'll be there in about ten minutes."

"Aiight playa'."

For the next ten minutes, Black watched to see if Solid talked to anyone in any other cars. He didn't, and Black could see that Solid was in the car by himself. A minute later he pulled up behind Solid, beeped his horn, and signaled for Solid to follow him, Solid nodded and fell in behind him. Twenty five minutes later they were pulling onto the backroad that led to the farmhouse.

What Black hadn't thought about was what Solid had been doing, which was giving Derrick detailed directions to the farmhouse as they rode. So as they turned onto the backroad, Derrick knew precisely where to go.

Black pulled up to the farmhouse and got out the Taurus as Solid was parking. Solid got out.

"What's good Bliz-Nak?"

"You playa'. Damn! I see y'all eatin'good in Schaumburg. How the fuck can I be like you?"

"Stop playin' man, we both know who the heavy is out here."

"I can't tell, my doors don't fly up and shit."

They both laughed.

"You lookin' good though." Black said and went on. "So you and Dee aiight down there?"

"Yeah man its gravy, the shop getting' plenty money and we constantly comin' up on clientele for the merch."

"That's good. Real good cause it won't be much longer. You ain't even seen what we come up wit' yet. Come on nigga' you finna' trip when you see all this shit."

"Straight up?"

"Fo sho', without a doubt. You finna' see exactly what you got comin' right now."

As they were walking to the barn they passed a ten by ten foot kennel cage that stood eight feet high.

Five pit bulls were caged, all of 'em solid muscle weighing a hundred and twenty to a hundred and twenty five pounds. One midnight blue and white, red nose, two all white, blue nose, one tiger striped with red nose, and one jet black, red nose.

"Damn nigga'! Them muthafuckas look good."

Solid said walking near the kennel. Immediately the dogs rushed the cage with ferocious barks and snarls.

"Naw, you don't wanna' do that playa'. The dogs only know me, Shy, and wifey. But don't trip, I'ma' let you check 'em out."

"Fo sho', fo sho'. I gots to get me some of them for the shop."

"Yeah. Well I'll tell wifey to holla' at her people because she got these."

"Aiight bet."

They walked to the barn and the bat was right at the door. Solid walked in first, Black grabbed the bat as he walked pass.

"Yeah man on the way down here, I was just thinkin'."

"About what?" Black asked.

Solid turned and Black swung the bat like Barry Bonds and smacked Solid right across the jaw. Solid's jaw shattered to pieces on contact. Blood flew from his mouth as his head snapped to the right sending Solid twisting off his feet twirling to the ground.

With an agonizing scream, Solid held his face as he squirmed spitting out blood and teeth.

Shy waked in the barn with the other bat in his hand and a blunt of Loud in his mouth.

"Look at that pussy ass nigga'." Black said casually.

"I told you that nigga' was a bitch. I should of gave it to his ass when he was here over a year ago. At least then Dee a still be alive."

Then Black raised his voice slightly.

"Yeah nigga'! I know Dee dead. I know about that, about Derrick, or D'man, Stan, his partner, and yo pussy ass comin' out here to get at me. You gon' wish yo ass was dead for a long, long time, but you know what? You ain't gon' die for a even longer time."

Solid couldn't do anything but hear the words and feel the pain as it shot through his body like jolts of electricity. He squirmed on the ground and prayed.

Black pulled out a .9 millimeter berretta, jagged it back and shot Solid in his left foot. Instantly blood turned his white ones red. Solid reached down to his foot screaming.

"Shut the fuck up bitch!"

Black stooped down, put the barrel of the gun in Solid's mouth and rattled it around. The pain of his broken jaw was excruciating and Black knew it.

He grabbed Solid by his get money fro, pulled his head back, looked into Solid's tear filled eyes and said with a face of hatred.

"I'm gon' tell you this one time and if you don't do it and do it fast, I'ma' shoot you in yo other foot, then yo left knee, then the right, then yo left hand, then the right, then both yo elbows - you hear   me?"

Solid nodded.

"Get the fuck out of all them clothes nigga', you got one minute, check yo Jacob if you need some help."

Solid immediately started scrambling out of everything. A minute later he was butt ass naked, chain, watch, earrings, Polo gear everything off. His foot had a hole through it and was bleeding bad.

"No head shots, you hear me Shy?"

"Yeah I got you G'."

With that they both commenced to beating Solid's body with the bats. They hit him everywhere except the head. After about two minutes they stopped because Black didn't want to kill him, he just wanted to break the majority of his bones for now so he'd feel pain and feel it for a while.

"We still got that rope in here bro'?" Black asked.

"Yeah."

Shy answered and walked to a corner of the barn and came back with five pieces of three foot rope. Black went to the farmhouse and came back with a chair. Solid was beat to the point that he couldn't move.

"Come on , help me put this fuck nigga in the chair."

They lifted him up and pain echoed through Solid's body as they sat him down.

Once he was in it, Black tied his hands around the back of the chair, and one foot to each of the two front legs of the chair. Solid sat there bleeding with his head slumped down.

Black pushed his head up by his jaw and said.

"Why you test my Gangsta' nigga? You been fuckin' wit me for years and you know I'm a nut. This ain't no muthafuckin' book nigga', this ain't no movie! This that real life shit. What you thought, niggaz was comin' back to see how the flick did at the show or somethin'? Well guess what punk, this a sneak preview and surprise, ain't no mathafuckin' Oscars, ain't no awards, it won't be no Emmy's. Because when you gone, you gone, you don't even get to see the credits roll."

Black shook his jaw and pain gripped Solid's body again.

"Dig pussy, this ain't New York or California, and I ain't no faggot ass nigga' hollering G Unit over no track. This Chicago bitch! And I'm a muthafuckin' Gangsta'. My whole fuckin' life is a fuckin' rap song, but you know what? I need niggaz like you. I need niggaz like you to - keep – fuckin' – tryin' - me. Because you bitches keep me motivated. But one thing's for certain and two things fo sho'. And that's one, you'll never try another nigga', and two, you ain't never gon' forget me!"

Black walked to the door of the barn and on the ground next to the extension cords and rubbing alcohol were some vice grips. He grabbed 'em.

"Now I would crush both of yo little ass nuts, but I want you to live long enough to see the pictures of yo people stretched out wit' bullets in their brains, so you can see how that bitch move you pulled fucked shit up fo' everybody. I tell you about these paper ass niggaz G'. Shiid if I had it my way, every snitch in the world would have his brains blown out his muthafuckin head - So they better be glad I don't rule the world. But since you ain't got no nuts anyway, here's what I'ma' do."

Black reached down, grabbed Solid's scrotum sack and clamped the vice grips on it and let 'em dangle. Solid let out an exhausted scream. After that, Black grabbed one of the bottles of rubbing alcohol, opened it, and poured it right in the bullet hole of Solid's left foot. The pain was enough to make him wish he was dead, but not enough to kill him.

"We"ll see yo bitch ass tomorrow."

And Black and Shy walked out the barn and closed the door.

CHAPTER 23

Lisa was in the lot of D's at eight o'clock sharp, looking like a bag of money patiently waiting for Black in her Benz.

As she was rummaging through her Hermes bag looking for her lip gloss, Black pulled up. He stepped out in a pair of electric blue Kenneth Cole slacks, a matching blue silk shirt, black Kenneth Cole square toes, the diamond studded Bulgaria watch Lisa bought him, his diamond earrings, and diamond set platinum chain.

"Whew! Sexy G.Q. man!"

Lisa said with a smile that lit up the night.. Being in Blacks presence made her identify even more with Alicia Keys' classic 'Fallen' as it hummed through her Bose speakers.

'What's happening baby girl?" Black asked as he sat down in the passenger seat.

As he leaned over to kiss Lisa, his Paris Hilton for men cologne danced up her nostrils arousing a pleasant sensational feeling within her. Lisa took a moment to take in the sight of her man. Because bullshit wasn't nothing, Lisa had laid claim to Black and at this point she would have endured whatever and just wait him out with the utmost faith she would get him in the end.

Black made reservations at the LaChateou' for dinner and a suite. Over dinner they discussed all the moves Lisa had made, the deal, her leaving the firm, and her reason for making her decision. Black was moved and truly feeling himself and Lisa.

He ordered a bottle of Champagne and Lisa casually sipped away the whole bottle. By the time dinner was over she was drunk with her shoes off massaging Blacks dick under the table with her toes.

After dinner they went directly to the elevator leading to their suite. On the elevator they couldn't keep their hands off one another.

While they kissed passionately, Black had Lisa pushed against the elevator wall with his right hand cuffed and lifting her by the ass. Lisa's left leg was propped up, partially wrapped around Black's waist with her hand down the front of his pants stroking him. Her dress was hiked up pass her waist with her ass exposed when suddenly the elevator door opened.

A black couple in their mid twenties waiting to get on the elevator got an eye full.

"Damn!"

The cute brown skinned woman said. Black and Lisa looked over and Lisa in her drunken state just giggled and laughed as Black let her down.

Her hand was still in his pants, she casually pulled it out.

"I guess this is our stop huh baby." Lisa said with her perfect ass exposed.

"Yeah, I guess so." Black looked at the guy and said,

"What up playa?"

The guy was still stuck on Lisa's stunning beauty, flawless body, and the hundreds of thousands of dollars in jewelry the two were wearing.

"Man, you the playa' dawg." He looked at Black good and added.

"Man don't you got the car lot on Main?"

"Yeah I do, come holla' at me." Drunk ass Lisa looked up and repeated,

"Yeah, come holla' at him. Excuse us." As she walked pass the couple adjusting her dress.

"Get at me." Black said walking off the elevator.

"Fo sho' dawg - No doubt."

Lisa trotted down the hallway with her heels in her hand until she reached suite '613'. As Black walked up, she put her left hand around his head and stuck her tongue down his throat while she grabbed at his dick.

"Get this damn door open before I burst." Lisa frantically spoke in between tongue lunges.

Black managed to get the key card out and slide it in the slot. The light changed from red to green, the door flew open, and they fell inside. Black caught Lisa before she hit the floor and let their momentum carry them to the bed.

Lisa sat down and immediately unbuckled Black's belt, unzipped his pants, pulled his dick out his boxer briefs and put it right in her mouth.

"Mmm, mmm, yeah, mmm, mmmm."

Lisa moaned as Black's hard dick slid in and out of her mouth. Black pulled off his shirt, kicked his shoes off and stepped out of his pants while Lisa maintained a perfect rhythm.

When he was done, he reached into her dress and cuffed her right breast. Lisa took his dick out her mouth and looked up at him with seductive aggression while she continued to stroke it in her hand. Her green eyes screaming fuck me as she occasionally licked his trophy in her hands.

Black grabbed a handful of her hair and pulled her head back. Lisa got an instant mini orgasm. Her breathing quickened as Black stood over her. She looked up like a submissive sex slave ready for duty. Black pulled her to her feet, and then lifted her dress over her head.

Standing there in her red laced bra, thong, and red heels, Black pushed her back on the bed; She quickly came out her thong as Black crawled on the bed, spread her legs, and began to lick her pussy. Lisa exploded into an orgasm as soon as his tongue touched her clit.

With her legs shaking in the air, heels dangling, body trembling, eyes rolled in the back of her head, she clinched the covers.

Black licked and sucked at her sweetness while he pushed his two fore fingers in and out of her. Lisa's pussy was dripping and squished each time his fingers went in and out.

"Put your legs back."

Black said with authority and Lisa immediately grabbed her legs and pulled them back as far as she could get 'em.

Her legs were back so far, she was practically on her shoulder blades with her whole ass in the air.

Black fingered her with the two middle fingers of his right hand and slid his left middle finger in her ass.

"Yess!"

Lisa moaned as she felt the finger penetrating her ass.

"Fuck me in the ass first please! Please! Please fuck me in the ass first!"

Lisa reached over, grabbed her purse and pulled out some strawberry K-Y massage oil. Black grabbed it from her and turned Lisa over.

He slipped out of his boxer briefs and squirted the K-Y onto his manhood and then on Lisa's ass and rubbed it in as he gradually worked his finger in and out her butt.

Lisa was on her hands and knees looking back at Black with a look of erotic pleasure. Her hair was wildly sexy over her face and back.

As Black moved his dick to Lisa's ass she braced and clinched the covers. Black slowly worked the head around the rim of her ass and slow and gradually worked himself in.

Lisa relaxed and continued to open up to him as she slowly pushed back. Once he was all the way in, Lisa rolled her ass around getting prepared for the ass fucking she had been yearning for. A couple minutes later she was hotter than hot and ready for her pounding. She shook her head wildly as her mind became in sync with her sexual mood and grunted out.

"Hell yeah! Get it! Get it! Get that ass nigga'! Get it!" While she rocked back and forth.

She smacked her hand down hard on the bed and grabbed at the covers while Black smacked her coco butter ass. The sting of his hand only intensified the pleasure of Lisa, who sexually strived for the pleasure of pain. Black slammed into her harder and harder and pants and moans became jumbled mutters of jargon expressing both their satisfaction.

Lisa put her hands on the headboard, propped her ass higher and took each slamming in stride with erotic welcoming.

"Yes! Yes! Yes! Yes! Yes!"

Her words shot from her mouth.

"Harder! Harder! Stop being a bitch nigga and get it! Get it! Slam it! Get that asssss! Yeeesssss! Get it!"

Black spread Lisa's cheeks apart and drilled her. She threw her head back and in an instant started bucking as an intensely hard orgasm erupted within her. Her words became slurred as she collapsed on the bed.

"More! More! More! More! Give me some more."

Black cuffed her around her thighs and rammed her until he felt himself wanting to explode. He began to grunt aggressively and Lisa knew he was ready.

"Do it! Do it! Cum for me baby! Shoot it Black! Shoot it right now! Shoot if for mommy! Do it! Do it right fuckin' now!"

And just as the words came out her mouth, Black came. As soon as Lisa felt the heat of his release shoot in her ass she wildly came again.

"Yesssss! Black yesss!"

At ten 0'clock that next morning, Shy and Black were pulling up to the farmhouse.

"I've been dreaming about this pussy ass nigga' all night." Black said.

"You too huh?" Shy replied.

They walked into the barn and Solid sat there like a beaten rag doll. His mouth, jaw, and body had swelled. Soreness had sat in, his legs were so numb from sitting upright, and he could barely feel them. The coolness of the September fall weather felt like February to his naked beaten body as he sat there all night praying for death. His eyes were black, purple, and practically swollen shut and he was bruised from head to toe.

At the sound of the barn doors opening he lifted his head.

"What's happening big pimping?"

Black said with the smile of a party host. Shy followed up with.

"Damn playa', it's safe to say that you den seen better days."

Solid thought the words 'I'm sorry,' but couldn't get his mouth and tongue to speak them.

Black untied the ropes from his arms and legs then kicked him out the chair. Solid fell over and once again pain traveled like currents through his body.

"Nigga' you been on my mind all night."

Black said as he grabbed one of the extension cords off the floor of the barn. Shy grabbed the other one and walked over to Solid, squatted down and said.

"You made me look bad. You made me look real fucking bad. I stopped that nigga' from knockin' yo shit back and this is how you do me. Man bro, what the fuck happened to you. You use to be thorough, on top of shit, trust worthy, but look at you now - A hoe ass nigga' wit' mo bitch in him than my bitch. And dawg, she can be a real bitch at times. But I guess like real niggaz do real things, bitch niggaz do bitch shit. But when bitch niggaz do bitch shit, real niggaz step up and give bitch niggaz what they got comin'."

Shy finished his speech, stood up and swung the extension cord. The sound of it cutting through the air whispered loudly until it came across Solids back wrapping around his ribs and stomach tearing into his already swollen bruised and sore skin.

"Aaahhh!"

Solid hollered as he flinched what part of his body that he could. Black and Shy beat him repeatedly for a couple minutes. When they were done his skin was bleeding and welted all over. Solid moaned in agony and silently prayed for death again. Everything on and in his body cried out in pain as he laid there defenseless as a newborn baby being attacked by wild baboons.

Black grabbed both bottles of rubbing alcohol, handed one to Shy and said.

"Damn playa' that looks bad, you need to get that shit cleaned up."

And they emptied both bottles on his scarred body. The alcohol may as well had been battery acid because it burned to his very soul.

Solid was done. He couldn't muster another lick of resistance, all he could do is lay there and wait to die.
Shy went in his pocket pulled out an ounce of Loud and pearled a blunt. He lit it and said.

"At one point and time me and you would have been blowin' this bad boy together, but now I wouldn't piss on yo ass if you was on fire."

And pulled on the blunt as him and Black walked out the barn. At one o'clock Latrice and Nia pulled up. Latrice had an envelope stamped Federal Express and a plastic bag in her hand. Black and Shy were standing at the dog cage checking the pits out. Latrice walked up, gave Black a kiss, and Nia did the same with Shy.

"Let me smoke wit' you baby."

Shy handed Nia a half of blunt and she fired it up.

"Here baby."

Latrice said handing Black the envelope.

"What's in the bag?" Black asked.

"The adrenaline shots and tranquilizer gun, plus a little somethin' for our boy."

Nia laughed. "More than a little somethin' girl."

"You know that's right." Latrice replied laughing as they high fived each other.

Black opened the envelope and looked over the pictures of the dead inside. All had bullet wounds to the heads lying in pools of their own blood. Most were in there bedrooms, only two were outside.

"Damn! Your man don't be fuckin' around do he?" Black remarked to Latrice.

"Nope. I told you he been doin' this for years. He got people on his team you pass everyday in the streets that you would never dream would be on this type of shit. My daddy use to do this and much more."

"Shit."

Black kissed Latrice.

"I hope you don't ever call me in."

"Well just so long as you know that yo ass can-be-touched."

Latrice patted Black on the butt as she responded with a sassy look on her face,

"But I couldn't do it, I'll just kick yo ass 'myself.'"

"Damn, good lookin' out ma." Black said jokingly.

"Where's the golden boy?" Latrice asked.

"In the barn. Let me get them adrenaline shots."

"Okay, now look. I only got five, so you can't miss."

"Like I miss or somethin' – stop playin'."

"Naw, I'm just sayin' baby. But you know."

Latrice showed Black how to load the darts and Black went to the cage and one by one shot each of the pits.

"It should take like ten minutes to really kick in she said, and after that they gon' be too charged for any of us to go near 'em. So come on so I can give our boy what we got for him."

"What you got?"

"Nia and I was thinkin', and us being women and all we know we become real bitches when we ain't getting' dicked the right way. We get to running our mouth and not givin' a fuck about what comes out even if it means getting' our ass whopped. So we figure, that must be the reason why the bitch came out of Solid. So we bought him a present."

Latrice reached in the bag and pulled out a twelve inch dildo about three and half inches thick.

"We call him the 'Bitch Tamer."

Shy and Black shook their heads and Black said,

"Hoes is scandalous."

Latrice poked him in the stomach with the dildo.

"That's aiight, you love me though."

Then with the excitement and smile of a kid at Christmas she ran toward the barn. They walked in and Solid was laying there welted, swollen, bleeding, and bruised.

"Damn playboy, you don't look too good." Latrice said. Nia pulled on the blunt and said.

"Naw girl, he just need some dick."

"I know. Ooohh, I can't wait to give him some. Pull his legs apart baby."

Black rolled him on his stomach and pulled his right leg as far as it would stretch until Solid laid there with his ass exposed.

"I ain't touchin that nigga'z ass!" Black said.

"Me either!" Shy followed.

"Y'all ain't got to." Latrice assured then said,

"Nia come on baby, spread his cheeks."

"Here, hold the blunt."

Nia gave the blunt to Shy then stepped over to Solid facing Latrice, who was squatted with the dildo positioned at Solid's ass. Nia cuffed and spreaded Solid's cheeks and said.

"This is for your own good baby, because trust me, I always feel better after some good dick."

"Me too girl, whew! It got my pussy hot just thinking about it."

Latrice put the head of the dildo right at the tip of Solid's ass, then rammed it halfway in. Solid hollered out in agony. Nia slapped him on his ass.

"I know, I know, it feels good don't it baby?"

Latrice worked it in and out turning it as she went along.

"Talk to me baby; let me know you like it."

Latrice said laughing as she worked it deeper and faster for a couple minutes. Solid moaned and screamed but couldn't move.

"Damn you got some good ass. Nia baby you gotta' get some of this."

Latrice moved and Nia took over. Nia pushed the dildo deeper in Solid's ass until blood and shit started to cover it, and then rammed him for a minute or so as she thought about Londa being dead.

"Yeah, he feelin' it now girl, look."

Black shook his head laughing.

"Aiight, Aiight, Aiight, y'all den did y'all thing. It's over wit'."

Nia turned around with pouty lips.

"But she got to hit it longer than me."

"Ooouuu, I'm sorry baby, was I ass hoggin'?"

Nia folded her arms across her chest, poked her lip out and said.

"Yeah, you know you was."

Then just as quickly she smiled brightly, shrugged her shoulders, and said.

"Fuck it. He a T.H.O.T. anyway and I don't too much like fuckin' wit' runners."

And snatched the dildo out, which was the first sigh of relief Solid had since his torture started. Black spread the pictures out in front of him, pulled his head back so Solid could open his eyes and see 'em.

"Well, one thing you don't gotta' worry about is nobody missing you, because as you can see playboy, didn't nobody make it."

Solid opened his eyes, saw the faces of his loved ones laying there shot dead, bleeding from their heads and then it was official, and he was ready to die.

"You did this. All this could have been avoided just by keepin' it gangsta'. But since you couldn't - Somebody had to. Help me get this nigga' up Shy."

They each put one of his arms around their neck and drug his limp body to the dog cage. The dogs were circling the cage growling and snapping at one another.
The adrenaline shots had kicked in. Black pulled out his .9 millimeter and shot in the air one time. The sound of the gun sent the dogs' scurrying to the back of the cage.

Once they were back there bumping around, they bit and snapped at one another as Black opened the cage and him and Shy picked Solid up and tossed him in.

Solid hit the dogs and that was all it took, they went in on him. Fueled by the adrenaline shots and the taste of blood the dogs ripped Solid's body apart.

Shy rolled another blunt and him and Nia smoked while the four of them watched.

At three thirty-three in the afternoon, Lisa had just gotten out the shower at the hotel suite and was sitting on the bed in a towel watching TV. Her cell phone rang, it was Derrick.

She didn't dare answer it because of what Black told her, so she just let it ring.

She put the phone down and started getting herself together. Twenty minutes later she was dressed, make-up done, and waiting for her hair to dry. She picked her phone up and saw it had one message.

"Well, he said don't talk to him, he didn't say anything about listening to messages."

So Lisa went into her phone and played the message.

"Lisa, I just want you to know that I know about your boy Black. Now I don't know what you know or what he got you thinkin', but just so you know he's the one who killed Tuko and took what was there. And while you running behind this nigga' suckin' his dick, you might wanna' know he thought you were gonna' be there too, and if you were - You would have been just dead as Tuko. Yeah, he was gon' kill yo dumb ass too. Get yo mind right." The message ended.

Lisa couldn't believe what she had just heard, but now it all made sense. Why Derrick was after Black and how someone knew where the money was.

Lisa flashed back to the conversation of her telling Black, and then to her showing Black where the dope was. Then she thought about him leaving town the same time Tuko was killed, and how he wanted so much dope now.

She was spinning and suddenly she felt sick. Tears welled up in her eyes and heart. She felt used, betrayed, and stupid. Her heart was shattered, she was confused and distraught. All she could hear was,

"Yeah, he was gon' kill yo dumb ass too."

Lisa shook her head.

"No. No. He couldn't, he wouldn't. He would never hurt me. He loves me, he has to love me. He just has to. I've done too much and we've shared too many good times. He has to love me - He would never want to kill me."

Tears began to flow from her eyes and just then Black walked in. Lisa was sitting on the bed in tears holding the phone.

"What's up baby girl? What's the matter?"

Black said as he rushed to her. He reached out for her and Lisa snatched away.

"Get away from me!" She screamed,

"Don't fuckin' touch me! Stay the fuck away from me!"

Black stood there, shocked.

"What's wrong? What's the matter with you? What's goin' on?"

"What's goin' on?!"

"What's goin' on muthafucka?! I'll tell you what the fuck is goin' on?!"

Lisa screamed at the top of her lungs with angry, hurt, and tear filled eyes. She set the phone up to play the message back again and tossed it to Black. Black listened to the message thinking to himself 'Damn, what the fuck.'

"Now! You tell me. What the fuck is goin' on!?"

Black looked at her speechless.

TO BE CONTINUED……………………………..

Scenes From "Da Block Two"... (Road to Riches)

"Damn G', who the fuck is this?"

Shy said to Black as they sat in the room under the barn counting money.

"I don't know."

The camera switched to another angle and zoomed in on the face. Shy stood up and walked to the screen.

"I know that nigga' G'. I den seen him somewhere before."

"Where at?" Black said anxiously.

"Give me a minute."

Shy stood there thinking, rewinding the video of his mind back until he saw it. He was sitting outside Lisa's condo waiting for Black and an old school Cutlass, clean and fresh to def rolled by. The nigga' looked at him and he looked at the nigga'.

"From Lisa's house. That's the cat them niggaz who tried to hit you stopped and hollered at outside her crib."

"You sure?"

"Positive. That's him bro."

Black knew off top that was Derrick.

"That's that police ass nigga'!"

"How the fuck he find us out here?"

"I don't know, but that bitch ain't gon' make it up outta' here!"

Black ran to another room and grabbed the A.K. and the S.K. He tossed Shy the S.K. and they ran to the steps that led to the barn.

"What's up G'?! What's the matter?! What happened!?" Shy asked rushing through the door of Black's house.

"It's Latrice."

"Latrice! What the fuck happened to sis!?"

"She got popped."

"What you mean she got popped?"

"Just that, she got popped G'. They caught her with five hundred bricks."

"Get tha fuck outta' here!"

"No joke G', she at the M.C.C. building right now.'

"Look bitch, you been in my way for too damn long. I don't give a fuck what y'all have together I'm sick of this shit and it ends right the fuck now!"

Lisa pulled out a ten shot .25 automatic and pointed it at Latrice.

David Silas   Da Block

I would like to take this opportunity to thank you for reading "Da Block" the first novel by David Joseph Silas. Please be on the look out for the follow up sequel " Da Block 2 Road to Riches " As well as recomended reading by Jamelah Thomas " Blood Brothers 1 & 2. " Follow us on Face Book @ David Joseph Silas & Jamelah Thomas. And stay connected with future projects through lelacanepublications.com.